Some Wine for Remembrance

Some Wine
for Remembrance

Edmund Keeley

White Pine Press • Buffalo, New York

White Pine Press
P.O. Box 236, Buffalo, New York 14201

This is a work of fiction. Names, characters, places,
and incidents are either the product of the author's imagination
or are used fictitiously, and any resemblance to actual persons,
living or dead, events, or locals is entirely coincidental.

Publication of this book was made possible, in part,
by grants from the National Endowment for the Arts,
the Foundation for Hellenic Studies,
the Leventis Foundation,
and with public funds from the
New York State Council on the Arts, a State Agency.

Printed and bound in the Uinted States of America

First Edition

Library of Congress Cataloging-in-Publication Data
Keeley, Edmund.
Some wine for remembrance / Edmund Keeley.
p.cm.
ISBN 1-893996-15-8 (pbk. : alk. paper)
1. World War, 1939–45—Collaborationists—Fiction.
2. Greece—Fiction. I. Title
PS3561.E34 S66 2001
813'.54—dc21   2001026727

Author's Acknowledgments

All the characters in this novel are of course fictional, but I have tried to create an authentic historical background for them so that the reader may enjoy the illusion—if the reader so chooses—that one or another actually lived in history. The following sources have helped me to imagine this background: Stephen Gallup, *A History of the Salzburg Festival*; Mark Mazower, *Inside Hitler's Greece: The Experience of Occupation, 1941-44*; correspondence between Professors John Iatrides and Hagen Fleischer, and an article by the latter entitled "The Question of Waldheim's Wartime Guilt in the Balkans"; Jack Saltman, *Kurt Waldheim: A Case to Answer*; and Robert Edwin Herzstein, *Waldheim: the Missing Years*.

The epigraph renders the concluding lines of the second part of the six-part World War II poem, *Amorgos*, that established the late Nikos Gatsos as an important voice in contemporary Greek poetry, one devoted in recent years to sophisticated and highly popular lyrics written for the composers Hadjidakis, Theodorakis, and Xarhakos.

Excerpts from this novel have appeared in *Antaeus*, *The Ontario Review*, and *Ploughshares*.

For Mary

It's enough if a plough and a sharp sickle
        are found in a joyful hand
Enough if there flower only
Some wheat for the festivals,
        some wine for remembrance,
        some water
          for the dust . . .

                —Nikos Gatsos,
                Amorgos, 1943

ONE

The troop abandoned the steam-driven truck on level ground well below the village because the driver said he wanted to make sure it was in good shape for the return trip to the city. On the way up the driver had stopped twice to stoke the fire under the boiler at the back, and now the boiler was low on water, so he'd said no farther the minute they reached the natural spring at the foot of the mountain. He said they had nothing to complain about really, the village was already in sight on the slope ahead. The scout master called the six scouts together in the shadow of the Byzantine aqueduct on the far side of the gully that ran beside the main road. He told them it was important that they walk the rest of the way in single file and try to stay in line, because even if the war had cost them their uniforms, it hadn't cost them their pride, and they ought to show it. They kept in line well enough until they reached the first houses in the village, though everyone except the scout master was out of breath by then and soaked with sweat. The houses on both sides of the road were burned through so that only the stone walls remained, no trace of the roofs, the walls blackened and broken here and there. The place smelled of smoldering charcoal. When some of them started to look around, the scout master made them line up again. At the first wide bend in the road that was now the main street, they were met by a gathering of men who had come down from the village square. The men asked who these schoolboys were and what they were doing up there, for God's sake. The scout master told them they were Boy Scouts from Salonika, on an excursion, but ready to help the village in any way they could. The men said there was nothing to help, the village was burned to the ground, and the dead were dead. The scout master decided to keep on going up to the square, he said there was without doubt a lesson in this. All around the square there were charred houses, and those that still had roofs were abandoned. One of the men pointed across the square to a sidestreet. That was the bakery down there, he said, where the Germans and their Greek collaborators had packed in so many of those who'd stayed behind in the village, mostly old men and some of the women and children, and had burned them alive. The scout master stood there looking at the empty side street. He shook his head. Then he said I guess we'd better get a move on. Instead of heading up the mountainside as planned, he led the troop back down to the main road below the village. The truck was gone. The scout master stood there gazing down the valley, then he told the troop that they were no longer boys after all, they'd survived the war and the German Occupation, they could walk back to the city, especially since it was all downhill. On the way down one boy asked the scout master why the Germans and their Greek collaborators had burned people alive in the bakery. Don't ask, the scout master said, don't even ask yourself.

Jackson Ripaldo had chosen his new studio apartment overlooking the Potomac partly because it was near the bar where he used to hang out with his radical classmates during his muckraking days at Georgetown University but mostly because he'd thought it far enough out of the way to be easily sealed against noise and well-intentioned intrusions. The answering machine he'd added to what furniture his estranged wife had let him take with him before their final settlement was a thing meant to make the seal tight. The trouble, he now realized, was that he'd decided to keep his old work number as a temporary expediency, and he hadn't yet trained himself not to notice recorded phone messages while he was still into what he considered a professional day's quota of pages for a middle-aged beginner in the art of mystery fiction. And once again he'd forgotten to turn the volume down on the machine, so that Wittekind's full-throated voice, with its quaint blend of American and German overtones, had cut sharply, implausibly, into his preoccupation with a scene involving people in high places negotiating a secret arms deal in Cairo.

"We need you, Ripaldo. I need you. Do you hear me? I call from

Vienna. What is this business about leaving a message after the beep? Why are you hiding so early in the day? We have serious affairs to discuss. Matters of international significance. This is your message from Wittekind."

The Cairo scene had fallen apart after that—and this just as Ripaldo was finally beginning to feel almost at home with the made-up corruption of imaginary politicians that had taken the place of honest if less-focussed government evil in the column he'd given up the previous winter out of a surfeit of righteousness and tired blood. He leaned over and cut the volume on the answering machine. Then he sat there gazing at his new portable typewriter as though that too was just waiting for its moment to talk back to him.

Ripaldo had first met Wittekind at a Columbia School of Journalism conference not long after World War II, while Ripaldo was beginning a failed attempt at graduate study on the G.I. Bill following his two-year tour on a destroyer in the Pacific. His Austrian friend had been introduced to him as Count Wittekind. Nobody, Ripaldo included, was at all sure that Wittekind had ever been a real count, despite the man's elegantly trimmed goatee and his grand style in clothes. The only thing he himself claimed to be beyond his name was a reformed Nazi with a passionate aversion to those who had difficulty facing the realities of their past. His past included an undistinguished war record as a Wehrmacht lieutenant who had been lucky enough to get wounded early in the campaign on the Eastern front. By the end of the war he'd become an anti-Nazi pacifist, convincingly enough to have earned himself a special fellowship from some American source that allowed for a period of State-side training in journalism that further cleansed him of his tainted background and gave him the right perspective and lingo to bring him work as a stringer in Europe for several American news journals. Some suspected that the fellowship signalled a C.I.A. connection, but Wittekind swore that he was clean in that respect too. In any case, he had managed to build himself a highly successful post-war career as an international playboy and joker, and an even more brilliant career as a meticulous if sometimes unscrupulous reporter, ready to go anywhere and do anything within the law to get his story.

Ripaldo had run into Wittekind again in post-war Greece during his apprenticeship as a correspondent covering the last phase of the Greek Civil War, but they'd come to know each other well a bit later, when both had found themselves in a relatively fallow period, a time when Wittekind had given himself over to cruising the Greek islands in a yacht he'd fitted out with a compressor and scuba gear for deep spear-fishing and for what he called his avocation of underwater archeology. He hadn't managed to indulge that avocation for long, because the Greek coast guard soon suspected him, not without cause, of raiding their waters less for fish and knowledge of ancient history than for Greco-Roman amphorae and Byzantine crockery to stock his private collection. But Ripaldo had come across Wittekind on several occasions at the high point of this hedonistic interlude for both of them, most memorably in a small harbor of one of the Northern Sporades at a time when Ripaldo still found the Aegean islands a plausible setting for a weekend tryst. Count Wittekind dropped anchor on that occasion with a new entourage—wife, mistress, and best friend—to create an evening of chaotic ribaldry at the taverna Ripaldo had carefully chosen for discreet dialogue with a young Greek lady who'd proven, up to that moment, almost too reticent to talk at all. Ripaldo had gone over to say a quick hello to Wittekind and his companions, then retreated to his table at the back end of the taverna.

"*Ouzo*, my American friend," Wittekind yelled at him after the new arrivals had settled into a table across the way. "You must give the lady *ouzo*. Even the gods in this country take it for an aphrodisiac."

"Did he say *ouzo?*" the lady asked Ripaldo. "One doesn't drink *ouzo* after dinner. Who is this loud friend of yours?"

"Just an acquaintance," Ripaldo said. "A journalist. Used to be a German officer, but now he's as American as I am."

"Ugh. I can't stand it. How does he have the nerve to return to this country after what the Germans did here?"

"He's all right now," Ripaldo said. "Clean of the wrong politics. In fact, a well-known pacifist in his own country."

"A pacifist. He seems to me more like a sexual maniac. Who are those women with him?"

"How do I know?"

"He keeps embracing one and then the other."

"Maybe they're his sisters," Ripaldo said.

"They don't look like sisters to me. The one looks like she's old enough to be mother to the other one."

"Well how about wife and daughter?" Ripaldo said.

"It doesn't look that way to me."

The waiter arrived with a bottle of *ouzo* sent, he said, by the table across the way. Ripaldo and his companion looked toward the front to see Wittekind raising his glass.

"From the goddess of love," he yelled. "So your lady will finally smile and agree that the world is really her oyster."

"What is he saying?"

"The world is your oyster."

"What does that mean? The man is a sexual maniac."

"It's just an American expression."

"Ugh."

After that evening Ripaldo lost the lady, but he became a close companion of the Count for a week on his yacht and, over the years, for a shared cruise every now and then or for a night on the town in any year that found the two of them in the same city. But fond of Wittekind as he'd become, Ripaldo was now more than irritated by the answering machine voice that had cut into his morning's work. It was an intrusion like any other. He was into a new life now, he told himself, a new freedom from obligations marital or otherwise, and had no intention of changing course. He'd turned his Wesley Heights house over to his wife and headed out on his own when she'd made it clear that his sudden impulse to become a freelance writer of mystery novels was more new insecurity than she was prepared to tolerate after a decade or so of tense financial brinkmanship, and she was right in her way. But so was he in his. Anyway, what counted now was the work, and no room for other temptations. Ripaldo stared at the answering machine again, then at the typewriter, then picked up the phone and called Vienna.

The matters of international significance that Wittekind had in mind seemed largely local on first hearing. It turned out that he had called Ripaldo on behalf of a recently-formed committee of

progressive Austrian journalists who were alarmed by the indiffer-
ence of so many of their fellow countrymen to the alleged involve-
ment in World War II atrocities of a leading figure in their government who was about to start his campaign for reelection to high
office. Wittekind explained that for years this distinguished statesman, with a strong background in international affairs, had successfully blanked out a portion of his war service as a Wehrmacht
officer in the Balkans through a series of lies that placed him far
from where he'd actually been. His political opposition had uncovered a more accurate account of his missing war years, as had the
World Jewish Congress and several foreign historians interested in
the case, but an official inquiry ordered by the Austrian government concluded that there was no specific charge that could be
brought against the gentleman as a result of either his wartime service or the inconsistencies in his account of things, which the gentleman himself simply blamed on a bad memory. The committee,
on Wittekind's recommendation, urgently requested that Ripaldo
join their effort to search out the truth about this distinguished
statesman's suspect days as a Wehrmacht officer in the Balkans,
specifically his term of service in Northern Greece.

"Why me?" Ripaldo said. "I'm really no longer in that kind of
business."

"You know the territory. The language. And yes, you have the
correct loathing of those in high places who have tried to hide their
unspeakable crimes."

"Only in this country," Ripaldo said. "I no longer meddle in the
unspeakable crimes of other countries."

"This meddling will give you great pleasure," Wittekind said.
"We're after the big fish. One of the great Nazi hypocrites of our
time."

"I know the case," Ripaldo said. "You'll never catch him. Look
at what he's gotten away with already. And anyway, you Austrians
seem to resent outsiders fishing around in your dirty waters."

"You're wrong. We want you, Ripaldo. We need you. And we
will catch the hypocrite. You will catch him. Think of the glory,
Ripaldo. The big fish."

"I don't know," Ripaldo said. "I've got other fish to fry these
days. Besides, fishing is your territory."

"It used to be yours too. What's the matter with you? Don't tell me you've given up the pleasures of the chase."

"I've given up the real world, Wittekind. I'm still in Foggy Bottom roaming the corridors of the mightily corrupt, but it's all made up. I'm into writing fiction. It beats reality."

"Then it is up to me to save you from making a fool of yourself. I'm giving you a chance to write history, Ripaldo. Together we will make the truth prevail."

"What truth is that, Wittekind? I'm wary of what passes for truth these days. Anyway in politics."

"The truth about what my people did in the country you and I used to have for our beautiful playground. Take the Hortiáti massacre, for example. You remember the massacre near Salonika at the end of the war, just before our army retreated north?"

"I heard about it. Along with some others in the area. What about it?"

"Well, our distinguished statesman pretends to have forgotten that Wehrmacht operation, though there are good grounds for believing he was there at the time. So this is one atrocity he may have trouble running away from. That is, if you help us hook him. And then you can write a book about it."

"What makes you so sure your so-called statesman was involved?"

"We know that during that period he was an officer at the Wehrmacht intelligence headquarters in a nearby village called Arsaklí and that his duties included counter-partisan operations."

"So you think he ordered that massacre?"

"That's for you to find out for us. You're the one who can do it, Ripaldo. Are you ready for adventure, for retribution, for setting the record straight?"

"I don't know. I'll have to think about it."

"Well think about it, Ripaldo. Think about Greece and what my people did to it. Think about the lost history you can give back to that place to pay for what we did."

There was the usual hint of self-irony in Wittekind's voice, but not enough to cover what Ripaldo heard as honest urgency. He promised to call him back at the same time the following day. After wasting the rest of the morning trying to shape a plausible meeting between an Iranian arms dealer and a retired American general on the banks of the Nile in a restored Mamluk palace that he could barely imagine, he called Wittekind again and asked for a further briefing on the Austrian case that had ruined his day's quota of pages. He could tell that Wittekind was pleased—too pleased for his own pleasure. He learned that Wittekind and his colleagues in Vienna had already turned up a number of documents from various sources: Wehrmacht organizational charts and job descriptions, a paybook, a number of photographs, and several army intelligence reports signed with a squiggle that could have been mistaken for a Greek omega tilted a little to one side. This, Wittekind said, would serve henceforth as their code name for the distinguished statesman with the conveniently deficient memory: Herr Omega, nicknamed by him "the Big O."

Wittekind went on to say that the research materials brought together in Vienna had allowed his committee to construct a fairly tight wartime itinerary for the Big O that showed his whereabouts from March of 1942 to December of 1944. They now knew that in 1942 he had been assigned to Yugoslavia during joint German and Italian operations that had resulted in a substantial number of murdered hostages and prisoners shot without trial, and during the same period he had been close to the Kozara region of Bosnia-Herzegovina when there had been mass killing and mass deportation of civilians. They also knew that in 1943 he had been an intelligence officer in Athens at a time when there was wholesale destruction of villages and the arbitrary execution of civilians suspected of helping partisans.

"But listen to this, Ripaldo. Listen carefully. In 1943 the Big O was transferred to the village of Arsakli in the hills above Salonika to become the 03 officer of the Ic/AO intelligence section of Army Group E. Have you got that?"

"I've got it, but what does it mean?"

"It means for one thing that he was in the area when there was mass deportation of Jews from northern Greece and severe retaliation against villagers, partisans, even captured Allied commandoes. What else it means will be for you to find out. This is exactly your mission."

"Don't push me, Wittekind. I haven't agreed to go on any mission."

"You will agree. I will make you agree."

Wittekind confirmed that nobody had yet come up with irrefutable evidence of the Big O's personal participation at the scene of any single atrocity, but he explained that it was among the functions of the O3 officer in intelligence to prepare reports for his seniors on all partisan activity or suspected activity in his region and to indicate possible counter measures. Exactly what this O3 officer in northern Greece had done at a given moment, or how much he had conspired with what others had done, remained to be demonstrated. Meanwhile, Wittekind said, the Big O continued to stonewall aggressively. When a member of the Austrian press corps leaked excerpts of the reconstructed wartime itinerary from a so-called reliable source and speculated on some of its implications, the Big O responded that he had known nothing whatever of anything that might be implied by this alleged itinerary. He stated that he had simply been a low-level officer in Yugoslavia, a mere interpreter for the Italians, with no authority to do anything on his own and no more knowledge of events than any ordinary soldier. And in northern Greece he was assigned to a village too far from the city of Salonika for him to have any idea about the tragedy that befell the Jewish community of that city, with duties that were those of a glorified clerk.

Wittekind laughed. Then he asked Ripaldo's permission to tell a little story that he felt would be useful as background:

His anti-Nazi juices had been so stirred up by this latest evasion that he'd dropped everything he was working on in order to arrange an interview with the distinguished hypocrite so that he could test the man in person—check out his responses face to face. He got the interview in his usual way when the prospect was difficult: through subterfuge. In this case it was by way of a high level member of the Big O's staff whom he knew from his days in the Party, and he pretended to this contact that he was interested in doing what he could as a journalist to repair the distinguished elder statesman's damaged prestige, along with that of other former officers who had served honorably in the Wehrmacht. This got him into the Big O's vast office, with only a single assistant in the background, pretending to be at work on some papers.

The interview had started out pleasantly enough, Wittekind said: iced orange juice to cut into the day's heat, and easy small talk about the years just before the war, when there was so much hope in the air for the generation he and the distinguished gentleman both belonged to, years of purpose and comraderie and a faith in possibilities beyond adolescent ambition that had gone hand in hand with the less fortunate aspects of the Hitler Youth movement. Far from the cool, aloof presence of his reputation, the Big O had been charming, accessible, almost sentimentally nostalgic at moments—that is, until Wittekind edged into the war years with a sly remark about how unfair to the Big O certain members of the press had been recently, especially those without any personal experience of the German side of the war, such as the young Yugoslav journalist who had seen fit to dig up that old 1947 file from archives in Belgrade, with its quite unjust accusations regarding the distinguished gentleman's wartime service in Yugoslavia.

"If I may say so, where is the justice in that?" he'd asked the Big O. "I mean to accuse any Wehrmacht officer of being a war criminal simply because he followed orders in carrying out the execution of resistance fighters. Including those pretending to be civilians."

That had made the Big O freeze. "The file in question means absolutely nothing. Everyone in the Wehrmacht who served in Yugoslavia during the war arrived on the Communist government's list of so-called wanted war criminals. Everyone."

"No doubt. I merely—"

"And using that file against me so many years ago was a political act. A plot against my efforts to establish democracy in Austria. Just as its sudden appearance now is a political act to influence the coming election."

"On the question of democracy, I'd like to—"

"And that isn't all. I want you to know that the so-called evidence from that file was the product of false testimony on the part of a petty criminal who was a German prisoner-of-war trying to save his own neck. Please. Hardly a believable witness to anything."

"I understand your position," Wittekind said. "I can assure you that I myself have suffered under similar accusations. In the aftermath of war, one easily becomes the victim of liars and hypocrites. And I am quite prepared to believe that the committee of journalists now preparing a new file on your case will come across equally questionable testimony. But may I nevertheless presume to ask—"

"What committee of journalists?" The Big O rose in his seat. "I know nothing about any committee of journalists. It is becoming an industry, this business growing up around my name. An industry run by fools and opportunists."

Wittekind had then assured the Big O that the committee was not commercial in any ordinary sense and had no other object than to uncover the truth about the distinguished gentleman's wartime service in Yugoslavia and Greece. This meant that the committee's work could only serve to exonerate him in the end, since all the evidence to date, at least concerning his time in northern Greece, pointed to his having been no more than a conscientious young intelligence officer who had to deal with undercover raids by merciless enemy commando units and a particularly vicious resistance movement in an area where the German forces were especially vulnerable to sudden ambushes, as in the case of the village near Salonika called Hortiáti, which unfortunately had to pay a high price for its partisan activities, as did certain commandos who were understandably subject to severe interrogation.

The Big O was still standing, his long face crimson. "Absolutely nothing of the kind. This committee of yours is quite wrong. In northern Greece I was assigned to a remote village. A place that I believe was called Arsaklí. I know nothing about ambushes and a village called Hortiáti."

"That is a village only a few kilometers from Arsaklí. I myself—"

"And as I've said publicly already, I had nothing to do with commando raids. If you care to know the truth, and I doubt that you do, I was nothing more than a kind of scribe assigned to keep a diary of military events and to write reports that were then passed on to others for study and decision."

"Of course," Wittekind said. "I fully understand. And on the basis of these reports, orders were issued—"

"I never issued orders. Others issued orders. I followed orders."

And with that, the Big O had moved toward the door. Wittekind followed him, trying to appear polite, even servile. He had not meant at all to insult the gentleman, he said to his back. He simply wanted to let him know that he still had a few friends among the corps of local journalists. And whatever the committee might turn up about atrocities in Yugoslavia and Greece, whether involving partisans, commandos, or civilians, the distinguished gentleman could count on a strong defense by at least one old Wehrmacht colleague who knew all too well the moral dilemmas that had confronted officers serving madmen in a lost cause.

The Big O stood there holding the door open. The secretary had already taken up his post on the other side of the doorway, erect, somber, his hands folded in front of him.

"Sir, whoever you are," the Big O said, "I can assure you that there is no moral dilemma here. The truth is quite simple. I did nothing more than serve my country honorably in time of war, as did so many others on both sides. And as far as I'm concerned, this interview, which was clearly solicited under false pretenses, is now over."

He offered Wittekind his hand almost civilly. Wittekind decided to take it.

The Big O smiled stiffly. "Your committee will find nothing. Search into the next century if you care to, but you will find nothing that makes me a criminal. Because I am not a criminal."

Ripaldo heard Wittekind laugh to himself again. Then there was silence, as though the line had gone dead. "

"Are you there?" Wittekind finally said.

"I'm here."

"Well, why don't you say something?"

"What's there to say? The son of a bitch is lying. Just a poor scribe is all he was, like the rest of us. Can you believe it?"

"Of course he's lying," Wittekind said. "The point is, will you help us prove it?"

"The son of a bitch," Ripaldo said. "Assigned to a remote village in northern Greece. Arsakli was on the outskirts of Salonika, for Christ's sake."

"Will you help us?"

"All right, yes, I'll help you. The son of a bitch."

Wittekind sighed. Then he told Ripaldo that he would be on his own once he got to northern Greece, free to follow whatever leads he himself uncovered, interview anybody he found who might be useful, and report back to him and the Vienna committee as he thought advisable. He suggested that Ripaldo take along a tape recorder and his portable typewriter so that he could go over what he recorded while it was still fresh and then translate and type up any interviews that he considered valuable for the committee's further investigation. These he could express-mail to Wittekind along with any other important documents that he came across during his work in the field.

"The crucial thing," Wittekind said, "is to find out first of all exactly what happened at Hortiáti and then to see if there is any clear link between the Big O and the massacre there."

"Well, don't we know what happened at Hortiáti? As I remember, the Germans burned the place down."

"Right, but the point is, we have to provide evidence that it wasn't simply a retaliation for partisan activity in the area. We have to demonstrate that it involved killing of innocent civilians. Simple reprisals for guerrilla activity were permitted under the Hague Regulations."

"Is it a simple reprisal when you burn a village to the ground, for God's sake?"

"Proof, Ripaldo. We need proof of what happened. Documents. First-hand accounts. Witnesses willing to testify as to who was involved. Whatever you can dig up for us that may be useful."

"I'm certain the son of a bitch was involved. Otherwise, why would he—"

"Proof, Ripaldo. Hard facts. Do you hear me?"

Ripaldo reached the village of Hortiáti by a newly-paved highway that angled across a tableland high above the city of Salonika, then climbed steeply toward the northern slope of the mountain that gave the village its name. On the drive up, he counted the years—almost half a century—since he'd last been up there for an outing in the family car on a dirt road crisscrossed by ruts deep enough to survive the rainless summers and break the springs of any moving thing less pampered than his father's black 1937 De Soto. The village had seemed as old-fashioned as any other in those pre-war days, crowded narrow streets following the natural contours of the hillside, the houses small, solid, undistinguished, though with a large measure of mountain stone, the churches carrying their years with some grace. Now, from a distance, Ripaldo thought the village had the look of the new post-war suburbs that circled the heights of the city. It had obviously prospered from Greece's entry into the European Common Market. There were several levels of recent villas set deep in the mountainside, some still under construction, no doubt summer homes for those who could afford the luxury of clean air and an unencumbered view as far as Salonika Bay.

Entering the village gave him a still different feel. What struck him after all these years was how ordered, how unimaginative the heart of it seemed, the houses small box-shapes that showed red brick between concrete columns where the stucco had worn through, few with any charm, any residue of history. And no school house built of stone, no neoclassical mansions bordering the central square, not even the few forgotten mud-brick remnants of poorer days that one normally found in villages that survived the war. And the aura of the place: too quiet, too few young people walking the main street, no old men sitting out in the central square, the side streets straight as though planned that way, wider than usual and barren of trees.

It occurred to Ripaldo that of course there was no history there. History for that village had suddenly stopped one afternoon just before the end of the German Occupation when Wehrmacht troops had climbed up that winding main street in their trucks or armored cars to create a wilderness that red brick and concrete, however stuccoed and whitewashed, were hardly likely to conceal even forty-odd years later.

Ripaldo's pre-war outing in the De Soto had taken place during the month before Hitler invaded Poland and the outbreak of war in Europe suddenly sent his family home from Salonika to Washington, D. C. His father, a middle-level civil servant on a special two-year assignment abroad, had taken out some of his resentment over ending up not in his beloved Italy but in the Greek provinces by shipping over what turned out to be the grandest of the few cars in town. When the De Soto climbed up through

Arsaklí to Hortiáti village that summer day in 1939, Ripaldo's mother had stayed behind with the driver, and his father had headed off above the village at his usual fast pace, waiting for no one. Ripaldo had followed well behind in the company of two of his schoolmates at the local American-sponsored high school called Anatolia College. He now remembered that when he and his friends came out above the last houses that afternoon and started up the mountain, the heat thinned out and the air turned sharply clear, so that the village on the slope below stayed in view all the way up. It had seemed to him that you could actually smell the sweetness of the green fields below the village whenever there was a break in the scent of thyme along their stone trail. And the only sound up there had come from the village pasture land where sheep were grazing, the tinkled waft of their bells fading and returning as though with a shifting breeze, though the air was perfectly still.

The memory of that serene landscape survived Ripaldo's return to the States and fed his nostalgia for a while, but what had brought him back to Greece after the war wasn't nostalgia so much as the new possibilities of the Civil War then still in progress and the chance to draw on his pre-war experience and remnant knowledge of the language to write that up in the image of young Hemingway reporting on the Asia Minor Catastrophe. During his first trip north he heard that the old village of Hortiáti and a number of other villages were no longer, just as the Jewish community of Salonika was no longer, gone with the forests and tended fields that had once made the mountains so green, gone with the broad open beaches along Salonika Bay that were now wired off because of uncleared mines and other wartime garbage. And he found that the old roads you used to take to high country were now closed because of the guerrilla threat or ruined beyond repair. He never managed to make his way beyond Arsaklí and up the mountain as far as Hortiáti village.

Now, when he came out above the village square to the villas on the upper slopes, he decided to keep on going so that he could check out the view from up there and see if he could spot the old trail he'd taken up the mountain with his schoolmates that afternoon in 1939. The view was disappointing. The broad curve of

Salonika in the distance below was barely visible now through the dark haze that seemed to rise from the city as though from a great smoldering fire, blocking out most of the harbor and dimming the sea as far as the horizon. And there was no sign of the trail he was looking for, though there was a new dirt road that had been cut into the mountain to leave a jagged scar under the nearest ridge, carrying the eye toward a giant radar station like a fractured crown on the mountain's peak.

Ripaldo turned his rented Fiesta around and went back to the central square. In the city they'd told him that the one place he might get some historical background on the village and a fairly accurate account of what had happened in 1944 was at the community office, where the people in charge were foreign to the village and therefore reasonably objective. But the community office, at the top of the square, was closed. He asked the man in the kiosk on the corner when the office was likely to be open, and the man in the kiosk told him he couldn't say.

"Maybe this afternoon. Maybe tomorrow morning. Why, are you in a hurry? If you are, don't be."

Ripaldo decided to be vague. "I was hoping to get some information about the village. What there is here for a visitor to see."

"There's nothing here for a visitor to see," the man said. "The place is a desert. Has been as long as I've been here. Though the lady in that community office will try to tell you that you shouldn't miss the Byzantine aqueduct off the main road that you surely missed on your way up here, because the truth is, it's nothing but a ruin. And the only thing important about that ruin is the German soldier who was killed there during the war and the fate he brought with him for everybody in this village."

"So it was just one German soldier who was killed?"

The man studied Ripaldo. "If that's what interests you, my friend, you can get all the information you need about that catastrophe from the patch of dirt floor that's left of the old bakery where they burned eighty people alive that day. Though the lady you're looking for will tell you that you shouldn't miss the new monument down the road here, where they have a list that mixes up those who were burned and those who were slaughtered elsewhere in the village. One hundred and forty-seven names in all, carved out nicely under a mosaic with big red flames that was put there by some modern artist they brought up here to make the whole thing look beautiful."

"Well, if that lady doesn't seem to get things right, who should I talk to about what really happened back then?"

The man shrugged. "Nobody gets things right these days. But talk to Vassílis Angeloúdis over there at the cafe. At least he doesn't lie much any longer. Not the way he used to."

Ripaldo had to wait until the early afternoon to meet Vassílis Angeloúdis, owner of the cafe in question, because Angeloúdis had gone down to the city on an errand. While he waited he managed to find a few village men, middle-aged and older, who were willing to talk to him over a coffee so long as what they had to say wasn't recorded on his machine. The village history he got that way was confusing. Nobody he spoke to had actually witnessed what had happened in September, 1944, because some had been in the mountains at the time or had moved to the village after the war, and very few seemed willing to speak openly to an outsider they didn't know.

One old-timer finally warned Ripaldo that he wasn't likely to get the whole truth out of anybody who had survived the World War or the Civil War. It depended on your politics, he said. Those on the left will tell you that what happened to the village was all the result of rightist collaborators who had planted the rumor that it was leftist ELAS resistance fighters who had come down from the mountain to ambush that German armored car when in fact it was the collaborators who had set up the whole thing in order to raid the village for booty and rid the place of what they considered communist sympathizers. Those on the right will tell you that it was the local communist sympathizers who had done in the village by telling their friends among the ELAS guerrillas camped nearby about the weekly visit of a team of German medical specialists to purify the water source below the village and that this had not only brought on the ambush and the German retaliation but had resulted in the death of some of those whose only crime had been to protect the village water from contamination. So where was the truth? The only truth, the old timer said, anyway the only truth Ripaldo might find both the left and the right agreeing on, was that the

German medical team and their Greek escort who'd been ambushed at the aqueduct had to be counted among the innocent. But, he added, don't say I said so.

Vassílis Angeloúdis proved to be the only old-timer who was willing to talk freely and at length into Ripaldo's tape recorder, but that had to happen over brandy in a back room of the cafe after it had closed. Angeloúdis was a man in his late sixties, large-bellied, with thin reddish hair and apple-red cheeks. He was referred to by some of his customers as Capitan Vassílis because he had commanded an ELAS guerrilla unit during both the Occupation and the Civil War. His cafe had once been a local gathering place for those who belonged to the political left, including both of the two factions that had split the Greek Communist Party some years back. More recently it had seemed home mostly to the left-of-center socialists who became prominent after the colonels' dictatorship. Now it appeared to have a completely mixed clientele of ardent cynics who had no use for any political party then on the horizon.

What Ripaldo came up with over more sweet brandy than his stomach found comfortable turned out to be something other than an interview in the ordinary sense. After his warmup questions to set a relaxed mood, he was barely able to ask Captain Vassílis his leading questions about what had happened during the so-called Hortiáti massacre and the possible role in it of the Austrian Wehrmacht officer now become a distinguished elder statesman before Captain Vassílis' response became an unrestrained monologue. Ripaldo decided to let it run its course, and after typing it up in rough translation and editing it only enough to eliminate his largely irrelevant proddings and some of Captain Vassílis' untranslatable guttural tics and hesitations, he decided that he'd better express mail his draft of the interview to Wittekind in order to get further advice, which would also give him the benefit of some free days to travel to his old haunts in other regions of northern Greece.

DEPOSITION: VASSÍLIS ANGELOÚDIS

Believe me, my friend, there is danger in what you ask of me. It is one thing to accept something the mind cannot escape seeing, and another thing to talk about it before a machine that will make it public and indelible. Once it is out of the bottle in this way, who can put it back in? And you are looking for things that have been buried for half a century, things that most of us in this country who are old enough to have known would prefer not to remember. We are told that one has to learn to live with the past, and I suppose few people would want to argue with that. But how one learns to do this of course depends on who one is and what past one has to live with. I know some who have a past that makes up their whole life and who would be lost if they had to let go of any part of it. And I know others who would do better learning to forget whatever they can of their past. And some who find that easy.

But surely you are not interested in listening to me philosophize, even if we Greeks have a reputation for it. You want facts. The truth. And I imagine you want it without the coloring that bad politics or a troubled memory gives everything one would rather not reveal in the clear light. My mother was a philosopher too, one of your home-made philosophers. I don't know how many times, when I would bring her some crisis in my life, she would say "Vassiláki"— am Vassílis to you and the rest of the world but not to my mother—"Vassiláki," she would say, "I don't really care what you do with your life, because I have to say that I don't expect you to do much with it. And I don't expect you to tell me or anybody else the truth all the time. But never lie to yourself. If you can help it." That was my mother, God forgive her—I mean the last bit, the reservation that allows you a way out. So I no longer lie to myself, and I will not lie to you and your machine. If I can help it.

To answer your first question, no one in this region will dispute that there was a massacre in the village of Hortiáti in September, 1944, or that it was a terrible thing. There is also no question about who committed the massacre—German soldiers under the command of at least one person of some rank carrying a sword and accompanied by Greek collaborators who belonged to the paramilitary group organized by the criminal rightist, Colonel Poulos. Both the Germans and their Greek friends were responsible for killing and maiming the innocent. And there were many innocent still in the village when the German trucks arrived to do their business.

You say you are interested first of all in the identity of those who were in charge of this slaughter. I can understand that. Especially if your purpose is not only to uncover the buried truth about these atrocities that keep showing through the surface of our history like the unknown and unwanted bones of the dead but also to make those still alive who were responsible wash the bones clean. Or, let us say, at least admit that there are bones still to be washed.

Good. But the question that has to be answered first from my personal point of view, accept it or not, is who was responsible for killing the German medical soldier that morning in 1944. And also important, who was responsible for allowing the driver of his armored car to escape with another witness among his passengers, so these two who were still alive could return to the German unit in the village of Asvestochóri to sound the alarm and bring about this unimaginable retaliation. This is the question you haven't asked. So I ask you in turn: how can we understand and judge these acts of so many years ago without seeing the beginning before we look for the end?

Of course the beginning is not entirely clear. What I can say—and I am willing to say it under oath even if this is only a voluntary statement—what I can say is that the guerrilla group I commanded in this region at the time was not responsible for killing that German medical soldier or anybody else involved. There are villagers here who will tell you otherwise out of their distorted memory, no doubt have told you otherwise already. Let me be exact about this. It is true that my guerrilla unit had joined the other *andartes* on the mountain above the village at the time the German medical team was ambushed. And it was certainly our purpose, as much as anybody else's in the resistance, to kill German soldiers even that late in the war, when those who had occupied our country for four years were finally preparing to leave. But our unit was not the one responsible for killing this particular medical soldier and the Greek escort from the Municipal Water Service who came ahead of him in their own car. And I will tell you why.

This is why. First of all, I am not stupid. And the others who were with me in the mountains were not—excuse me—retarded from masturbation. We would not kill those of our own who were providing an essential service for our people. Our group was made up mostly of local *andartes*, men from the village of Hortiáti and other villages in this region. And the truth is, those Greeks from the Municipal Water Service were sent here to purify the water that served our village, as the German medical team was sent to make sure that they did their job correctly since their people depended on the same water source. Of course the Germans were no doubt interested in protecting their own water more than ours. But without that purification, who knows what diseases might have ruined this village long before German troops came up the main road in their trucks to destroy it.

You smile, but you must understand what water means to us— what it meant to us in those difficult days, before the village could be supplied from the main sources that now supply us and before we had electricity to provide the power. All that progress came much later under the dictatorship of the colonels, I suppose the only good thing those fascist buffoons did along with all the terror they spread. Especially among those of us who were sent into exile for being faithful to our belief. But forgive me, that is another issue.

Let me just say here that everything in war soon becomes relative, however it may begin. Believe me, both good and evil come to live a healthy life for a while on both sides. I'm not saying that in the end there isn't likely to be more evil on one side than on the other, and that was surely the case during the war that interests you, but nobody can claim to be entirely pure during a war. I do not claim that for myself. Not for a minute. I have done things, I have killed in cold blood, many people, too many innocent people during the later phase of our civil war. And though it pains me to say it, there were times when I couldn't truthfully say that it was only because I was an *andarte* captain following Party orders. Of course I was very young, and of course I was under pressures of more than one kind, which I must say were—. But you have not come to this village to listen to my confession, especially since there are others here who are quite ready to confess for me. You want facts about the ambush and what it brought with it. Here are the facts that I know.

There were no true witnesses to what happened at the place called Kamara below our village, where we have our water source and where there is a Byzantine aqueduct. The people in the village heard some shooting, that was all. They knew it meant trouble of course, but they didn't know how much trouble. It has been reported that one of the ELAS *andarte* units under the command of a junior officer had come down from the mountain to wait below the village in case the Germans came in that day or the next to gather up our animals for their own uses, as was their practice on occasion. And this unit under inexperienced leadership was supposedly the one responsible first for the ambush that failed to kill the driver and second for leaving their place of hiding immediately afterwards without warning people in the village about what had happened.

I cannot deny this report. But if it is true, it should free my *andarte* unit of any suspicion, because I can guarantee you that, had we been given this assignment, there would have been no idiocy or effeminacy under my command that would have made it possible for that Hun of a driver to escape alive or any others with him. But at the same time, I am not ready to say that I could have found it in my heart to kill any Greek who'd been sent here that day for no other purpose than to purify our water.

You will also hear a report that this ambush was the business of rightist plotters who hoped to use the Germans and their fascist collaborators to punish the village for the support it had given throughout the Occupation to those of us in the mountains fighting for our country and the liberation of its working people. I cannot deny that report either. It is of course entirely believable, but I have to say honestly that nobody has offered any evidence beyond a firm suspicion, born of what I'm afraid is political hatred. Even if there is reason for that hatred.

In any case, the fact is, somebody came from somewhere to kill the German medical soldier who was among those supervising this team of Greek water purifiers. In my personal view, that ambush may well have been an amateur operation. And of course taking place so close to the village insured that our villagers would be the ones to suffer the full reprisal. Which came quickly. Our men on watch along the ridge above the village sighted the trucks full of German soldiers crossing the plain below the village at noon—a whole convoy, some say as many as fourteen, but I didn't count them personally. Anyway, there were enough of them to make me immediately dispatch messengers from our unit to warn other comrades on the mountain.

Of course we knew those trucks would be coming up the road before they actually appeared, because by the time they were sighted most of the men in the village and some of the women had fled up the mountainside—those who had the freedom or the youth to leave everything they had behind once the news of the ambush reached them. And a few of these had already arrived at our camp to tell us what they could about the attack on the German medical team.

There couldn't have been many in the village who didn't know that they would be made to pay for this ambush, but there were some who thought the Germans might settle for burning a few houses or at worst rounding up a few men unlucky enough to be selected for retaliatory execution. And there were also some who gambled that there would be no reprisal once the village President and the priest explained to the Germans that the village had not been responsible for the ambush, that it had happened well below the village, on the main road to the city.

So there were even a few entirely sound men who chose to stay behind to protect their families and their property as best they could. After all, we had been forced to house German soldiers in our own homes for many months, and we had learned to live with them peacefully. Why should they choose to harm the innocent so late in a war they were now doomed to lose? And the President had been good at bargaining for favors with those in command of our region, providing them with wood for the winter and feed for their animals even beyond what they demanded, while also making sure that enough was left behind to take care of our own needs.

But they say that when the Germans arrived in their trucks, the President barely had a chance to speak, and the priest had no chance at all. The retaliation was quick and efficient. The trucks came up the hill and lined up below the village square, and when they had discharged their troops, they loaded the trucks with what things of value they could gather from the houses nearby before they began to burn the village down house by house. Some say the German soldier in charge and the two leaders of the Greek paramilitary group who worked for him interrogated people in the cafe that the President owned on the main square, but others say there was no interrogation because when the President came out to greet these visitors by extending his hand, the German in charge slashed his arm with his sword.

You don't believe he would have had a sword? That is what they say in the village, but I wasn't here to see whether this was true or not. What is certain, though, is that the President still made an effort to explain that the village was not at fault for what had happened and to plead for mercy, and whatever it was that had caused his wound made him faint from loss of blood before he could finish his plea. After that, the priest was shot in cold blood, though not before he was allowed to witness the killing of his two daughters and the others who had gathered around him for protection.

The few witnesses whose fate it was to survive and drink for the rest of their lives from this bitter cup of memory blame what happened then more on the Greek collaborators than on the German soldiers they served. It is, I suppose, one curse of our race that we sometimes come to hate each other during wartime more than the strangers who do us harm, for example not only during our civil war, which goes without saying, but even during our failed campaign against the Turks and even during this war against the Italians and Germans that we finally won. In any case, if the witnesses who survived the massacre can be believed, it appears to be true that it was a leader of the collaborators named Kapetanakis who told the Germans that they should stop wasting their ammunition by spraying the gathered villagers with bullets. It was more practical, he said, to guide them into the local bakery not far from the square and then burn that to the ground.

And that is what happened, though it embarrasses me to say so openly. Embarrasses me as a Greek, I mean. But I'm sure you don't want to hear about what I may feel or not feel as a Greek, you want facts about what happened, and the fact appears to be that some of those collaborators brought together by Colonel Poulos—fascists, bums, cold-blooded murderers, call them what you want as long as you don't call them Greeks—were the first to press the villagers forward into that bakery. And those who were slow to move, especially the children and the elderly, were killed on the spot, their throats slit. Quickly, no emotion, no fuss, as you would slaughter a goat or a lamb. And those who were laid aside this way would be left there on the ground for the German soldiers to shoot dead. Until one of the Germans in charge of soldiers burning houses farther away put a stop to that. So there was no longer mercy for the wounded even.

I can't say if this was the Austrian officer with the long nose and weak chin who interests you most, because nobody described the man exactly. The only German or Austrian in a position of command whose name has been spoken by the witnesses who survived was one Schubert, the hated Wehrmacht soldier with the sword who was said to be not an officer but a high-ranking sergeant in a special unit for dealing with partisans and who knew enough Greek to swear at those he was about to kill in language that would embarrass me to use in front of most men, let alone women and children. You know, calling his victims passive queers, ass lickers, communist pimps, and I don't know what else.

You may be interested to know that this sergeant made the mistake of returning to Greece after the war as a tourist, a thing that allowed us to provide him with the same fate that he had dealt out to so many others, though of course in his case by way of a legal execution. As happened with Colonel Poulos as well. But these two were the only people I can remember being executed for war crimes in our region, which shows you how terrible they must have been, since there were enough fascists in the post-war government to protect your ordinary murderers and thieves who worked for the Germans. In any case, whoever the other officer or soldier who moved in to stop the bloody business outside the bakery, I imagine he thought that this Greek way of slaughtering people was not the German way. The rules of reprisal maybe called for more military discipline, more thoroughness, without the jagged edges left by knives and bayonets and the mess of wounded bodies.

What happened afterward was told to us late in the evening of that day by one of the few survivors who escaped from inside the bakery and climbed the mountain to our hideout. This woman reported that the German soldiers were not rough, in fact they were sometimes gentle with the women and the children, but they were insistent and of course they had bayoneted rifles. And it seems that some of our villagers thought they were being crowded into that bakery for their own protection now that the burning of houses was almost complete and the shooting seemed to be over. That is, until one of the Germans in charge came to the door and ordered people to stand back so that two of his men could spread some kind of yellow powder along the inside of the bakery's front wall. And when the powder was lit and burning well, the soldiers shut the bakery door.

The woman who survived could not talk easily about what happened then. All she could remember was the sound of the panic in that place and her own luck. She had managed to climb up to the platform at the back of the bakery where there were tables for kneading the bread and a window that opened to the back of the building, and as flames rose from the space below and smoke made the air too thick to breathe, she clawed her way up the back wall and hurled herself out of the window. She landed on others who had done the same thing and were lying there wounded, but she didn't stop to see who they were, she crawled away and fled until she was clear of that place and the houses near it and finally the village itself.

Believe me, the gods usually see to it that there is some leak in man's efficiency, whatever his purpose. This was one of the few leaks that day from what was then known as the Gouramanis bakery. When our villagers who had run away came down from the mountain and the hills some weeks later, after the Germans had left our country, all they found in the ruins of that bakery were ashes and pieces of bone.

You asked if I knew whether those responsible for this massacre were German or Austrian. How would I know? German, Austrian, what's the difference? We had both kinds in Macedonia, and you could never tell one from the other when they were in uniform. They all behaved the same, at least from the distance we saw them, and the only time we in the mountains came close enough to see what they might really be like was when they were dead. Besides, wasn't Hitler Austrian? So if you think there may be a difference in how those officers or soldiers conducted their business of slaughtering the innocent, you won't get anything useful out of me, though others will tell you that the Austrians were better than the

Germans. And I can assure you that you will find some who will tell you the opposite.

Of course these soldiers were following orders. That is what you read these days in the newspapers whenever someone is brought back out of hiding from that war to explain why he did this or that. But were their orders to burn every house in the village and kill every living thing they could catch so that only ashes and fragments of bone were left for burial and nothing else to feed the village memory? If it was simply a matter of orders, how is it that even most of those who stayed behind but managed to escape to the edge of the village were shot before they could break away? What harm would it do to allow a child to go free or a woman whose time was near? It seems no one was given that gift of life. No one earned any mercy, not even one woman who had the courage to try and strangle the Greek collaborator who took her child from her when she refused to follow others into the bakery and thereby lost most of her face to a bayonet. What, my American friend, makes you think you will now find a single officer— German, Austrian, whatever mixture—who has the courage, or maybe just the bad conscience, to admit having ordered the things that happened in Hortiáti that day?

I say this with passion and I believe it, but at the same time, I again feel embarrassed in saying it. I am forced by what I say to confess something, even if it is beyond the facts you may want about what took place so many years ago. I myself have followed orders when it came to killing innocent people. You are a foreigner, so you can't know all that went on here, and I don't mean only during our Occupation but in the years that followed, after the Germans left our country. I have told you that I was an *andarte* captain during the period of our civil war and that I was young—barely twenty, to be exact. And at one point when things were turning too much against us and the monarcho-fascist army of those years was clearly winning the war, it became our Party's policy to eliminate its enemies, or possible enemies, by the most simple and direct means. The purpose was to assure a following even if it meant doing so by means of terror.

I didn't object to the policy. I let myself think that others knew better than I did about the virtues of one political strategy over another. I was ignorant in those days. I hadn't yet taken advantage of the education provided me after the war by the rightist government that sent me to prison on the island of Makronissos, where there was much time for contemplation and debate and even secret reading. I'm not speaking of the official education they provided in their attempt to cure my diseased mind by way of their nationalist propaganda. I'm speaking of the hidden school I attended in the prison barracks, where books were passed around unseen and the debate was sometimes in a private language, I suppose the way our forefathers educated themselves under the Turkish Occupation.

But long after Makronissos I was still ignorant enough to think that the Party knew best, so what might one have expected of a twenty-year old? In any case, I have to confess that during the civil war I followed the Party's orders to commit murder. I would go with my men into one village or another and gather up those in the area who had money or authority and who were not on our side, and I would supervise their execution. I even shot people myself. Ten, fifteen, I never stopped to count. And of course the policy proved a disaster, because each of those we shot had a family, and friends of the family, who repaid us by their hatred until there were many villages in the region we occupied where we ended up with almost no supporters at all.

So much for following orders. So much for learning to live with the blood on one's hands. But I can see that you are not interested in our civil war and the passions we Greeks still have to face whenever someone mentions that godless time. You want to know about Germans and Austrians and who was in charge of these ruthless killers who massacred our village in the year 1944. I can tell you something you may find useful, but I cannot tell you anything certain about the officer who seems to interest you most. What I know for a start is that the Germans had their headquarters in two places. The group that was supposed to provide intelligence about where and how the resistance was operating in our region had its headquarters in the village of Arsakli, in the elementary school house. But the main headquarters of the occupying forces in our region was at the American school you will find a short distance below the village of Arsakli—you know that school? and the village? In any case, as you see, it is no longer a village now but almost a suburb of the city, and it is no longer called by the name given it when it was settled by refugees from Asia Minor but by the high-class name Panórama.

So, you know Panórama too, and you know that the American school was called the College though it was actually a gymnasium of some kind. Fine. How can I be sure of what headquarters was there during the Occupation? It's simple. My wife worked at the American College as a cleaning woman, though she was not my wife at the time. She was a girl of eighteen. And a truly beautiful girl in those days, even if I am the one to say it. Beautiful and smart the way village women are who know themselves entirely and who have an extra eye in the back of their heads. Her name is Marina. My point is, she knew much that went on among the Germans and Austrians both in Arsaklí and in the headquarters below the village—not everything, but enough to make her of possible value to those of us in the resistance, which is how I first came to know her. You might say that I was sent to recruit her, only the truth is, I sent myself.

Forgive me if I tell you the story. It may amuse you. Even if it may also appear to be at my expense. I knew about Marina because she lived with her family on the upper edge of Arsaklí, and her father was one of us. That is, until he was killed during a skirmish with the enemy on the far side of Mt. Hortiáti early in their campaign to root us out. Of course we did what we could to stay in touch with the families of those who lost their men, but it wasn't always possible in the case of Arsaklí, so close to Salonika, with German officers in the village school and housed below it in the few villas that had been built by the city's rich along the main road during the dictatorship of General Metaxas.

I had seen Marina for the first time not long after her father was killed, God forgive him. Maybe a month or so after that fated skirmish, I managed to make my way down to her village with two other men during the night and return her father's few personal things to the family. Which at that time of night meant her mother, while the rest of the family hovered out of sight in the background. That is, except for Marina, the oldest, who was allowed to get dressed and bring us our teaspoon of sweet and a coffee on a tray, her hair loose, almost to her waist, and her eyelids a little puffy—

but what dark almonds those eyes were if you caught sight of them as they passed over you. Though I have to say that she barely looked at us, either because she was pretending to be shy or didn't find much worth her while to look at. I assure you on the other hand that I saw enough of her to keep my teaspoonful of cherry preserve from sliding sweetly down my throat the way it should have. Still, that isn't the heart of the matter. The heart came later.

I learned from her mother that the girl was working at the American College, where the mother had also once worked, in the days before the school was taken over by the Greek army as a hospital and then by the German army. I didn't make much of this at the time. I suppose I was too absorbed with the girl herself. But I thought about it later, as my men and I made our way back to our hideout in the mountains. We knew that the College buildings were being used as offices by the staff of the main headquarters, in fact, at one time we had hoped to blow up one or another of those buildings if we could somehow manage to get into a place so well guarded and so close to the outskirts of the city. We hadn't managed it, and for a while I thought that was a good thing, because as long as the place remained occupied, there was a chance we might find a way to learn our enemy's plans for destroying what they could of us and our city before we got around to destroying them.

Marina was the way I found. But let me tell you, it was not easy. Once I'd thought this idea through, I took it upon myself to persuade her to help us, and for her protection as well as mine I did so without telling anybody else, not her family, not my comrades, nobody. This is how it happened—the persuasion, I mean. She walked to work in those days   what else could she do?—through the village and down the hill on the main road until that ended where the Germans had cut it off with barbed wire to protect their headquarters. I made sure of what she did at what time by scouting that road early one morning from a point just below the village, watching her make her way down almost as far as the guarded opening in the barbed wire enclosure around the American school.

It was over a month later before I got back to her village, because we had business farther east with another guerrilla group of the

Right that was giving us more trouble than the Germans in those days—but I can see from your expression that such internal political problems don't interest you now. Why should they when they were so easily forgotten by our own people, especially those who came to power once our struggle was over? In any case. To return to my story.

Marina of course knew nothing of my plans for her and so expected nothing. My God. I can't believe what I did to her that day. I found a place to hide along the main road not far below the village, a ditch that had thick brush between it and the road, enough to keep me concealed from those who went by but not enough to prevent a quick move when the moment was right. I had plenty of time to watch her approach around a bend in the road, and the distance to the next bend was short enough to give me confidence that I could do what I had to do without being seen by anybody coming from either direction if I did it suddenly and swiftly. I let her get just past me, holding my breath, and then I pounced.

I knew what to do to seal her mouth. I'd had some practice by then. But of course since I couldn't slit her throat, there was a problem as to how long I could keep her quiet. She struggled like a demon. Still, I managed to drag her back into the ditch and hold her down there with one arm and the pressure of my body, my hand still over her mouth. The one time I got a flash from her eyes, it nearly unmanned me. I held her there and talked quietly into her ear, told her not to be afraid, I had no intention of hurting her, I just wanted her to calm down so that I could talk to her about very serious business. The fuzz of her hair against my mouth was damp, and she gave off an animal odor, not pleasant but not unpleasant either, a mixture of sweat and fear, I would say, and her own personal odor, that I came to know so well later on. In any case, the more I talked to her, trying to keep my voice steady and slow despite what was going on inside me, the more she relaxed. I finally decided that I could release my hold and back away from her just a little.

That was a mistake. The minute I was off of her, she swung around and clawed at me, like a rabid cat, so that I had to hold her hands tight and swing her around again to get her hands behind her, which made her call out. "Please don't fight me," I said to her.

"I don't want to hurt you. But I'll have to if you don't keep quiet, because it could be the end for both of us if we're heard by the Germans or their friends coming along the road." She was panting, but she didn't say anything, and gradually I got her to settle down so that I could hold her from behind without having to worry about protecting my eyes and cheeks and who knows what else. And that was when I told her what I had in mind.

It took her a while to believe me. I explained that it was necessary to ambush her that way because secrecy was essential. I said that for her own protection I didn't want anybody to know that we'd met to talk about what I needed to talk to her about, even if it wasn't exactly a normal way of meeting and even if she hadn't chosen to hear what I had to say. And then I told her that I wanted her help—more than that—her pledge to keep an eye and ear open for anything she might find out from the Germans she worked for that could be valuable for our group in the mountains and the resistance movement. She looked at me as though I was without the slightest doubt insane. "You are quite insane," she said. "Now get away from me." And she tried to break free, so that I had to grab hold of her again, more fiercely than my heart would have wanted. Then I said: "Think of your father. Don't do it for me or my men. Do it for him."

The gods had inspired me. Marina became relaxed again. Then she began to cry. When I tried to hold her to comfort her, she thrust her elbow into me so that I lost my breath. "Leave me alone," she said. "You're not a man, you're a filthy animal." That hurt me. Really. I loosened my hold on her. "All right," I said. "Go ahead. Go work for your German friends. And hope that your father is not watching you from his grave." She got up and brushed herself off. "You better hope he's not watching you," she said. "He would cut off your head. And the Germans are not my friends. I have no choice but to work for them now that my father is dead. Who is supposed to take care of us? You animals who took him off to be killed in the mountains?" That made me lose heart completely. I let Marina climb back up on the road. "If you change your mind," I called after her, barely loud enough for her to hear, "you know where to look for me."

It took her another three months to do that. And she didn't

approach me directly but through one of my men. It was in the late summer of that year, anyway after the Feast of the Holy Virgin as I remember, the days getting shorter, and we had just come back from another engagement in the west and had begun to set up our fall quarters on the mountain. I had sent some of our men out to the neighboring villages to stock up on provisions so that we would be prepared for the colder weather and simply to keep them occupied. Men get restless between engagements, when the anticipation and the excitement are gone, so it is best to keep them active doing something, even if only a raid here and there and a chance for a moment of domesticity. In any case, one of my men returned to our camp from one of these outings and asked to see me in private. "I have a letter for you," he said when we were alone, and he handed me an envelope with nothing written on the outside of it. I asked him where it was from. "Arsakli," he said. "It was given to me by a girl." I studied his face. "A girl from the village. Not a girl I know," he said. And when I opened the letter, what I found in it was not anything written for my eyes, but a curious document, a thing I couldn't understand because it was in a foreign language, written on a typewriter.

So, my friend. You can imagine my surprise on receiving such a letter, and my confusion. What was I to make of it? From the shape it seemed an official letter of some kind, with no heading but with a date that the numbers showed was in July, 1944, and no signature except for a handwritten omega. That is, what looked something like an omega in Greek, a bit slanted, but turned out to be a letter in German that we don't have in our alphabet. This I found out when I went to the one person I knew who could give me some explanation, a school teacher in Kavalla, who was one of us and who had some knowledge of foreign languages.

It took me almost a week to reach this man, and what he told me was that he could not entirely explain the document except to say that it was in fact a document, written in what he understood to be German from the little he knew of that language. He also said that it appeared to be a report concerning English commandos on some island that I didn't recognize. He said the names and some other words appeared to be in English, the one language he knew well from his pre-war schooling at this American College where Marina worked.

No, unfortunately I do not remember the English names or any other names connected with this document. As I said, the thing was unsigned except for this one initial, and it was a thing I could not read. So I cannot speak about names. And I must admit that at the time, once I decided the document did not have to do with our activities in the mountains but with those of some foreign group on an island, what interested me most about the thing was the unspoken message in it from the girl who had arranged for it reach my hands. Clearly Marina had finally given in to my persuasion, even if it had taken her some months. The question now was what use I could make of this.

So, my American friend, as is true of so many things in the life of this country, fate answered my question. I had no sooner returned to our new camp near Livadi than we were brought under pressure by a German unit that had somehow learned of our being there and came out in force to find us. We had to move deeper into Chalkidiki, into the mountains above Arnea, and then gradually work our way back to Mt. Hortiáti. It was September by the time we returned there. No chance for me to get myself to Arsaklí before that. Then, on September 2nd, unforgettable date, the massacre of Hortiáti village that I've described took place. We had more than we could cope with during the days after that, with so many who escaped from the village just ahead of the slaughter now arriving at our camp for help. And by the time things settled down enough for me to ease my way into Arsaklí, Marina was gone from her home.

This is perhaps of little interest to you, but it was of vital interest to me at the time. Marina had moved to the city the day after the Hortiáti massacre. I was told that she had gone there to live with her aunt, who was sick and needed attention, but even then I didn't believe this was the only reason. And when I learned that the aunt had been sick for months, I became convinced that Marina's sudden move into the city had to do more with the massacre and less with the aunt. But it took me some years to learn the exact truth, years after our marriage, because it was not a subject Marina cared to discuss. What she told me was that after the ruthless burning of that village, it became impossible for her to continue working for the Germans, not for an hour, not for a minute. And this meant she also had to leave her village and go into the city in case those animals from the German headquarters at the American College came after her for abandoning her duties without a word. That is what she told me, and to this day I have not felt the need to question her about it.

You can understand that of course the immediate result of her move was devastating for me. Not only did it spoil my plans for gathering further information from the Germans she had worked for, but it spoiled my plans for seeing more of Marina. Yes, I will admit that my motives in all this were confused. As I have mentioned, I was only a little over twenty at the time, and our national struggle was not the only thing on my mind even if I was an *andarte* captain in the field. How could my imagination not remember what I had seen of that dark girl? How could my skin not feel how close to her I had been, even if only for minutes and awkwardly? Her look, yes, her smell—they haunted me in the mountains. And so did the beautiful meaning I gave to the fact that she had sent me that secret document.

Where is the document now? I'm afraid that is a thing you will have to ask Marina, as I will explain in a minute. I see that you are restless to hear more facts about our terrible history and less about my personal life, so I will not go on to tell you how I persuaded Marina to be my wife, a thing that—believe me—required almost ten years. Let me just say that getting her consent was a task that nearly exhausted me—I mean in a spiritual sense. You may hear from others that by the time she agreed to the marriage she was an easy target because she was not so young any longer. And of course some will say that she was deeply scarred by the difficult moment in her past when she worked for the Germans. That is all nonsense. She was not an easy target. She was in fact the same at twenty-seven as she was at eighteen, desirable enough to drive any normal man out of his mind but almost impossible to handle. Not only by me but by others who had her best interests at heart. And what in her case had happened or not happened with the Germans was long forgotten by the time my intermediary finally came to an agreement with her mother.

You look surprised, but that was the way of things in those days.

Though I can't say that this agreement was exactly the last of it. It was the beginning of the end, and if you are interested you can hear from Marina herself about what followed and why she decided finally to give in to her mother's persuasion. You can also ask her whatever else you want to about those days in 1944 that now seem so important to you and the people you work for—or, for that matter, about the days after the war. And as for documents that were once in my hand, part of the marriage agreement was that I return to her whatever I still held that pointed to her having worked for the Germans during the Occupation and that I keep my mouth sealed about that period in her life.

All I care to say concerning our days together since the time that interests you is that we have made a reasonable life for ourselves against the odds. We have survived our country's bad politics and our own foolish belief that a new world order was possible. I myself had two opportunities for a long vacation to look at the world while on prison islands in the Aegean, once under the king and once under the colonels' dictatorship. I learned much of value gazing out from behind the barbed wire during those vacations, much about national loyalties and human patience and the mythologies of belief. If the purpose of making me an exile in my own country was to cleanse me, I suppose I can say that I am cleaner than I once was. Certainly clean of illusions. Certainly clean of hatred for anyone who has suffered from forced exile, whatever the supposed political crime, whatever the party loyalty that caused the crime.

My friend, I assure you that I am not deliberately avoiding further discussion of German or Austrian officers and the atrocities that, without question, they committed during their occupation of my country. I no longer have any need to protect either myself or my wife by pretending not to know things I know for certain. So I can tell you in all honesty that I myself know nothing specific about this particular officer who concerns you most. Whether Marina knows more, I am not in a position to say. Perhaps she does. As I said, you are free to ask her yourself. I might just add that I have not followed the gentleman's subsequent career as an important political figure, because by the time he rose to take his place on the world stage, I had walked out of the theater, so to speak. No more interest in either domestic or international politics. My only political activity since the treachery of the colonels' dictatorship has been talking more than I should while managing my cafe in this village and supporting my friends—friends of the right kind, of course. Friends who are as disgusted with politics as I am.

In any case, you will have gathered by now that my knowledge of what was going on during the period of the German Occupation was somewhat limited because my operations in this area were confined to the neighboring hills and mountains. Except for a few sorties into the outskirts of the city, such as the one to recruit Marina. And once the Germans were gone from here—but that is another story. Our civil war clearly has nothing to do with the crimes that interest you. But I want to say just one thing more about the issue of crimes committed during wars. I say this: do not be too quick to judge. The issue is complicated.

At the same time, don't misunderstand me. You will never find me defending those who were responsible for this German policy of reprisal, of going into a village and killing ten Greek men and then fifty Greek men and then one hundred Greek men for every German soldier killed. That is hubris by the self-proclaimed master race, that is idiocy, insanity, call it what you will. And of course the more men killed under such a policy, the fewer remained in the villages, because those still alive would run to the hills to join the resistance, whether ours or our political opponent's. And it wasn't long before the Germans had to fulfill this—what shall I call it?—this hydra-headed quota of theirs by killing women, and the very old or the very young that the women were left to care for. I've told you what happened in Hortiáti at the end of the Occupation, when the war was no longer theirs to decide. What more is there to say? Madness. Evil hungering after evil for so long that it turned back to feed on itself.

I will tell you something else. Political policy is one thing, a person's action is another thing. From my point of view, there are few of us who are so pure as to have earned the right to pass judgment on others so long after the moment, especially if one has never been in a war. Of course there are those who have clearly earned the right, those who have suffered from the depravity of others and who are themselves pure at heart. Which is why I do not mean to speak for you, my friend, and the people you work for, who must surely be among these. Even if your country and others besides Germany have not been so pure in the role they have played in our recent history—certainly not Italy, which hoped to invade us under Mussolini, nor England under Churchill early in our civil war, nor America under Truman with its terrible Helldiver airplanes late in that war that defeated the already defeated, meaning me and my comrades. But forgive me, perhaps I speak out of a private bitterness that still distorts the way I see things. I really mean to speak only for myself when I say that I do not have the right to judge. Let me explain why. Or better still, let me tell you a truthful story. About myself.

I've mentioned this policy I was made to follow during our civil war. It was sometimes a policy of retaliation, sometimes of terror, and in the end it was both evil and unproductive. And since of course evil breeds evil, as all of us learn in school, we Greeks especially, no good came out of this for anybody. As no good came out of the White Terror that was unleashed against us resistance fighters of the Left by those in power on the Right after the Varkiza Agreement. Enough about that. I speak of things that have no meaning for you. By way of example, let me simply speak of this one episode I lived through late in our civil war.

There is a village in this area which I think it best for me not to name, a village that has had the usual political history, half right, half left, half in between. But during the third stage of our civil war, it was considered ours more than theirs or anybody else's. We had friends in that village, no doubt about that, and it was often a source of supplies for those of us who were then in the mountains once again. Still, we had enemies in the village as well, though never openly declared—not in those days. This became obvious when some of my men reported to me what they had found when they went to that village one night to collect wine and raki from the local grocer, the local grocer who was one of us. What they found at the cafe opposite the grocery store, resting on a plate in the middle of an outdoor table, was the grocer's head.

What was I to do with this news my men brought me? Ignore it? Pretend that this crime hadn't happened? Allow what friends we still had in that village to consider us unfeeling cowards? We depended on their good will, on their allegiance. And my men depended on me to be strong in my command. So I had no choice but to go back to that village with five of my men and find a head to put beside the one outside the cafe. That was the style of war in those days, the expected thing.

This action took us part of a night and a day. To make our point, we chose the richest farmer in the area, a man whose land we had sometimes raided because he had more fields than he could handle and even a cow from the nearby farm school, also run by Americans before the war, like the school where Marina once worked. We ambushed this man at the morning milking, early, while he was alone, and to muffle his cries we put the half-filled milk pail over his head.

Again, it embarrasses me to speak of this now. A disgusting business. I remember the mixture of blood and spilled milk on the stable floor and it makes my stomach turn. Of course since I was in command, I had to sever the head, and I made a mess of it because my knife was too small. And when it was done, one of my men wiped the blood off the man's face with his handkerchief, as though that made a difference to the poor man—or to us. We propped the body against the wall and put the milk pail where the head had been, and then we put the head in a feed sack so that we could march with it into town, as arrogant as you can imagine. When we reached the village, we found a plate and set it on the cafe table and put the head on it beside the other one that was rotting there. And then we went back to the hills.

I have not been in that village since. The army appeared a few days later to guard it, so it was no longer of much use to us during the civil war. And by the time I returned from my first unplanned post-war vacation at government expense on the prison island I mentioned, I had other reasons for not going back to that village. But the memory of that necessary action stayed with me. What had this man done to deserve such a fate? I couldn't even be sure what his politics were because I didn't know him and he didn't know us. He was simply well-to-do, maybe from his own labor, maybe not. But one morning it is suddenly all over for him. Instead of finishing his work and maybe going to the cafe to gossip with his friends, he ends up there with his head on a plate. And I end up with his head on my conscience.

So much for crimes during our civil war. Some of them will never disappear for some of us, whether we speak about them or not, and most of us no longer choose to do so. That is a personal matter, one lives with one's God as one has to. Forgive my digressions. I will try to say something more about this officer who interests you most—all I can personally tell you in answer to your specific question about what he may have known or not known concerning what the Germans did to the Jews of our city. I'm afraid that I can speak only in general terms, but I think I can do so with certainty. If he was at the German intelligence headquarters in Arsakli during the summer of 1942, he would without doubt have heard about the registration of all male Jews in Eleftheria Square in July of that year because it was a scandal. Worse than that. A disciplined torture. Ten thousand men were made to stand in the heat and perform exercises, like school children, some too old to walk well let alone bend and squat and jump in place with their arms flopping this way and that. No hats allowed under that sun. And as the day drew on, those who fainted were kicked alive again, or revived by cold water in the face, so that they could go on with their exercises, while the German soldiers who were humiliating them in this way laughed at their awkwardness. And so did a troupe of German actors and actresses who had been brought in to entertain the local German army and who watched this spectacle from their hotel balconies above the square. I don't exaggerate. Though I didn't see this myself, there are more personal accounts of it than you would have the patience to listen to. From survivors and observers alike.

But of course this was nothing compared to what happened in the spring and summer of 1943. Again, if your man was in this region, what happened then could not have escaped the notice of anyone within five-hundred kilometers of Salonika, to say nothing of Arsakli on the edge of the city, where the stench of what the Germans did—I speak metaphorically—would have been unbearable for many days. Over 50,000 Jews of all ages were sent out of our city, their city as much as ours, in less than six months. Maybe 2,000 returned from Poland after the war. So, if the officer who interests you was in Arsakli during that spring or the months that followed, how could he not have smelled the stench of what his own army did? And if his long nose was so insensitive, would not his large ears have heard about it from others? An officer in German intelligence? Five kilometers away? I assume you have asked this question knowing the answer already.

But let me say one more thing. All German officers are not the same. Those of us in the resistance during the Occupation have a way of thinking they were because of course for us the enemy had to remain impersonal while we were killing it, and the evil we were fighting had to be single. Which in reality it generally was. But what I now have need to say comes from information that reached us by way of the Jews themselves. There were some Jews who escaped to join us when it became clear what end the German policy regarding their people was leading them towards—not many Jews from Salonika, who were the first to go north to Poland, but those from regions to the west of here, from Yannina and even Corfu. By the time the Germans came to gather up these communities for shipment north, the Jews had some idea from the silence of others who had gone ahead of them that they would never return if they took the long train ride to the new life that was promised them.

This is what I learned from one who escaped this fate and came to us via Yannina. Like other Jews who joined the resistance, he had more book knowledge than most, and he was not only smart enough to have saved himself but slowly to have become a leader in his resistance group. What he told us you may not believe, but it is true. It was verified by other witnesses later and by historical documents. This man was originally from Corfu, and he said that the German officer who was in charge of that region had done everything he could to convince his superiors that sending the Jews away from the island would create great unrest among the Greek population. Though this was late in the war, the spring of 1944, his superiors were not moved by his arguments. They had orders directly from Himmler, they said. So special envoys were sent to Corfu to investigate the situation there and to make plans for sending the Jewish community to the mainland and from there to oblivion beyond our borders. At the last minute the officer intervened again, insisting that there were no ships available for transport of local Jews to the mainland. Besides, he said, the local population would consider such transport immoral. He used that word. A German officer. So there was at least one man occupying this country who did his best to remain clean—not that it made much difference in the long run. Enough ships were found, and in the end only one in twenty belonging to that Jewish community returned to Corfu after the war.

My friend, forgive me for suggesting that this officer should interest you as well because he tells you something about others who say they could do nothing during the war but follow the orders of their superiors. Think what it must have meant for this German to argue against his country's policy, against the officers above him in the army, even against Himmler himself? Where did he find his courage? And did he survive his war or did he disappear into oblivion as well? Of course he did not become an international figure like your man, but even if his fate remains obscure, what he did should give you ammunition in making your case against the officer with the long nose and the large ears once you find out exactly what he knew and what he did while he was in our country. And, my American friend, let me hope that the gods are good enough to help you with that. I myself can do no more.

TWO

Vassílis Angeloúdis' deposition, express-mailed to Count Wittekind, prompted a long phone call to Ripaldo's hotel in Salonika. Wittekind told Ripaldo that the 1944 document Angeloúdis had described in an off-hand way and that had been of no interest to him because it apparently had to do with English commandos on some unspecified Greek island was in fact of great interest to his committee. Not only did it carry the familiar initial, but the substance of it could prove crucial because it might establish beyond doubt the connection between the Big O as the young Ic/AO intelligence officer in Arsaklí and certain so-called interrogations at the headquarters there that had resulted in the murder of uniformed commandos, a blatant violation of the Geneva Convention. Getting hold of that document was now Ripaldo's first order of business.

"But of course we are interested in any other documents the good lady may have," Wittekind said. "And any information about what Wehrmacht officers were where at what time when massacres occurred in the region under the command of Arsaklí intelligence."

"Well, I've got to warn you," Ripaldo said. "There's no guarantee she still has that document, let alone anything else useful."

"Of course there is no guarantee," Wittekind said. "There never is in this business. I just ask you to do your best for us."

"I will do my best. But the lady may not want to speak to me at all."

"You have to make her speak," Wittekind said. "We are counting on you."

"How am I supposed to make her speak?"

"Flattery, Ripaldo. Persuasion. Bribery. You know what works best in that country."

"Not with a village woman who has eyes in the back of her head."

"In any case, you will also want to find out how this Marina Angeloúdis came by the commando document that must have been prepared by our distinguished statesman at the intelligence headquarters in Arsaklí when she was not actually working there but at the main headquarters down the road. Just a small detail I picked up from the deposition. But maybe important."

"And a detail I picked up is that this woman may be especially sensitive about what she was doing where during the war. Her husband was a little cagey on the subject, as though there may be wartime secrets even he didn't know about."

"If anyone can find out the lady's secrets it's you, Ripaldo. I've told my people here you are a genius at that, so please, do not let me down."

"You're the one who's a genius at that, Wittekind. All I know is what I learned from you."

"As always, just be gentle but firm, my friend. And remember that we are after the real truth, not the convenient truth of those with a hollow memory. Am I coming through clearly?"

The extended village that used to be called Arsaklí and is now called Panórama lies on a slope below the tableland that carries the highway leading to the village of Hortiáti. Panórama was where Vassílis Angeloúdis now lived with his wife Marina, in the two-story concrete house he had built some ten years previously to replace the humbler one that had come to him as his wife's dowry, along with the second-hand Jeep that he had used for some years to travel back and forth to his Hortiáti cafe. The Angeloúdis house was on a narrow street in the older section of the village, not far from the school house that in 1944 had served as the Ic/AO intelligence headquarters of Army Group E, the northern command center for the Wehrmacht's anti-partisan activities late in the

German Occupation.

Ripaldo followed up on his conversation with Wittekind by driving up from Salonika through Panórama to Angeloúdis' cafe in Hortiáti village because that was the only way he could get through to him, his cafe phone apparently out of order or in a state of delinquency. When Ripaldo arrived there he found Angeloúdis just coming out of his afternoon siesta in the back room, his eyes narrow, distant. Was there any chance, Ripaldo asked him, assuming it was not an intrusion, that he might follow him back to Panórama whenever it was convenient for him to take a break and arrange for him to spend an hour or so with his wife Marina to clear up a few questions that had come up, as Angeloúdis had been good enough to suggest might be possible during their interview the previous week.

Angeloúdis asked him to sit down, he'd have to think about the matter. Then he called his waiter over and told him to bring two medium coffees. Then he asked Ripaldo to please call him Vassílis and to please drop the formal plural and use the familiar singular in addressing him since he considered the two of them to have become friends. But about the matter of his wife, he felt that might be a thing that would take some time, maybe a day or two. Marina was not very comfortable with strangers, he said, and she was sometimes touchy when it came to talk of the war years. Ripaldo would have to wait until there had been time to soften her up a bit, ease her into the possibility.

"Not that Marina has anything to hide," Vassílis said. "Not anything I know of. But in general, for her the past is the past and the present enough of a problem to keep her mind busy without using it to dig up old memories."

"I understand," Ripaldo said. "I don't want her to dig up anything that would make her uncomfortable in any way. Nothing personal. Just whatever public documents she may have kept. And I'd like a chance to check out some facts of local history that she may be able to verify for me."

"Aha, local history. That is really my enthusiasm more than hers. What local history in particular?"

"I was thinking of her village. The village the two of you now live in. But back when it was called Arsaklí."

"So," Vassílis said. "I suppose that is a history worth your time, though I'm not sure why. Would you like to know how it became a village for human beings, even if only Asia Minor refugees, out of a hillside meant for sheep and goats?"

"I had in mind more recent history. During Marina's lifetime."

"Well, I have to tell you that Marina was among the first to be born in the village of Arsaklí," Vassílis said. "She once told me that the only good thing about being there in those early years was the air she breathed—clean, sweet, the kind that makes your mouth water. Especially when there's too little else to fill it."

"It must have been hard on her. I mean trying to make a decent life out of good air alone."

"Life was hard for all of us," Vassílis said. "Especially since our parents had the refugee mentality that God will provide come better or worse. But I myself can remember days on this mountainside when the air was clear enough to let you count the caiques in Salonika harbor. Which was about as much as any of us up here saw of the city in those years, because the only way you could reach it from my village of Hortiáti or Marina's village of Arsaklí was by the one truck that traveled our one dirt road, and that happened only on days when the truck owner found it profitable enough to test both his fate and yours in that insane way."

"Well, it looks like God provided in the end," Ripaldo said. "Driving through Panórama these days, all you see are villas."

"That began with the new road they built before the Germans arrived," Vassílis said. "Once the road was paved, some of the rich who used to come up from the city for mountain air in the summers decided to stay the year round like the rest of us. And when they did that, of course they made the villagers find themselves a new name that had no refugee flavor in it. Which is why it's now Panórama instead of Arsaklí."

"About the Germans arriving," Ripaldo said, "I know the village was still called Arsaklí during the German Occupation because of the intelligence unit stationed there, and I wonder if any of the villagers still living from that period might—"

"The Germans," Vassíli said. "What did the Germans care about what it was called? They arrived on their motorcycles and in their trucks by way of the new road, took over the school house for their headquarters, put up some soldiers in the better village houses, and turned the villas into officers quarters and clubs. That was all they cared about. The heart of the village was still too poor to be of use to them, so they went their way and didn't bother with it. And the village went its way."

"But people must have known what the Germans were up to in that school house."

"Maybe yes, maybe no," Vassílis said. "Most people kept to their own business. If you didn't bother the Germans, they wouldn't bother you is what most people said. But of course some of the villagers had too much pride to leave it at that."

"What did those with too much pride do?"

"Took to the mountains," Vassílis said. "Along with some others who were out for adventure. And some others with the wrong politics but the right heart."

"And what about those who had less pride and less heart?"

"They worked their fields as they always had."

"Though I gather some worked for the Germans as well," Ripaldo said.

Vassílis studied him. Then he shrugged. "Of course some worked for the Germans. Why not collect wages from the enemy since he can conscript you to work for him without wages anytime he wants to?"

"Sure," Ripaldo said. "Why not?"

Vassílis was still studying him. "You know, life in those days wasn't only a question of pride. One had to survive. You understand what I'm saying, my American friend?"

Ripaldo had planned to feel Vassílis out on those in Arsaklí besides his wife who had worked for the Germans and who might have information to give him out of personal knowledge, but he realized he'd touched a raw nerve, so he let the subject drop. He decided he'd have to scout the territory on his own while he waited to see if Vassílis could arrange the interview with Marina that Wittekind thought might prove crucial. Vassílis promised to call him at his hotel as soon as there was news of a kind that might interest him, and on his way to the door he put his arm around Ripaldo's shoulder and tugged him in close, bringing on a ripe odor of sweat and garlic that jolted Ripaldo back, with some nostalgia, into his post-war years in Greece.

On his way down to the Salonika Ripaldo decided to take a walk through Panórama to look for the old Arsaklí school house and see if there was anything else leftover from the war years that might provide a context for his approach to Marina Angeloúdis. He found the school house not far from the main road. It was a square hulk two-stories high that might have been impressive when surrounded by mud-brick cottages but now seemed disappointingly commonplace, with no aura of mystery in its bland facade, nothing ominous behind the neck-high fence that closed in its paved yard. And beyond the school house there was little left to define the heart of the old village, only a few pre-war cottages without any connection to each other and even fewer unpaved spaces. The one remaining patch of open ground did have a plane tree in its center that was of a size to suggest a certain long-standing authority. A middle-aged man hunched over on a bench there reading the back page of a newspaper identified this patch as the village square. He was wearing a cap stained with whitewash. Ripaldo asked him if he knew of any old-timers in town who might help him with a bit of local history that interested him. The man looked him over, chewing on a twig that he rolled from one side of his mouth to the other.

"What bit of local history might that be?" he said.

"The war years," Ripaldo said.

"What war years do you have in mind?" the man said. "There are wars and wars and years and years. A few too many of both for our health, I'd say."

"You've got a point there," Ripaldo said. "I had in mind the Second World War in particular."

The man leaned back. "Well, you won't find many old-timers who know anything about that war. Not around here. And those who do aren't likely to want to talk about it. Anymore than they're likely to want to talk about the war that came after that one. I mean, even if they have enough mind left to talk about any history as old as that."

"I was just hoping there might be somebody in town who lived here under the Germans and who might be willing to do what they could to help set the historical record straight."

"Well, if there are any, you won't find them sitting out here in the open sunlight."

"Where might I find them sitting?"

"You might find them sitting outside the cafe over there across the road, where there's at least an awning overhead to cover their sins. And you can be sure most could use a lot more cover than that."

The cafe was at the back of an empty lot off the square—a post-war brick box with a flat roof, dwarfed on both sides by newer buildings of bare concrete. There were two marble-topped tables set out in front of the door. At one of them two men had opened up a backgammon box and were setting up the pieces. A third man was sitting at the table opposite, gazing out at the square. All three were white-haired and weather-beaten, but as Ripaldo hovered there deciding which one to approach, each had a particular way of looking at him or beyond him. One of the backgammon players had eyes that were constantly in motion, as though he had to keep a steady lookout over the full stretch of the territory in front of him. His opponent looked up once while Ripaldo was standing there, but his look went right through Ripaldo's gut. The man sitting alone had eyes that seemed to find something amusing in whatever came into view, deepening the crow's-feet the sun had cut into his face above his cheeks. He sat there sipping a small glass of raki, glancing at Ripaldo or the square in the distance as he chose.

Ripaldo decided that was his man. He went inside the cafe and got a beer and brought it out with a glass over its neck. He stood in the doorway working hard to kill the sudden sense he had of being an unwelcome intruder. When he motioned at the empty chair beside the man sitting alone, the man finally made a gesture offering him the chair. Ripaldo filled his glass and sat there trying to figure out the best way to get down to business. He heard Wittekind's image in his mind's eye say that he had no choice but to come out with a lie to cover himself, so he told the man opposite him that he was writing a history of the Second World War and wondered if the man or his friends there knew anyone in town who'd lived in Arsakli during the German Occupation.

"You're a foreigner," the man said. "A German. But you speak Greek."

"I speak Greek but I'm not a German," Ripaldo said. "I'm an American."

"Aha," the man said. "A Greek-American."

"No, just an American. I've lived in Greece now and then over the years."

"What's your name, if you don't mind my asking?"

"Ripaldo. Jackson Ripaldo."

"That's not an American name," the man said.

"Well, there really isn't any such thing."

"There must be such a thing," the man said. "How can there not be such a thing?"

"We're a mixture," Ripaldo said. "Americans come from every-where. Originally. My background happens to be Italian."

"But since you speak Greek like a Greek and have lived here, why do you have to know about the German Occupation?"

"I wasn't here during the German Occupation," Ripaldo said. "I went back to America during the German Occupation."

The man was still looking Ripaldo over, his eyes smiling the whole while.

"You're sure it wasn't Germany you went back to? Or maybe Austria? I mean before you ended up coming back here with the wrong army?"

Ripaldo shook his head. He was trying to keep his irritation under control. When he pushed his glass aside and started to stand up, the man apparently decided to trust him rather than lose an audience. He touched Ripaldo's arm.

"So what would you like to know about the German Occupation, my friend? I can tell you anything you want to know. And what I can't tell you, my friends here might be willing to tell you. That is, if you promise to take their picture and put them in your history book."

What Ripaldo learned about the German Occupation in Arsakli was that nobody seemed to remember the details in exactly the same way—at least no one of the three in that cafe. It was true that there were German officers in the school house, but were they with intelligence or transportation or supplies? And the only officers housed in the village were either housed in the old olive factory on the upper road or in the upper stories of the old restaurant that became the new Nereida Hotel or in the abandoned villa that belonged to the tobacco merchant who never came back after the war was over—maybe in all three at one or another time. It was hard, they said, to know exact dates and places after all these years.

And this particular officer with the long nose and large ears? Who knows? The name seemed familiar but it couldn't be put to a face. Wasn't that a name that was famous in Germany or Austria? That could be why it seemed familiar, from seeing it in the newspapers. But as for the German Occupation, who could remember a face that far back? Especially that of a young officer who probably stuck to his own and went his way without bothering anybody, as was true of German officers in general in the village of Arsaklí.

The only face of a German soldier that all three could remember clearly belonged to one Friedreich—a thick, jolly face very red from drink—an ordinary soldier who was billeted in the home of the village baker and who fell in love with the daughter of the house, so that the two had become engaged, so to speak. When the Germans were set to leave the region in October of 1944, Friedreich decided to stay behind, being much in love with the daughter and even more so with the local wine. The baker covered his blond hair with flour and hid him under the floorboards of his bakery. A bit later the Communist andartes came into the village and despite the baker's objections took Friedreich off to the mountains to fight on their side in the Civil War, but they finally brought him back as a hopeless guerrilla, who had no understanding of politics, no heart for firing a rifle, and who drank more wine than five healthy men. Friedreich ended up marrying the baker's daughter without a dowry because the only person in town who would hire him for a wage and provide him the wine he needed was the baker himself.

"That daughter was one of the lucky ones," the man at Ripaldo's table said. "Her husband's liver didn't hold out very long, and the daughter died young of a broken heart, but at least that German soldier didn't cost her father anything. And he restored her good name in time."

"Others weren't so lucky?" Ripaldo asked.

"Some were, some weren't," the man said. "What others do you have in mind?"

"For example, others who worked for the Germans. Or got involved with them in some way."

"Not in this village," the shifty-eyed man playing backgammon said. "Not our women."

"I thought some people worked for the Germans as a way of survival. For example, at the American College down the hill."

The man with the deep crow's feet was studying Ripaldo. "Could be," he said. "Who told you that?"

Ripaldo shrugged. "Vassílis Angeloúdis, for one," he said.

The two men at the backgammon table looked up, then went back to their game.

"Vassílis Angeloúdis is a special case," the man sitting opposite Ripaldo said. "Some things he knows and some things he doesn't know. Besides, he has a past."

"I had in mind what he himself told me about his family," Ripaldo said. "His wife, for example."

"I know what you had in mind," the man said, looking into the distance. "But I still can't speak for what he may know or not know."

"And what about what his wife may know?"

"I can't speak for that either," the man said. "And you won't find anybody else around here who can."

His look turned toward the square, where it stayed.

When the phone call finally came through with the news that Vassílis Angeloúdis would be pleased to receive Ripaldo at his home in Panórama the following afternoon, Ripaldo suspected that there were difficulties ahead: Angeloúdis' tone was too formal, the invitation too precise, no mention of his wife Marina, no talk about anything else beyond the directions for reaching his house in the village. And when he arrived there, Angeloúdis met him at the door, shook his hand, then stepped outside to speak to him under his breath.

"Let me explain," he said. "You must understand that Marina is not used to being alone with foreigners. She'd rather speak to you with me present. At least at the start."

"Fine," Ripaldo said. "Whatever you think best."

"Please. It's not what I think best. It's what Marina thinks best.

The woman has a mind of her own. Always did have."

Marina proved to be a woman with the usual plump excess that was meant to signal a prosperous village life, but she was still beautiful in her face, with clean features and sharp, almond eyes. Her thick hair, pure white, was held in close by a perfectly shaped bun. She was sitting in the living room on the edge of her chair, and she barely looked up when Ripaldo went over to shake her hand. Then she got up immediately and disappeared into the hallway. Vassílis motioned Ripaldo to a seat, then sat down himself and stared at the floor. Marina came back with a tray that had a glass of water on it and a dish holding a spoonful of cherries in thick syrup. She smiled without really meaning it as she bent to offer Ripaldo his sweet.

"Vassílis says you're an American," Marina said. "But you speak Greek."

"That's right. Bad Greek. Village Greek."

"What other kind is there?" Marina said. "If you're true to who you are. Do you speak village American as well?"

"Not exactly," Ripaldo said.

"I didn't think so," Marina said. "You don't look like you really come from a village."

"It's different in America," Vassílis said. "People don't live in villages."

"What do you know about America?" Marina said, turning to face him. "You've never been anywhere but the other side of Hortiáti mountain."

"I know what I know," Vassílis said to the floor.

Marina turned back to take Ripaldo's dish of cherries and offer him the glass of water.

"Vassílis tells me that you want to know about our war with the Germans," she said to her tray. "Why does an American want to know about a war as old as that?"

"It's a little complicated," Ripaldo said. "I'm trying to get the history of it straight. Set it straight."

"You never will," Marina said. "There is no straight way to look at that war. Everyone looks at it from one's own point of view."

"I'm sure that's right. But at the moment all I'm trying to do is get a few facts straight. After talking to Vassílis here, I think you might be able to help me."

Marina raised her eyes to stare at Vassílis. He stood up and moved toward the door. Marina called him back to take the tray she was holding, then sat down opposite Ripaldo, on the edge of her seat.

"Whether Vassílis stays here or doesn't stay makes no difference to me," she said, "though he seems to think it does. In either case I'm not prepared to talk to you about that war. But since you're a foreigner and a friend of his, I thought it only right that I tell you so myself, especially since he seems to have promised you more than he should have without my knowing it."

"Let me clarify things," Ripaldo said. "I don't mean for you to talk to me in a personal way. All I want is to ask you a few questions that you can answer or not as you choose."

Marina gazed at him as though trying to read his face, then she studied the floor. She seemed to be thinking it over. Ripaldo groped in his jacket pocket to get his tape recorder out, then flicked it open to check the cassette.

"You can put that thing away," Marina said. "I refuse to talk into a machine."

Ripaldo put the tape recorder back in his jacket pocket.

Marina sighed. "If you've come all the way from America to ask me questions, you must have a good reason. And I don't want you to think me a difficult woman. But I have my reasons for not wanting to talk into a machine that others can listen to, and that includes Vassílis."

"Well maybe I can just ask you some questions and take notes on what you say and then let you see the notes. And I swear nobody else you know here or elsewhere will ever see those notes."

Marina shook her head. "No. You may write your questions on a piece of paper, with the help of Vassílis if you don't know how to write our language. I want him to see that even now I don't do things behind his back. And when he's given me your questions, I will then decide whether or not I have anything to say to you."

"Fine. Good. Only how will I know what you've decided?"

"You will know," Marina said. "I will find a way for you to know. Whether through Vassílis or some other way."

Ripaldo delivered his questions to Vassílis' cafe in Hortiáti the following morning in an unsealed envelope so that Vassílis could correct his thoroughly casual spelling while assuring himself that the questions were general and impersonal enough not to be offensive to his wife Marina. After a five-day wait that fully taxed Ripaldo's patience, a large white envelope appeared in his hotel box, sealed all around by adhesive tape, with an almost undecipherable Greek version of his name on the front of it. He was grateful to find that the Greek script inside was clear and beautifully shaped. And since it was, he felt certain that the envelope and its contents were Marina's work. He read it through, then decided that he'd better translate it as best he could and send off a typed draft to Wittekind without delay.

DEPOSITION: MARINA ANGELOÚDIS

Your questions tire me. I've read them, and thought about them some, but it doesn't suit me to answer them one after the other as though I'm in a schoolroom taking an examination. I've decided not to pay much attention to your questions but to say what I must in this private way. The reason I've decided to answer you at all is this. You will hear much about the past in this village that is not true. You will hear much that serves somebody's need to harm somebody else but that does not tell you about things as they were. I am sure you have already heard things about me and my husband Vassílis that are not true and other things that may be true but that should no longer see the light of day. The questions you ask are about a time of war long ago. Those times have been followed by other times that had their own evil days, but none were so confused for me as what happened during the days that interest you. And none have remained so strong in my memory. I have decided that I must try to make sure that you, a foreigner, do not see those days only as others in this village will paint them for you. There are things that even Vassílis doesn't know, though he knows more than most. About me during those days he knows almost nothing. And what others know is mostly an invention of cruel minds.

If you think me a difficult woman for refusing to talk to you in person or to your machine, you are free to think that. I will nevertheless tell you why it is necessary. My husband Vassílis believes that I am not at ease with foreigners and shy. I'm sure he told you that. He knows only what he knows. He also believes that I always tell the truth. I do not always tell the truth, especially when speaking to foreigners and sometimes when speaking to him. That is why it is more likely that I will tell you the truth if I do not have to speak either to you face to face or into your machine but while I am alone and in this way. It may seem strange, but knowing that this will be read, and read by a stranger, makes it easier for me to say what I have to say.

I've come to an age when I have no need any longer to protect myself from the past, and this even includes the memory of my young demon. What would be the point at this stage of my life, so late in the century? But it is my past, it belongs to me, and I refuse to allow others to make out of it what they choose. Also, I must admit that I now find pleasure in remembering, even the details that still cause pain. But of course the days that interest you are long gone, most of those who matter are dead or have disappeared, and I can only make do with what recollection the Lord has left me. At least you can be sure that what I remember is free of hatred. And since I have no choice but to trust your promise not to let anybody in this village or anybody else I know see what I have to say, which also means my husband Vassílis, I will tell you the truth as honestly as I remember it. Then you are free to decide whether you can trust my memory of what happened as I write it down here.

I will begin with the day it became clear to me that there was a demon inside my young body, even if it was not clear then that nothing I might do or anybody else might do would rid me of it soon enough. It happened during the second month that I'd been working at the American school which the Germans had taken over for their headquarters in our region during their occupation of my country. I had just entered my nineteenth year. Those first weeks at work had been very difficult for me, not only because in those days I was a bit shy with strangers, but because the strangers were our enemy. Of course I didn't actually see the enemy often. My work in the morning was cleaning one of the new buildings that the Germans had put up across the main road opposite the school gate. This building was used as a dormitory for ordinary soldiers, and for this reason I didn't begin to clean it until the place was empty of people. Also, in the late afternoon, when some of the offices on the other side of the main road closed for the day, I helped to clean those too.

Still, even if I saw the German soldiers only from a distance and never spoke to one during those first weeks, their presence was a humiliation for me. And this was so though I knew that I'd been left no choice but to take my mother's place among the cleaning women at that school after my father was killed in the resistance. There was too much for her to do at home taking care of my younger sisters and brothers, and the war had made us too poor for me not to work as I could, being the oldest child and finished with school. So I did my work as I had to. But it was not work that pleased me, and I never spoke to anyone while I was inside that barbed wire enclosure except some of the other women who worked there for the same reason I did.

The day my demon came to me began like any other. I had cleaned the dormitory bathroom and swept the floors and made up most of the beds. With only the laundry chores left for that morning, I was nearly ready to go across to the kitchen for a coffee with the women who worked in the main buildings when there was a great commotion outside my dormitory. Suddenly a German officer and several ordinary soldiers came through the front door carrying a man who looked as though death had closed his eyes and then opened them again after showing him what he should prepare himself to expect in the next world. This man was not in uniform. He looked like a villager, and he smelled like one. They laid him out on the first bed in the dormitory, and I was pleased to hear him moan, because that meant he might not die after all and leave an evil spirit behind to make trouble for me in the days that would follow his passing.

But that man was not the cause of my difficulty. I learned later from the other women I worked with that he was in truth a farmer from the village of Kapoudjida on his way to the market in Arsakli. He had been climbing the hill beyond our barbed wire enclosure with a cart full of ripe tomatoes when his donkey was startled by a military car coming out of the bend ahead of him at great speed, so that the donkey felt it had to bolt off the side of the road, overturning the cart on its owner. The poor man was knocked unconscious and woke up to find himself covered with what he thought was blood and pieces of torn flesh from himself or his donkey. So he screamed and fainted again and only woke up when those in the military car tried to carry him inside the enclosure and found from his cries that he had not only cracked his head but had broken one arm at the elbow and one ankle. The donkey only scraped himself deeply and so survived for more life of misery and pain.

It was while this man was lying on the dormitory bed recovering from the agony of his trip there that the demon possessed me. I am told that people in Anglo-Saxon countries do not believe in demons, and that is your right, and maybe your luck, but in my country they are real, as anybody who has lived in a village as long as I have will swear to you in the name of the Holy Virgin or the Lord Himself. My demon came to me that morning by way of the soldier who was assigned to act as the wounded man's doctor. He was not exactly a doctor, just a medical soldier, not much older than I was, a soldier I'd never seen before on my side of the main road. And he came from a world I hadn't seen either, someplace where they are blond, Oh my God, so very blond, not the darker kind or the painted kind who go by that name here. And his eyes a pale blue like that of no living race we know, and the skin so white and soft that one is afraid one's look is enough to cause a dark bruising. This soldier was not only something else to study. He was gentle as a woman when he did his work, holding that villager's ankle and binding it up as though it was a bird's crushed bones. And when he came to the elbow, he eased it into the sling he'd made so slowly and carefully that even the villager from Kapudjída seemed to feel cheated of the pain he could no longer show.

The pain had moved on to the demon that this soldier brought into my life. I found that I couldn't take my eyes off the kneeling blond creature, so hard at work that he didn't glance over at me even once. That was a thing that would have stopped my heart. And when the officer in charge said "water" to me in my language, I didn't hear him until the second or maybe the third time. I ran out of there like a frightened schoolgirl, across to the kitchen, my heart beating so fast that I had to rest outside the kitchen doorway and talk myself into coolness before going inside to fill a pitcher at the sink and face the curious women who gathered around me to hear the news I carried in to them. I was much too calm. I heard myself telling about the scene in my dormitory as though soldiers arriving there suddenly with a broken man was just another every-day event to be expected in time of war. And of course no mention of the kneeling figure that I knew even at that moment had changed the center of my life.

I won't pretend that he was the first man to make me too aware of myself. No young woman in a village so close to the city who walks out of her home for work or fresh air or the evening stroll will take very long to learn that she is attractive to men. And attractive in a certain direction once she has filled out, even if it is nothing more than discovering the new way men sometimes look at her. But that is beginning to know what one can do to others whether one wants to or not. I speak of what others may do to one's self simply by being there, without even looking at one—what happens when one's body is under the spell of something it cannot control and when that turns the mind against itself. This is what that blond creature did to me. And I don't mean the man himself. How could he have known what was going on inside me as I watched him gently put that villager's ankle back together? I mean the demon in him who became my demon.

The soldiers didn't stay in my dormitory any longer than they needed to. When the villager was cleaned and bandaged enough to move again more easily, they carried him away, God knows where. And it was exactly because the soldiers left so quickly and I no longer had reason to give my mind to any one of them that I knew something foreign had come inside me. I couldn't eat anything that noon. And I was difficult with the other women the rest of that day—sometimes withdrawn, irritable when anyone spoke to me, everything at fault. One of the women finally told me that some-one had given me the evil eye and that I should go home and stay there until it went away so that she and the others could have some peace.

There was no evil eye. There was the demon, and the mania, the stupidity that he had brought into my life. I couldn't eat again that night or sleep. I turned and turned in bed, my sheet damp, curs-ing myself for being still a child or worse, for allowing my head to see what it had no business seeing. I finally threw off my night-gown and lay there naked in a sweet panic because the idol of that young German was with me all that while, looking at me again and again without any shame, and I was feeling something very personal I had not known.

The next day I resolved to visit our village priest and ask for his help. I had no other choice, because I couldn't speak about it to my mother—how could I expect her to understand this possession by a thing living in one of our enemy? And it was in any case the priest's business to accept confessions and perform exorcisms. So I went looking for him. I found him sipping a coffee at his usual cafe, but when I went over and stood in front of him, the demon sealed my lips, and I all I was able to do was bend and kiss the priest's hand. "Bless you, my child," he said, absently, barely looking at me, as though my coming over to stand in front of him and kiss his hand was simply the expected thing. I turned and left him there, and I didn't go back to him, not that day or the next day or the day after that. It was too late by then anyway. Instead of seeking out a cure, I had begun to welcome my secret, to protect it, to hide from others every sign of what I was feeling. I carried the sweet pain of it silently through the days and nights that followed. And when I learned from one of the women later in the week that my blond soldier was part of our own guard unit, assigned there to distribute medical supplies and provide first aid, I became shrewd, then lawless.

Lest you think that this was entirely my own doing, let me explain that I was ordinary in those days. I won't say innocent, but during the many months since my father died my mind had been on my duty to my family as the oldest child. I had little time for daydreams or any other kind of dreams. The center of my life was my work both at home and away. I was also a person who believed in proper behavior, not out of a schoolgirl's belief in rules, or even my mother's strict teaching, but out of my own pride—too fierce pride sometimes, I admit. I would not allow myself to be weak as other young women I knew, and I would scold myself when I did things that I knew were wrong. So what showed me without a doubt that my mind had turned on itself without my having willed it was the pleasure I began to take in my lawlessness. It is one thing to feel that you are acting against your sense of what is right, even to feel that you cannot help it, and quite another thing to feel a satisfaction when you do it. My God. Why does it hurt me to say this even now? And why does it still give me pleasure to remember what I did?

In any case, what I found myself doing nobody who knew me would have believed. Like a hunter, I stalked that man of my days and nights. That is the only way I can say it. When my afternoon work was done in the buildings used for offices, I would say good-bye as usual to the women I worked with there and cross the old road toward the guarded opening in the barbed wire enclosure that put one on the road to my village—but I wouldn't go all the way out. Instead, I would cross back over the old road where the trees surrounding the school grounds became a forest, and I would make my way through the trees to the back of the school grounds. There was a deep ravine back there to protect me on one side and still enough trees to hide me from the building I had just cleaned and the one next to it. The passageway between those buildings gave me a view of the armored cars and trucks that the Germans had lined up where there used to be athletic grounds for the students to play their games. But from one corner I also had a view of the courtyard that led to the school's main gate, so that I could see most of those who might come and go across the old road.

I knelt there unseen among the trees and watched. And there was more pleasure than I could understand in doing that. The men in uniform would come out of the buildings that we were not allowed to enter at the far end of the courtyard and cross it toward the lined-up vehicles or disappear out of sight on their way to the main gate, crossing usually in pairs but sometimes alone, quickly, standing up straight, their legs so long and no looseness in their walking. And there were moments when I could hear their strange floating talk, their exchange of greetings and their laughing with each other, but what held me most as they came into the courtyard from one direction or another was the way they carried themselves until they spoke, a manner so severe, so foreign to our own.

Of course there was danger in what I was doing. I couldn't imagine what would happen to me if I was caught hiding there. Maybe that was part of the excitement I felt, but I was never really afraid or even nervous. My mind was sharpened for my purpose in being there, for the chance to see my blond soldier again as he passed in front of the parked vehicles or crossed to the main gate. And as I waited, watching became my private cinema. Though he didn't show himself while I was there that day, the parade of others was enough to keep me kneeling where I was until the sun came low, so that when I turned away and hurried through the trees to climb the hill toward home, I had to make up the first of the lies I told my mother. I told her that I'd been given more work to do by the Germans and that this might make me late some evenings in the days ahead. Maybe many evenings. There was no way of knowing how many, I said.

It was late during the evening of the third day that I suddenly saw my blond soldier from my hiding place in the trees. He came out of the building next to the one I helped to clean in the afternoons and he crossed to a low building made of wood rather than stone and with a metal roof. It was one of the new buildings the Germans had built. He had his back to me and only a fringe of light hair showed below his military cap, but I knew who he was the second I saw him. I could feel it. Unmistakably. And not only because his walk seemed different from the others, less stern, less careful. When he reached the building with the metal roof, he turned to speak to somebody before going in and I saw his pale face to tell me what I knew already. Two minutes out of so many hours of watching, but seeing that face made my breath short, and it made me stay there uselessly until it was almost dark. I couldn't sleep again that night, and when I looked at myself in the morning, I was ashamed of the shadows around my eyes and the darkness inside them.

I decided the next day that there was only one way left to rid myself of this demon. I made up my mind to exorcise him myself by cursing his presence face to face in the man who was carrying him so that he would leave my troubled spirit alone. Of course going to the church near our home and lighting a candle before the icon of the Holy Virgin would have been the sensible thing to do, but I told myself that this would only draw attention to what I was suffering and maybe bring on gossip. This foreign presence would in any case be out of me soon, I was certain. What was the point of marking myself in that public way and endangering my good name? I told myself that my pride wouldn't allow it. And as I did, my mind began to plan how I might get close enough to that sweet face to cross myself, spit three times, and turn away once and for all from this lawless pleasure it had brought into my life.

It took much cunning and boldness to get myself near that man. Even if it had been acceptable for me to try and use some language of the tongue or hands to speak to one of the enemy, we who worked for the enemy knew he was forbidden to speak to us except when giving orders. And to meet that young soldier alone was beyond thinking, beyond imagining. That is, until I discovered the way.

I found out from the woman who was in charge of cleaning the offices that the wooden building with the metal roof was a storehouse for supplies—all the special supplies that the Germans kept for themselves, special foods and medicines and I don't know what else. That told me what business my blond soldier had in going there, but I also had to know where he took the things he gathered from the storehouse. This I learned from another woman, an older woman I sometimes helped late in the day when her chores in the main office building were too much for her to cope with alone. She showed me a room in that building, a small room with only a desk and a chair and a sink against one wall, the place the officers and soldiers went to get their personal soaps and ointments and medicines that came in bottles. And where they went if they needed to cure a fever or fix some small wound. This told me where my soldier spent his days.

I suppose some people would say it was the devil in me that made me do what I did next, but that is not true. It was to challenge the devil, I can swear to this. And I was very calm about it, very certain of myself, not at all possessed at that moment. One day that week I went into the kitchen where the women came together for our noontime meal, and while cutting a piece of goat cheese for my lunch, I quietly sliced through two fingers of my left hand, deep enough to make a mess of the sink. The women gathered in there shrieked as I turned away from the sink dripping blood, there was a great commotion, but I remained calm and just sat down at the luncheon table, holding my hand in front of me so that the blood dripped freely onto my black skirt. I was straining not to faint, and I didn't.

They wrapped a dishtowel around my hand and took me across the courtyard to the office building with the room that gave out medicines. My soldier was there, as I knew he would be. He barely looked at me before he sat me in a chair and kneeled down to give all his attention to my hand. He removed the dishtowel carefully, shaking his head at the sight of what I had done, then quickly wrapped gauze around the fingers to stop the blood that had begun to flow freely again. Then he got up and tried to tell the women crowded round the desk that I would be all right, talking to them quietly in German but really speaking with his hands, and finally he motioned them out of the door.

That pleased me, but I killed the thought of it. When he turned back to me, I closed my eyes and sat there stiffly trying to give myself the courage I needed to reach into my blouse and bring out the cross I wore around my neck so that I could hold up my Christ against the evil spirit that this man had brought from his country to torment me and no doubt others like me. He had a bottle in his hand now. He put that down on the floor and was kneeling in front of me again, unwinding the gauze he'd used to stop the blood. When he had it unwound, he held my hand turned up in his and looked up at me to ask me something I didn't understand. But his eyes told me that he was asking about pain, and whether I was ready for the thing he had to do next. What came into me then I can't entirely explain even after all these years. Instead of reaching inside my blouse, I reached down with my free hand and touched his face with my fingertips.

I'm sure you know as well as I do that there are things one does that one has difficulty explaining even to oneself but that nevertheless create a border one crosses with no chance of turning back. I am certain that I could not have had the courage to wound myself and use that wound to put myself in front of this man if I had not believed truthfully that this would give me the chance to rid myself of him and what in my heart I felt he carried. And though I was still not much more than a child, I had the pride of a grown woman. At that time, had I been in control of myself, I would not have exposed my feelings to any man, least of all to one of the enemy. Still, when he looked up at me to ask about my pain, I touched his face. And in that moment I understood not only that the tender mark I had made on his face would stay there but that if it was a demon that had made me do it, this demon was surely carried not by him but by me.

This knowledge brought my hand back to me as suddenly as it had gone out to him. But it was too late. I could tell from the way he looked down after a single glance at me that he understood a thing that put fear in his heart. He opened the bottle and cleaned my wound, so gently that I felt almost nothing beyond the sting of the white fluid fizzing in the wounds. And when he was done, he still held my hand, palm open, studying it as though a gypsy reading my fate. I finally reached down to touch his face again just to get his attention, to tell him it was all right, I wasn't really hurting, but he still wouldn't look up at me. Then he took up new gauze and bound up first the fingers and then the whole hand. And when he was done with that, he touched the bound fingers to his lips, quickly, as though sealing his work with a kiss, and gave my hand back to me.

You have asked me to tell you what I can remember of my days with the enemy, what I may have learned about who they were and what they did. I learned more than I dare tell you about this one soldier, but you must understand that it was not easy for me in the beginning, and this may be why I remember it so well. We had no common language, no common alphabet even. I could neither speak nor read his language, and he could neither read nor speak mine. In the beginning we came to each other like two deaf mutes. We had to speak to each other with gestures, with pictures, and in the darkness, entirely with our hands, like the blind.

When I remember how that first meeting in his work room ended, it makes me smile at the childish comedy of it. He wanted to tell me something when I stood up to leave, and he tried with his silly language, with gestures I couldn't understand, then went to his desk and took out a piece of paper to draw a clock. He gave me the drawing with the clock set at seven, then took my wounded hand and touched the bandage. Of course I understood him to mean that I should return at seven, I suppose to have the bandage changed. But did he mean seven that evening or seven in the morning? I took the pencil from him and drew a line across the page below his clock, then a circle for the sun above the line and an arrow beside it pointing both up and down. He studied my ridiculous drawing, looking hard at it, and finally circled the arrow pointing down. I found myself thanking him in my language, more than was necessary, stupidly. Then I moved quickly to the door. I turned to see him crumple up the drawing we had made into a small ball so that he could put it away in his pocket.

When I came back to him that evening to have my bandage changed, we were both very careful in our manners. Our eyes hardly met. At least not while he was changing the bandage. It was late enough in the day so that the building was empty, but spring had long since begun to rise toward summer, and it was light outside well beyond that hour. I realized that he had come there to take care of my hand after his regular duty was done, and I could tell that he was nervous about it because he kept the door open. When I first came in he nodded at me shyly, then went right to work on my hand, doing that so much more quickly than he had in the morning. The wounded fingers looked awful to me, and they were painful, but I didn't make a sound except to draw in my breath when he cleaned away the old blood and this time put horrible iodine on the wounds.

As he finished the new bandage he said "Zo" with a sigh and stood up to lean back against the edge of the desk. His eyes were turned toward the door. Suddenly he reached over and took my good hand and put it to his face. He held it there lightly, and when I didn't take it away, he moved my fingers to his lips and held them there, his eyes not on me but again on the open doorway. And then he looked at me in a way that was unmistakable, a way that made me take my hand back and glance down at my feet. But only for a second. It was too late for shyness now. I raised my eyes and looked back at him just as boldly as he had looked at me, until he was the one who turned his eyes away.

I watched him move around to the far side of the desk and open the drawer to take out a blank piece of paper as though preparing to send me to the pharmacy. What he did instead was draw another picture. He drew it slowly, oh so slowly, using a ruler so that all his lines were straight, with perfect little boxes of different sizes set here and there, some tiny ones with wheels, and trees with branches that had no leaves. His mind was so much on what he was doing that I could get my fill of his young face without his noticing me. He was so light-skinned, his eyebrows almost invisible, everything that made his face his own, the cheekbones, the nose, the jaw, all clean in their lines, all as though cut out of stone. He looked up suddenly to catch me watching him, but I didn't lower my eyes. Then he motioned me to come up to the desk on my side, and he placed his drawing so that I could have a closer look. I really couldn't make any sense out of it. I watched him draw some short arrows between two of his parallel lines, and when he made the arrows turn a corner, I finally understood that this was a kind of map he had sketched and that his arrows were meant to guide me somewhere. He put an X in one of his boxes and a smaller X where the arrows ended, and before he handed me the map he'd made, he drew in a clock and set the hands at seven again.

That map is my one souvenir from those late spring days in 1944, the only one of the various papers—what you call documents—from the war years that I still bother to look at once in a while. It's barely readable now, and it's coming apart where it's folded. In any case, that map led toward catastrophe. But not right away, and I suppose that's why it's the one thing in the box of my papers from those years that I still bother to hold in my hand. At the start it led me to an hour and sometimes two of darkness while the sun was still up, in a place that allowed me to discover pleasure beyond a girl's imagining. Maybe not any girl's imagining but surely what might come into the mind of an ordinary young woman like me in her nineteenth year living in the village of Arsakli. And even an older woman living there. Who am I to say?

The place my soldier had marked on his map for our rendezvous the next evening was a shed for storing winter wood that the Germans had built on the far side of the warehouse I'd seen him enter that secret afternoon earlier in the week. The shed was at the edge of the school grounds at the back, just above the steep hillside that ended in a ravine. There was an overgrown garden beyond it and then trees as far as the barbed wire on the lower rim of our enclosure. This made the woodshed completely private on two sides at least.

I didn't once follow his map to get there. I don't know what he had in mind with his arrows, but I could not have crossed the courtyards of that school in daylight, however late in the evening, to meet a man alone where others could trace my path as I went there. When I had studied the map thoroughly and calculated exactly where I was to go, I got there by way of my own route, through the trees on the border of the school grounds and along the edge of the ravine at the back. But what I found at the end of my route made the journey there seem hopeless.

The place he had marked on his map, the only possible place, was a small building that had no windows and no doors that I could see. If it was the right place, how was I to get into it without being seen? I knelt in the underbrush and studied it, completely confused, trying to pretend that I was strong enough not to care, not to weep over this ridiculous situation I'd put myself into. I was perspiring so that my underarms were soaking wet. Then I suddenly saw part of the wall on the garden side of the shed begin to move enough to show a patch of darkness and then a face—that sweet face. I don't think it saw me, but I didn't wait to find out. I ran low through the weeds across the open ground in front of the shed and pushed the sliding door aside enough to squeeze through, then pulled it shut behind me.

I cannot tell you everything I remember of that first hour of darkness. It is not something a woman should tell to a stranger. And in any case, it is a thing to be known, not talked about. What I can say is that the senses in my body came to life then as they haven't often since, enough to make some things impossible to erase. The odors of that room for example. They return to me whenever their kind come near me again. The resin from the left-over pine logs stacked at one end, and the scent of thyme that clung to some of them, and the earthen floor we lay on. My God, and my own odor mixed with his. But another thing—the darkness in that room. This gave me a new understanding of light, not only how much one can learn to see as one's eyes get used to what little there is of it, but also how the tone of the light changes with what one feels. And I learned that one has to try to see the rhythm of time in a new way, because there were moments when one was carried beyond time, and other moments when there was a beautiful lingering that could not be measured. One had to learn to come back into time while there was still enough light outside to get one safely home.

My understanding of this new rhythm was not good at the start. Often I arrived in the village when there was no dusk left and had to explain myself to my mother as coldly as I could. But I managed. And as the days moved toward the end of spring and the light outside lasted longer for us, we found that there was time to sit quietly with the door open just enough to let us see each other clearly. We used those moments at first to learn to name the parts of our bodies, each in the other's language. And then we taught each other some words to show our pleasure in what we were naming, and this we would practice in the darkness, so that words could begin to mix with the other sounds we made. And when that was learned well enough, we turned to things outside ourselves, naming whatever we could see around us in that slanting light.

One day Martin—that was his name, what he said was his name—brought a pad of paper with him that he used for his accounts. This became our school book. We would sit side by side where the light came in through the narrow opening in our doorway and we would draw pictures of whatever it was that we wanted to teach the other to say. Martin drew slowly but well. I drew childishly, so I soon let him have the pad except when I needed to ask a question. He could not only draw men and women with faces, but he could dress them so that I understood what they were—soldiers and officers and nurses and cooks and farmers. And when the clothes he drew no longer spoke clearly, he would give his men and women tools that told me who they were. And then houses and their parts and even the names of towns in a map he made of his country to show me where he lived.

I learned so many words during that time that I've now forgotten completely. But these pictures were all of things. When we tried to reach for what was in our heads, our school became difficult, sometimes impossible. And that was true also of trying to say what we were feeling, at least what I knew I was feeling and what seemed to be growing so quickly in both of us during those first days. Only a few words made sense and then really not enough, so we often found that we had to return to the language that had done for us before we arrived at words.

I have to admit something now. During all of this time, though I was learning to speak Martin's language at least as a young child might, a language quite foreign to mine and with a very different sound, I did not once think of Martin as the enemy. Maybe it was our having to be so secret, so completely alone. And with the coming of the summer heat, so naked when we were alone, like children hiding together for their games out of the sun with no thought for the country of men and women somewhere else. But even when I would help Martin dress so that we could sit near the light for the day's lesson or when I would tidy his uniform before he went out and turned away in the direction opposite to the one I would take through the trees, he didn't change into the enemy. The war was not ours then. The war belonged to another place.

And that is where it stayed until the day we became bold enough to move outside. That was near the end of our second month. It was my doing, and the reason I gave for wanting it was the rising heat in our room as we approached the heart of summer. The air became so heavy at times that it could kill one's breath, and at other times it was so still and thick that it weakened the will outside sleep. But the truth is, one could get used to that, or at least learn to accept it, just as one had to with the dying light and the pressure of time as the days seemed in a hurry to grow shorter.

The real reason was something else. I began to feel imprisoned in that shed. I became restless about having to conceal myself every passing minute we were together, and never a chance to be open to the sky even if it had to remain a nighttime sky. I suppose most unlawful lovers must long for a few moments of freedom from the need to hide, a few moments to be as natural and honest in the open air as they are to each other in secret. What I was too young to understand was that our hot prison gave us all the freedom there could possibly be for the two of us. And I think this was a thing that Martin knew with certainty but could not teach me.

In any case, it was the cause of our first quarrel. And I won only by being so stubborn that Martin had no choice. I told him I was going to look for a hidden place in the hills outside my village where we could meet some evening as it turned dark and maybe sit out for an hour or two under the night sky to breathe the cooler mountain air and study the stars. Martin laughed when I made him understand what I had in mind. Then, when he saw that I was serious, he became equally serious.

I couldn't make out all the words he used to try and argue against me, but what I saw clearly was that he thought this a very dangerous bit of girlish foolishness. And of course he was right. But I insisted. Not that day, but two days following, after I failed to show up the next day for our usual meeting without warning him. This was a thing I did not so much to show him my mind as to spend that time searching the hillside beyond my village for the kind of place I was now certain I needed, we needed, in order to feel normal, whatever danger might be involved.

What I found was an empty sheepfold almost a kilometer beyond the edge of the village, one of the sheepfolds from before the war that hadn't been used recently and wouldn't be used until peace came and shepherds again had flocks to put out for grazing. It was off the road leading to Hortiáti mountain but not easily seen from that road by anyone who didn't already know where it was. I could get there by a path that went in that direction beyond the village, one of the many paths that one would use for gathering wild herbs from the mountainside and therefore not open to suspicion if one walked it alone.

It seemed to me the perfect hiding place for us, with more room than our woodshed and a thatched roof at least partly open to the sky. I told myself that it would be cool, and natural, mine and Martin's as much as anybody's, and no barbed wire between us and the world outside. When I got back home, I spent a good part of the night drawing a map for Martin to use in getting beyond the village and on the right path—a map almost as good as one he might have drawn.

He didn't say anything when I gave it to him the following evening at our usual meeting in the woodshed. He looked at it almost as though he didn't want to see what it was, then put it away in the pocket of his shirt. When I reached to take it out again, he held both my hands and made me sit down beside him so that we could talk. He tried again to tell me that my idea was foolish, but it was too late for me to be reasonable. I didn't want to hear any more arguments. His going to that sheepfold to meet me had now become a test, a way for me to learn if his feeling for me was as deep as mine for him, worthy of the same risk that I was willing to take, that I had already taken day after day.

I couldn't tell him that. All I could do was show him how firm my mind had become. And I did this by making him understand that if he wanted to see me again, he would have to do so by following my map to the "X" that marked the hiding place I'd found. He took out the map and studied it. Then he put it away again and looked at me with an expression so sad that I couldn't help but lean over and kiss both his cheeks. But that was all. When he tried to hold me, I broke free and stood up. Then I left him to sit where he was and decide our fate on his own.

The next day I went to the new hiding place after my work was done and I waited until after dark, but Martin didn't come. It was not a comfortable place, at least not if one had to be there very long alone. The thatched roof was coming apart in many places and so was the circle of branches that made up the wall of the fold, which meant that one had to choose carefully where to sit in order to be protected. And there was a mixture of straw and dung for a rug, both old enough to leave only a quiet odor but not pleasant for lying down. I spent that first evening cleaning the only space I could find that was well sheltered by the roof, and some space beyond that for sitting in the open, and then I spread what I'd cleared with a light covering of straw that I'd shaken clean. I sat there until the stars came out completely, but I didn't stay to study them.

When Martin didn't appear the second evening I went there, I had bad thoughts. I wanted to believe that his not coming wasn't his fault, but if that was so, it meant that something had prevented him from leaving his place of work and climbing up to my village to follow the map I'd given him. We had never talked about the life he lived when we were not together, what restrictions he might be under, because there was no life for us outside our woodshed. And I hadn't given him a chance to tell me what difficulties he might face in doing what I had insisted he do. The only way I could learn that now would be by meeting him again in our usual place.

But what if his not coming to the new hideout I'd found was his own choice, whether out of fear or his own kind of pride? How could I swallow my own pride now and crawl back to him? I couldn't bear to think of that. But at the same time I couldn't bear to think of losing him. I sat there in complete misery. Then I decided I would give him one more chance to come to me, and if he didn't, I would give myself one more chance to go to him.

Martin came the third evening. He arrived out of breath, in his uniform, and he sat down beside me without saying anything. I watched his eyes move from me to circle the inside of the sheep-fold. When he took off his cap and I brought his head next to mine, I felt his hair damp with sweat. He got up suddenly and went over to the opening that had let him into our new hideout and he stood there a minute gazing out at the path that had brought him there. Then he came back and sat beside me again. When I asked him what it was, why he looked the way he did, he tried to explain in language I couldn't really understand, though I gathered he was afraid somebody was following him, or might follow him. I told him not to be afraid, that I was sure it was going to be all right, but that just made him get up again and check the path outside the sheepfold.

When he came back to me, he took my head in his hands and told me it was no good, we couldn't meet this way, he had come to me because he knew he had to, but it was too dangerous, he couldn't do it again. I held his head in turn, caressed his hair, kissed it where it was damp, held him as close as I could to show him I understood what he had done for me. When I released my hold so that I could kiss his face, I saw that he was weeping, freely but without a sound. I tried to kiss his eyes dry, but he couldn't stop.

We made love in that place, and though it was tender, it wasn't right for either of us, not the way it had been. While we sat there side by side waiting for enough darkness to cover our return, I told him he wouldn't have to come there again if it was so difficult for him. I would come to him as I always had, and maybe the time would arrive soon when there was no longer a war to keep us from being as free as lovers ought to be. He said he was sure that would happen before long, the war was not going well for his people. And then he turned to look at me and said that even if he had to leave my country sometime soon with the German army, he would come back to find me when the war was truly over. To show me that he meant this, he made a cross with his finger first on his chest and then on mine. It wasn't the way we make the sign of the cross in this country, but I believed what it said, and I kissed his hand to tell him that I did.

I didn't know it at the time, but the sign he made that evening killed the demon inside me. That is, it killed any chance that it would possess me in some shape that was not the shape of this blond German soldier. Martin and I had left the sheepfold apart, he ahead of me, and he must have walked swiftly, because he was already swallowed up by the village by the time I came out to the main road. I went to our usual woodshed the next evening as I'd agreed to do, and all I found there during the hour I waited was darkness and heat. When that happened the next evening as well, I knew Martin wouldn't be coming there again, though I went back one more time just in case, after I'd put off doing that as many days as I could bear. I refused to believe he had simply chosen not to see me again. I decided that he must have thought our old meeting place too dangerous now as well, that he was trying to protect me and would soon find another way for us to meet. When this didn't happen day after day, I began to find it difficult to accept what I wanted to believe only on faith, and the new pride rising in me made me bold again. I decided to go to him while he was at work, a thing I hadn't done since that day so many weeks before when he'd taken care of the fingers I'd wounded for him.

I knew it wouldn't be wise to use the same trick to get to him again since it would involve the women I worked with, so I tried another. On the way from my dormitory to the kitchen during the lunch hour the next day, I stopped to pick up a branch from a thorn bush on the edge of the forest and I scraped it against my left arm until there were long bloody streaks there. I rubbed dirt over the arm so that it would seem I had injured it by falling, and then I made a sling out of the bandanna I always wore when I walked outside. I went on across the old main road to the court-yard that led to the building where they gave out medicines, walk-ing quickly. I kept my eyes always on the ground when I passed people on the way, my wounded arm held out in front of my breasts. Nobody chose to stop me. When I reached the room with the medicines, Martin was not there.

The soldier behind the desk was an older man, fat and bald. The top of his head was pimpled with drops of sweat. I stood in the doorway staring at him, and he stared right back at me. The desk was stacked with papers on one side, and though there were still medicines in the cases behind the desk and a sink with bottles beside it, the room had a different look and a different smell from what I remembered. I didn't know what to do. I finally raised the arm in its sling and thrust it out in front of me as though offering it to him. The soldier shook his head. When I still didn't go away, he came around to the front of the desk and took the sling off to have a look. He shook his head again as though my coming there was a mistake, it was none of his business. When I didn't move, he finally went over to the sink to pick up the bottle of fizzy water that Martin had used to clean my wounded fingers. I let the soldier wipe my arm with cotton dipped in that water, though he didn't do it gently enough, but when he went back to pick up the bottle of iodine, I turned and ran down the corridor outside and kept on running until I was out of that building and as far away from it as I could get while my breath held out.

It must have been a week later, when my arm didn't look so terrible any longer, that I found the courage to show it to the woman who took care of that building as an excuse to see if I could learn anything from her about why Martin hadn't been where he was supposed to be. I told the woman that my arm had been cleaned by the soldier who was in the room where they gave out medicines, but that this soldier was much rougher with people than the young one who had worked on my cut fingers, and I wondered what hours that soldier worked there. The woman shrugged. She said she hadn't seen the young soldier for days and assumed he had been sent elsewhere. "Where is elsewhere?" I asked her. The woman just looked at me. "How do I know? Elsewhere could be anywhere you want it to be."

I knew there was no hope after that. And I also knew what had happened was surely my fault. If Martin had been sent away, it meant he had done something that couldn't be forgiven, and I was sure now that this had to do with his coming to find me in the sheepfold beyond my village. He must have gone outside our barbed wire enclosure without permission and somebody must have turned him in for doing that. Or somebody must have reported seeing him go into the countryside or coming back from there, maybe one or another of his people in my village, where the Germans had another headquarters.

I was certain none of his people had seen him with me, because that would have meant my being punished in some way I couldn't bring myself to think about. But there had been an evil spirit with us in the sheepfold that evening, and he had felt it there the moment he arrived. I remembered how afraid he'd been when he first came in to sit beside me. He had said from the start that we couldn't meet like that again. And later he had said things that I now realized were his way of telling me that he could no longer see any life left for the two of us, at least not until the war was over.

I didn't go back home that evening right after work but went to sit by myself in that horrible sheepfold. It was a place I hated now, as I hated myself for having insisted that my German soldier come to me there. And I suppose I went back there to make myself suffer for what I had done. But sitting alone in that sheepfold soon stirred up my pride so that I became defiant, and my understanding had moved in a different direction by the time I reached home. I saw then bitterly but clearly that it was the enemy and their war that had cost me Martin, and this made my hatred cling less to me and more to his people. The change in me became complete a few days later, when I decided to do what I could to help my own people by gathering what information I might steal from the Germans I worked for.

My husband Vassílis has told me that you already know how this came about. He didn't say just how much you know, but I believe he was honest enough to tell you about his attack on me one morning from the side of the road below my village. I can smile about it now, but when it happened, I really thought it was my end, at least the end of my virginity, because I was sure that is what he had in mind. And this was several weeks before I met Martin, when I was still pure. What I remembered most after Vassílis' attack was his odor, almost unbearably a man's odor, and a man who had spent too long in the mountains. And I remembered his voice, so quiet and sure of itself as he spoke into my ear, so different from what I was told by the force of his holding me against the ground with all his weight and with his hand sealing my mouth. He was so young then, so strong and slender that you wouldn't think he could become what he is now, with his belly hanging over his belt and his cheeks marked with red veins from too much raki and cognac. But the voice is the same when it's quiet. And there's still gentleness in this man. Maybe even some wisdom.

But let me finish with the business about my trying to help the resistance, which seems to be what interests you most about me, along with what documents I may still hold. I had not given Vassilis a chance to tell me just what he wanted from me because at the time of his attack I had no intention of giving him anything he might want. Three months later, when my hatred had turned toward the enemy and my shame had become defiance, I wanted to let him know that I was ready to do what I could for the partisan group my father had joined in the mountains. But I still had no plan. And I didn't know exactly where he was or how to reach him. The only way I could imagine telling him what I had in mind was by sending him something, something that I might steal from one of the offices in the building where Martin used to work and where most of the German officers spent their days. I didn't know what I might steal, but it had to be something written in German that looked official, so that it would tell Vassilis it had come from the enemy's hands.

This was not an easy thing for me to do. I often helped to clean that building after my work was over in the dormitory across the main road, but I was never allowed in there while the German officers were on duty, and when they were gone from the day's work, everything of any value in those offices was carefully locked up. I would need Vassilis' help, or somebody else's help, to learn how to steal from locked cabinets and drawers, but for the moment I simply wanted one official paper to show him my good intentions.

I remember that it was a few days before the Feast of the Holy Virgin in mid-August when luck came my way, if one can call it that. I had made a habit of helping to dust at least two of the larger offices in that building every late afternoon, and as many of the smaller ones as I could get to in time, but not once had I found anything lying out on a desk or table that might be useful to me. There were German calendars here and there, sometimes a photograph of someone's wife or family, nothing with writing, nothing that looked official. One office attracted me more than the others because it was by itself at the back of a much larger office with several desks in it. This more private office had its own large desk and bookcases and a row of cabinets made of nice wood against one wall. I was certain it belonged to an important officer. But what drew me there was my being able to dust it quickly while the other women worked in the outer office. And as I dusted that room from one end to the other, I could check every drawer and every cabinet in my path to see if one or another had been left open by mistake.

Then a strange thing happened. One afternoon while I was in there working quickly before the other women joined me, dusting all the cabinets and checking to see if any one of them might be open and then dusting every surface of the desk and checking each drawer in that as well, the German officer who worked in that office came back after hours. I suppose he came back to pick up something he'd left behind, at least that is what I thought at the time. He didn't come in right away, and I was too intent on my work at his desk to notice him standing in the doorway until he actually spoke to me. "What are you doing there?" he said to me quietly in German, and I felt my heart come up into my throat.

He was an older man, maybe twenty years older than me, with hair that was turning gray at the sides. His nose was like a hooked knife and his eyebrows were at an angle, so that his face looked as though it was made for sorrow, as one sees in some dogs. I didn't know how long he'd been standing there, but however long, I was certain he must have seen me testing the drawers of that desk and maybe the cabinet doors as well. I stood up straight behind the desk without answering him. How could I admit that I knew some German? Then I came around the desk and picked up the trash bag I carried. I crossed quickly to go out the door as though that is what was expected of me now that a German officer had come into the room. He barred me from going out the door with his arm, smiling as he did so. I backed away and stood against the wall. I was sure he was going to accuse me of trying to get into his desk. But instead of that, he just stood there with his arms crossed studying me without saying anything, as though seeing how long I could stand his gaze without breaking into tears. And I stood there gazing back at him just as firmly because that was the only weapon I had. Then he suddenly uncrossed his arms and went over to the desk to pick up the wastebasket beside his chair. He brought it over and handed it to me. "You forgot this," he said. "You must not forget this tomorrow. You understand?"

I understood the German, but the truth is, I didn't understand what he meant, because I hadn't forgotten to empty the wastebasket. There was nothing in it. Wastebaskets were always the first things I took care of in my cleaning. I didn't simply empty them into my trash bag but always checked what was there just in case something I could use had been thrown away. There were never any papers, only trash—cigarette boxes, paper handkerchiefs, peelings, scraps with numbers on them sometimes, but nothing to be read. The Germans were too careful for that. I just stared at the empty wastebasket, thinking this German was trying to humiliate me in some stupid way. Then he took the wastebasket out of my hand and returned it to the side of his desk. "Tomorrow," he said. "You must not forget this tomorrow. You understand me?"

How was I supposed to understand him? I gazed at him as firmly as I had before, not afraid any longer if he saw the hatred in my eyes. Then he did something very strange. He unlocked one of his desk drawers and turned over some papers in there, slowly, one by one. Then, without looking up, he discarded one of those papers into the wastebasket. He locked the drawer again. "You understand now?" he said, pointing at the wastebasket. Then he sat back in his chair, leaned back as though waiting for an answer.

I studied his face. He wasn't smiling, but there was something soft in his look, certainly nothing that seemed a threat. I went over and picked up the wastebasket and emptied it into my trash bag with only a glance at what was there. It was a sheet of paper with writing on it, that was all I could tell. The officer said "thank you" as I turned toward the door. Then I was certain I heard him say "tomorrow" in Greek. I turned to look at him. He said it again, half-smiling now, as though the Greek word, or his way of saying it, embarrassed him. Then he stood up and walked stiffly past me out of the room.

What in God's name was I to make of this? I couldn't wait to get to the dump cart with my trash bag to see what it was that he'd wanted me to carry away. But when I dug out the sheet that he'd discarded into his wastebasket, it said nothing to me because it wasn't in my language. It seemed to be a balance sheet or chart of some kind, with a list of words or names and then numbers with periods between them in columns that looked like dates, and next to those, other numbers with letters beside them. There was no stamp on it or anything else to show that it was an official paper. In any case, I was sure this officer would not have thrown out anything of importance, especially not in front of me.

But then why had he thrown it out at all? If he'd wanted to pretend that I wasn't doing my work properly and ought to do it better tomorrow, why would he thank me at the end for doing the unnecessary thing of emptying a wastebasket that had been empty until he chose to discard something into it? And why bother trying to humiliate me with this stupid little game when he could have reported me for testing the locked drawers in his desk? That was a thing that would have caused my dismissal at the very least and probably something worse.

I decided it would be best not to mention what had happened to anybody until I could work out what it meant. It wasn't until late that night, after I'd lain awake too long worrying about what had happened, that certain thoughts came to me with enough force to seem true. Maybe this officer's little game wasn't stupid at all. And maybe the last thing he wanted was my dismissal. It seemed to me that the only way what had happened made sense was if he had understood exactly what I was trying to do and meant to make it easy for me. But why would he do that? I could think of only one reason. Wasn't it possible that, like my Martin, he wanted his war to be over? And also like my Martin, might he not believe, as so many others did that summer, that the war was no longer going at all well for his country, that his country would soon have to begin a retreat to the north? And if this was so, might he not now be looking for a way to save himself from the disaster ahead of him by turning himself over to our people, to someone who could help him reach the partisans?

This may seem to you just the fantasy of a frightened young

woman with troubled thoughts. Not so. Our village had heard about one Austrian officer who was said to have come over to our side earlier in the summer, not one of those assigned to the head-quarters where I worked but to another group of officers who had taken over the school house in Arsakli. This news had caused much talk both in the village and among the women working with me at the American School. That Austrian officer was known in the village as a man who was good with our children and some-times allowed them in to see the films that were shown in the school house for the entertainment of the Germans serving there. One day he simply disappeared from that school house. Though there had been much commotion among the Germans, much roar-ing of motorcycles through the village and searching of houses and the rest, the officer was never found, at least not in Arsakli. We assumed he had been hidden by one or another of our resistance groups and had eventually been taken far from the city. And it was said by those who pretended to know about such things that he must have come to the resistance with something valuable enough to earn the protection he was looking for or else he would have been returned to his own people with his throat slit through. I finally went to sleep that night quite certain that my gray-haired officer hoped I might somehow help him escape his war in the same way.

The test of my thinking that night lay in the wastebasket the fol-lowing afternoon. It took much courage for me to go back to that office as though nothing had happened, but I did it. The office was empty, and everything was just as I had left it the day before, but one look at the wastebasket told me that my thinking was right. It was full of things that had never been there before, mostly maga-zines and newspapers. I emptied it carefully into my trash bag, and dusted the desk as usual. The drawers were all locked. I didn't bother to check the cabinets but dusted them quickly and went out to tell the women working in the outer office that I had a terrible headache and would be going home now. At the dump cart in the back of the building, I went through the newspapers and maga-zines page by page until I found what I knew would be there. It was a page covered on both sides with German writing, and a date at the top, and a scribble like an omega for a signature. I had no doubt that it was official. It was certainly official enough to serve for my message to Vassílis. As soon as I got home I put it in an envelope with his name on it, and then I decided I might as well also put in the other paper with dates and numbers on it .

It took me some days to get this envelope on its way to where it was meant to go, and those were difficult days for me. Vassílis himself was somewhere in the mountains, nobody knew where nor was supposed to know. The only way I could reach him was by going to those in our village who had been political associates of my father and asking them to send me any one of Vassílis' men or women who showed up in our region for one reason or another because I had an important message for him. I said nothing more, and since my message was for Vassílis, I was asked for no more than I gave out. The man who finally came to me was hardly older than a boy, but I could tell that he was a true *andarte* from the terrible smell he brought with him off the mountain and the confusion of clothes he was wearing, half some kind of uniform and half rags. I had no choice but to trust him, so I gave him the envelope and made him swear on his mother's life that he would personally hand it to Vassílis without opening it.

The days I waited to hear from Vassílis brought no peace to me, as they surely could not have to my German officer. He became my new torment, not because of any demon in him or me, but because of the new danger that he had brought into the war we still had to share. Though enemies, we were obliged to speak to each other now that I knew he was trying to leave his side to join ours, yet we couldn't speak directly. He never showed himself during those days, I suppose because he was afraid to be seen with me until it became absolutely necessary. And this meant that we could talk to each other only in a ridiculous way, through his wastebasket.

I knew he was waiting for me to send him a signal of some kind, because as I continued to clean his office I uncovered things in the wastebasket that made this clear. Two days in a row I found more official papers between the pages of a discarded newspaper, nothing that I could understand but surely of some value if he chose to send them out like that. Of course he couldn't be certain that they were going where he wanted them to go, but at the same time, since they might truly be useful to Vassílis, I couldn't bring myself to send them back as a signal that I had indeed received them but that he should stop this business that was so dangerous for both of us until I had news to send him in return. The third day I found some German money between the pages of a magazine. The money was useless to me, but it embarrassed me to receive it nevertheless. I had no difficulty sending the money back in the same magazine, and I did that by leaving his wastebasket full the next day and using the magazine to cover all that I'd failed to remove.

My officer understood this message. The wastebasket was completely empty the next day, and the day after that. I don't know how he managed to get rid of his trash during those days, I imagine by dropping it in wastebaskets outside his office, but his doing so didn't liberate me from him. I kept thinking about how desperate he must have been to have risked what he did to reach me, and how desperate he must be now that I'd silenced his wastebasket. And then it came to me that in truth he may have taken heart from what I'd done, that however he may have understood my returning his money to him, at least it told him that his discarded papers and the message they carried had reached me safely. But of course I couldn't really be sure of his thinking anymore than he could be of mine.

What followed was silence. I assumed that while I waited to hear from Vassílis, my officer waited to hear from me, and though his wastebasket was no longer empty during working days, I didn't find any newspapers or magazines in it. Then one day, at the end of the month, the magazine that had carried the money came back into the wastebasket, only this time what I found in it was a photograph of two young girls. They were maybe ten and eight years old, both with blonde hair in pigtails and wearing those full skirts that northern people sometimes wear, tight at the waist. Those girls were like porcelain dolls, with very white skin, pale blue eyes, not a hair out of place on their heads, and teeth as perfect as they are made. Each had an arm around the other, barely touching, so that only the fingertips showed. Their color made me think of Martin. For a second that photograph caused tears to come, but only for a second. I pushed it aside quickly, just as I had pushed aside the officer's money.

Of course I understood this meant that my officer was getting restless, maybe truly desperate, and that he was trying to reach the woman in me to see if that might make me do something to show him that I was still listening. And though I resisted this at first, when I hadn't heard from Vassílis by the beginning of the following week, I felt that before I could free myself from this German, I had to prove to him that I was at least honorable, whatever he might be, and that I had as much courage as he did. I decided I would give him a chance to meet me just once so that I could tell him I was waiting to hear from those he wanted to find and he should leave me alone from then on until I had news for him. I hoped in this way I might release myself for a while from the new fear that he'd brought into my life, whether or not he had the courage to face me again.

There was only one place I could think of for us to meet in secret that might be acceptable to him because it was inside his enclosure, though I found no relief in the thought of returning so soon to the woodshed that had been my beginning and my end. I couldn't possibly give this officer the map that Martin had drawn to guide me there—it was the only thing of his I had left—so I drew a careful copy of it, with a clock saying seven and a sun below a line for the horizon. This I sent to the officer's wastebasket inside the magazine he'd sent me, clipped to the back of his porcelain children.

The officer did not come to the woodshed. The first time I went there by my usual route, I stayed among the trees at a distance because I found the door shut. I waited there for an hour, but the door didn't open, and there was no sign that anyone was there. The second time I waited an hour again, then decided to leave my hiding place and cross the barren garden in front of the door to open it, though that sent a tremor through me that cut my breathing short. There was no officer waiting for me, but he had been there at some point because what I found on the ground just inside the door was the same old magazine that we had passed to each other before, only there was nothing in it this time. When I had finished leafing through it, I realized that it was there merely to give a name, even if unknown, to the small bouquet of wild flowers that I'd found lying on top of it.

I stared at those wild flowers as though they were the officer's severed head. What in God's name did he mean to tell me by this ridiculous gift? Had the poor fool misunderstood my map to mean that I wanted to meet him for romance? Was he now completely out of his mind? Or had he come at a time when he knew I wouldn't be there to leave this final offering because he was afraid I was setting a trap for him? How could I do that within his own barbed wire enclosure and how could I do that without condemning myself? Or was he just too much of a coward to take the chance of being seen with me and chose what he thought was a gentlemanly German way of saying that? If this was what he meant to say, how was I supposed to answer his cowardice?

There was a simple answer, of course. I could return the flowers and the magazine to his wastebasket, and that would surely send him a message that he could not fail to understand. But what if Vassílis then came to me, or sent one of his people, expecting to do business with this German deserter? I decided to leave the flowers and the magazine where I had found them, only with the magazine turned upside down. The officer could make of that whatever he wanted. And if Vassílis did reach me, I would let him figure out what to do next. I had done enough for him and his *andartes* in my father's name. I was through playing dangerous games with the enemy. I lay the flowers in the center of the magazine, and as I stepped back to shut the door, the feeling came to me suddenly that I was shutting out the light from someone's tomb.

The next day I learned that my officer had disappeared from our headquarters the previous day. He had disappeared just as the Austrian officer had from the headquarters in Arsaklí. There was great activity among the Germans in our enclosure and talk of nothing else among the women I worked with. I tried to appear calm in the midst of all the disturbance, but I was frightened to the bottom of my soul. It was no benefit to me to discover that my view of this officer, of his truly being a deserter, had been correct from the start. I wondered now if he had become so desperate waiting for me to send him the message he wanted as to turn entirely reckless. Or had he thrown out anchors in several directions all along, and one that wasn't meant for me found a hold someplace else to reward him? That was the best hope. But what if his people caught up with him now and made him reveal that I was one of those with whom he had played so shamelessly trying to arrange his desertion?

I wanted to leave my enclosure that very day and go into hiding somewhere, but I didn't see how I could do this without creating suspicion even among the women I worked with. Then, the following day, a thing happened that made it easy for me. The resistance killed my soldier, not the officer, but my Martin. At least that is what I then believed beyond any doubt.

You have asked about the massacre at the village of Hortiáti, and Vassílis has told you what happened there in the same words that he has told me, as have others, not once but more times than I care to hear. Vassílis will say that no one can be sure who killed the German doctor and wounded the others who were ambushed near the aqueduct, but what he does know is that those bullets did not come from men in his resistance group. I am willing to believe that now—what choice do I have?—but I did not believe it that day of the massacre or in the days that followed. What I believed then was that the papers I had sent Vassílis, especially the chart with dates and numbers on it, had been the cause of that *andarte* ambush. And I also believed that this German doctor, who was called a good man by so many of those villagers and who was said by the women I worked with to have been called blonder than Alexander the Great and as gentle in his manner as men are made, was not a doctor at all. He was a medical soldier, the one I knew as Martin, assigned to this position of protecting the water source for that village and all the territory below it after he had been forced to leave his work in my headquarters because of what I had made him do.

Why was I so sure? I will tell you why. What I understood at that moment was this: the meaningless chart with dates and numbers on it which the deserting officer chose to leave in his wastebasket that first afternoon after searching through other papers in his drawer was not so meaningless to him. I understood for the first time that it must have meant two things to him. One thing was that it had something to do with Martin, maybe a chart of the dates that the water source needed to be purified and the quantity of whatever chemical our headquarters supplied for the purpose. And another thing was that he knew or maybe suspected that I also had something to do with Martin and he was trying to tell me this because it was useful for what he had in mind for himself. Of course it may have been just a momentary thought on his.part. Even if he did suspect that I was the woman who had been involved with Martin, the one he had gone to the countryside to visit, how could he really expect me to understand what his chart was supposed to show me? In any case, I did finally understand, though by that time it could serve no useful purpose for him or me.

I am sure there are those who would say that this belief of mine was a girl's hysteria. That could be. God knows I had reason for hysteria in those days. But I felt it to be the truth as no other truth I knew. Of course I couldn't swear that the chart with dates and numbers on it had anything to do with my Martin and the purifications of his new assignment, but it seemed entirely logical to me that it was so. And there were things reported that helped my belief, not only the way people described the dead German who was the cause of the massacre, so like my Martin, but the fact that this new assignment was the kind of work he could easily do and might even have wanted to do.

There was something else. This belief told me how Martin's war had ended—how our war had ended, and with it, our possible life. One can say that I made up his death in this way to explain to myself why he didn't return to me that summer or anytime after the war. That could also be so. What I know is that my belief was strong enough to put me into silent but deep mourning. And though that lasted longer than it should have in a young woman, it worked to cure me of the war entirely. Even of the guilt I felt for having put my German soldier into such danger. But it did not cure me of Martin. And that is a thing I have told nobody until this day.

I left the enclosure where I worked immediately after the massacre of Hortiáti village. And as soon after that as I could gather my things, I left the village of Arsaklí. I did that by lying to my mother again, that is, by telling her only half the truth for a start. I told her that for three months now I'd had a lover. This was a thing that didn't seem to surprise her at all, though I could see it hardly pleased her, especially when I told her that the lover had now deserted me. And then I told her a straight lie, that I now had the signs of being pregnant, and for this reason I thought it best for me to go away, maybe to the city, maybe to my aunt's place in the old section of the city near the prison towers. Nobody need know where I had gone, I said. My mother looked at me as though I'd come to her to announce that I had leprosy. She stared at me and said nothing, the sorrow in her face struggling with disgust. But when I began to gather my things, she helped me silently, which was her way of saying that what I'd decided to do was the best thing.

I think I have written enough in answer to your questions. What followed in my life is of no interest to anyone but myself, and, I suppose, to my husband. It has nothing to do with the war and the German occupation that now interest you and other foreigners. Though maybe that is not quite true. Maybe one could say that I finally agreed to marry Vassílis so many years after the war because he had been part of the history of those days I couldn't entirely escape, the part that remained so strong in my memory. Even if he himself doesn't remember receiving the chart that I am still certain helped to kill my lover. It is possible of course that he discarded this piece of paper as less important than the other one he kept, and that the chart then fell into other hands working for the resistance. It's also possible that somebody removed it from the envelope I sent him and gave it to those who arranged the ambush. I am ready to believe that or anything else he prefers. Ready for his sake if not mine. Ready in any case to let the past we talk about be what he wants it to be for the sake of necessary peace. But one thing I can still be sure of is that my memory of those days does not lie, whether or not you choose to believe it.

THREE

Vienna: even with its remembered music, this Vienna, Ripaldo decided, was not among his favorite cities. It had been once, some thirty-five years earlier, after he'd come there for the first time during the Grand Tour that he'd arranged for himself after his G. I. Bill money ran out but before he'd splurged most of his savings yachting with Wittekind in the Aegean. Vienna in those days was the city of the Third Man. There was zither music everywhere, Orson Welles and Joseph Cotton and Trevor Howard look-a-likes drinking Kaffee mit Schlag at the next table and the beautiful Valli walking alone and away down the path of one or another public garden. The giant Ferris wheel was also there in the distance, lit up after dark to show that pleasure in the Vienna of those days easily crossed the boundary between day and night. But there was a difference. In the black and white movie it had been a city that seemed to carry a left-over aura of defeat in its air, with dark streets and underground passages and stark ruins against a dusky sky. By the time Ripaldo arrived for his fist visit, there was little trace of the war to inhibit the city's emerging hedonism. The enemy was dressed in lederhosen, and Vienna had the look of a vast playground, full of open spaces for games where the war ruins had been cleared away, full of parks where midgets rode toy trains and long-legged girls danced lean and careless. The four-power occupation forces appeared to be on holiday. Ripaldo had run into a Russian soldier standing alone on a bridge over the Danube Canal, and sometime later a French officer kissing his girl in the dark alley that had once hid all of Harry Lime except for the tilt of his ironic and corrupt head, but their war seemed long over too, crime of another generation if only a few years gone.

Vienna had been the high point of Ripaldo's grand tour. And over time it remained an image of careless pleasure that seemed impervious to the relentlessly modern progress that Ripaldo read about during the post-war decades. But when he returned for the first time after so many years to meet Wittekind and his local committee, the city had the wrong feel. Day or night it seemed dull, heavy, the old buildings as arrogant as much of their history, the newer buildings stark, even taller, without the charm or threat of any history at all. It seemed largely a commercial city now, expensive, the music mostly canned, the cafes set up for business transactions and tourist traffic. And the politics of the place had begun to go bad again. Skinheads were said to roam through underground regions waiting for a signal to crack the skulls of foreigners and refugees. And above ground old Nazis were coming out of hiding to train new Nazis in the political process. The giant Ferris wheel on the edge of the Volksprater seemed unchanged, but the largest shadow in that city was now cast by the Big O's unconfessed past.

Ripaldo's sudden return to Vienna had come about after another urgent phone call to his Salonika hotel from Wittekind. He learned that the Big O's political campaign had begun to heat up alarmingly, and with or without his solicitation, forces on the Right, including those in the neo-Nazi movement, were now working hard and with growing success to increase support for his candidacy, especially in the provinces. Wittekind thought it vital now that his committee come up with the kind of evidence that would discredit the distinguished statesman once and for all and that this happen soon. He remained convinced, after reading Marina Angeloúdis' deposition, that she was still their best hope for finding the right evidence, and that meant Ripaldo had to go back to her village immediately to talk to her again.

"Never mind any longer what she remembers or doesn't remember," Wittekind said. "Just get her documents. And then bring them to me."

"How am I supposed to do that when I can't even get her to talk to me directly?"

"Promises," Wittekind said. "Make promises."

"Like what? I told you, she's not the kind you can bribe."

"I'm not talking money," Wittekind said. "I'm talking sentiment. Go for her heart."

"That's your territory. I'm no good at that. A registered failure, in fact."

"I don't say you should try to make her fall in love with you. We're not that desperate yet. Work with her memories of the boy she loved in the trenches."

"What trenches?"

"The blond soldier. The one with the tender heart."

"And just how do I do that, Wittekind? Especially when the soldier is dead."

"Ah, but do we know that for a fact? And even if he is dead, would she not like to know this for certain? Know for certain, anyway, what really happened to him?"

"Maybe. But I doubt it. I get the feeling she'd just as soon leave things as they are."

"Well, try it. Promise her that you'll find out the truth. But only if she gives you the documents first to help you get there."

"So I'm to bribe her into giving up what she clearly won't want to give up with a promise I can't even be sure I can keep?"

"Please," Wittekind said. "This sudden puritanism is making me uncomfortable. It isn't a bribe if the woman simply helps us find a necessary truth that will also help her. Remember our mission. Catching the big fish."

"I don't get the connection," Ripaldo said.

"The point is, the documents are what will bring her the truth about her lost lover, which can only do her good. Help her live with her past. And they will also set us on the right tack for catching our fish by hooking her lover's Wehrmacht boss. Do you follow me?"

"Not really. You mean the officer with the wastebasket? The deserter?"

"Correct, Ripaldo. You bring me the lady's documents and I'll give you her lost lover for you to do with as you please. Is it a deal?"

Wittekind had gone on to explain what he was driving at. He'd

become convinced by Marina's deposition that she was right to suspect that the deserting officer knew about her liaison with Martin
before he took the chance of using her as a possible messenger to
the resistance movement. And if he knew about that, the officer
was very likely to know what had happened to Martin after he'd
left the American School enclosure on another assignment. But
what really interested Wittekind was the possible connection
between the deserting officer and other officers at the intelligence
headquarters up the hill from that School. The document having
to do with British commandos captured on an island in the
Aegean that the officer had passed on to Marina could have come
from one source only: an officer at the Ic/AO intelligence headquarters in Arsakli.

"And we know who was such an officer in the summer of 1944,
don't we?" Wittekind said.

"The lieutenant with an initial like an omega."

"Right. And we now know for a fact not only the full name that
goes with that initial but most of the war it tried to hide. Our committee has strong evidence of exactly where that Wehrmacht lieutenant traveled and how he spent his days."

What the committee had uncovered recently from sources in
Italy, Germany, and Austria itself was not only proof of the Big O's
proximity to those regions of Bosnia-Herzegovina where there had
been cleansing operations by the occupiers but new evidence that
brought him intimately close to atrocities against civilians in
regions of both Epirus and Southern Greece. But the evidence so
far consisted mostly of reports, sometimes initialed and sometimes
not, that the young Wehrmacht lieutenant had issued from the
security of his army unit's office in Athens. And the reports were
in laundered language, converting known atrocities into what were
called counter-partisan operations against pockets of armed resistance. So the Athens phase of his duty in Greece was still largely
under the cover of subterfuge. The committee was now basing its
strongest hope on finding the direct evidence it needed from
records and witnesses who had served with the young Wehrmacht
lieutenant while he was the O3 intelligence officer in Northern
Greece toward the end of the Occupation. There were new
grounds for believing that during the period in question, it had

been the lieutenant's section of Army Group E in Arsakli that was responsible for the deportation of Jews from Corfu, Crete, and Rhodes to Auschwitz. There were also grounds for believing that it had been his section of Army Group E that had supervised the interrogation and torture of captured Allied commandos before handing them over to the SD security police for execution in accordance with Hitler's secret order of 18 October 1942 calling for the "special treatment" of uniformed commandos, in criminal violation of both the Geneva Convention and German military tradition.

The documents in hand left no doubt about what methods the Wehrmacht had used in trying to contain resistance activities and commando raids in the last days of the German Occupation, and Vassílis Angeloúdis' account of the Hortiáti massacre had helped to fill in a gap in this connection since that massacre had remained buried deeper in the history of the war than other like reprisals. But his account was still not that of an eye witness, and the link between that massacre and the Ic/AO intelligence unit in Arsakli still remained speculative, though there now seemed little doubt that this atrocity and others in the region had been ordered at a time when the Big O was one of the two O3 officers in that unit. More documentary evidence and an actual eye witness might clinch the case, Wittekind told Ripaldo, and that was why Marina's documents could prove crucial.

"I promise you a long cruise either alone or with a lady of your choice along the southern Turkish border if you bring us what we need," Wittekind said before hanging up. "I've been told the fishing there is as good as it was to the west in our younger days, and the winds of hope are still very sweet, even for those with gray hair. Do you grasp my meaning?"

Ripaldo had concluded that his prospects of getting what was needed from Marina Angeloúdis might improve if he went back there and faced her without the intercession of her husband Vassílis. He had also decided that her way of seeing things called for him to be as direct with her as diplomacy permitted. When she came to the door in answer to his ring, she stood there looking at him for a moment as though her eyes had to adjust to the glare of his image before she could tell who he was. Then, without a word, she stepped aside to let him in. She motioned him into the living room, then sat down on the edge of the settee.

"So. You got my letter. So many pages, but that isn't enough for you?"

"I got the letter, and I'm very grateful to have it," Ripaldo said. "I thank you for it. Most warmly. And I promise to keep it to myself. But I'll be honest with you, Mrs. Angeloúdis. I need something more."

"Well, you can't have more. What I gave you is already too much."

"I don't mean anything more that's personal," Ripaldo said. "The people I work for have need of the documents you mentioned in your letter. The official papers. What you gave your husband from the German officer who deserted. And anything else you may have from the war years."

Marina shook her head. She didn't say anything.

"Let me explain," Ripaldo said. "We're trying to find out things that are still important in Germany and Austria. For example, who was responsible for the massacre in Hortiáti village. We think those documents will help."

Marina shook her head again. "Why should I care about that now? Those papers are of no value to anyone but me."

"They may be of great value," Ripaldo said. "For one, they may help us identify the German officer who ordered that massacre. And other atrocities."

"You don't understand," Marina said, without looking up. "Those papers are all I have left."

"I do understand. I wouldn't think of keeping them. I just want to borrow them for a while."

"Why should I let you have them even for a while? Why should I trust you with them?"

Ripaldo gazed at her, then looked away. "They may help with something else," he said. "They may tell us what happened to Martin."

"Us? Who is us?"

"Just you and me," Ripaldo said. "No need for Vassílis to know."

"But this is ridiculous," Marina said. "I know what happened to Martin. He was killed at the aqueduct below Hortiáti village."

Ripaldo stood up and began to pace. He couldn't look at her.

"Maybe," he said. "But maybe not. We don't know that for sure. And I think I can find the officer who would know."

"What officer?"

"The officer of the wastebasket."

Marina didn't say anything. When Ripaldo finally looked over at her, she was staring at the floor, shaking her bent head.

"I know what I know," she said. "Martin died that day."

"You may be right, of course. But wouldn't it help you to know for certain? Wouldn't that make it easier for you to live with what happened?"

"I've lived with it all these years," Marina said, looking up. "Why do I need to know more than what my heart tells me?"

Ripaldo gazed at her. "I can't answer that," he said. "I just thought knowing the truth with certainty might free you from the wrong memories."

"Martin is dead. That is the certainty I know. And my memories—my memories are what they are."

Ripaldo went over and stood in front of her. He reached down and let his fingers touch the side of her head where the hair tightened toward the bun at the back, then took his hand away. Marina didn't move.

"I'm sorry," he said. "I really meant to help you. If it turns out you think I can, you know the hotel where I'm staying."

Ripaldo didn't call Wittekind. He decided to go off to the Chalkidiki peninsula and spend a few day on the border of Mt. Athos in a pension by the sea. He was tempted to keep going down that finger of the peninsula and visit what monasteries he could along the coast, but at the pension they told him that the rules for touring the Holy Mountain had become very strict of late, only five foreigners granted passes on any given day, and in any case he would have to fill out the necessary permission papers in Salonika. He decided to save the monasteries for the following week, assuming that by then his work for Wittekind would in fact have come to the dead end that it seemed to have reached already.

Back in his Salonika hotel lobby three days later, Ripaldo spotted the large white envelope in his mail box on his way up to the desk to ask for his key. He waited until he was in his room to open it. The report on the commandos captured on an Aegean island was there, and some other official papers that looked authoritative but didn't make much sense to him on first glance. There was no handwritten message from Marina, but in a separate envelope inside the large one, she had included the fragile map her lover had drawn to set up their first tryst in the spring of 1944. Ripaldo took that to be her message, her way of granting him permission to uncover what he could about her Martin and bring that news back to her along with the map and the other documents she'd been moved to lend him after all. He folded the map carefully and put it away in its envelope, then decided to seal that one shut with a lick.

Wittekind's committee, after reviewing Marina Angeloúdis' documents, determined that these called for some intense follow-up research. The report, signed by an initial, clearly the same "omega" scratch that appeared on some of the reports of counter-partisan activities which had come out of the Big O's Athens office, confirmed that the same kind of service had been rendered by the young Wehrmacht officer after he was transferred to the Ic/AO intelligence unit in Arsaklí. And it confirmed that the commandos of several nationalities captured on the Aegean island in July of 1944 had in fact been handed over to the security police, presumably for the fatal "special treatment" designated by Hitler's secret decree. But the follow-up research had determined that several of the British commandos identified in that particular report had not only survived the war but, in recent statements solicited during a British inquiry that had reviewed their case when the issue of commando torture and execution became public, had testified to their relatively reasonable treatment while in enemy hands. The other documents in Marina's envelope proved to be either local instructions meant to increase security throughout Army Group E in Northern Greece or reports on Wehrmacht operations in a broad area extending into Montenegro and Croatia, including counter-partisan activities in the region, but not specific enough to serve the committee's purposes conclusively without substantial further research.

Ripaldo heard the committee's response to Marina's offering while he and Wittekind were having an iced coffee at one of the outdoor tables of the Schwarzenberg on the Karntner Ring, both of them sweating freely from the sudden heat wave that had come into the city with the change from July to August. Wittekind had a handkerchief knotted around his neck to take up the sweat below his goatee, still neatly trimmed but totally white now, and he kept running his finger along the upper edge of the handkerchief as though tracing a scar there.

"Don't look so downcast," Wittekind said. "We still have work to do."

"I guess we can say we've at least got the son of a bitch cornered now," Ripaldo said. "Since we know exactly where he was that summer in 1944 and since it's obvious what he was up to."

"Correct," Wittekind said. "But we still don't have the smoking gun."

"Well, another thing we know is that we're never going to find a smoking gun in one of his documents, so we can give up on that. I told you from the start the man is too subtle to have put anything really incriminating in writing."

"But that is where you're wrong," Wittekind said. "The documents are still everything. Which is why I insisted you get your hands on them."

"I thought your people found them inconclusive."

"Of course in one sense they are. But in another sense they are essential."

"How is that?"

"Because as I told you over the phone, the documents are going to lead us to our necessary witness. The one who will point to the smoking gun."

Ripaldo took out his handkerchief and wiped the sweat off his face.

"I guess the heat is making me dense," he said. "I don't see how that follows from what we have in hand."

"Think a minute. Your friend Marina's officer of the wastebasket was working at her headquarters at the American School. How did this officer come to hold documents that were surely not his property but the property of the Ic/AO headquarters in Arsakli, as we've now established?"

"I don't know. I suppose they were distributed to him."

"Intelligence reports about the disposition of captured commandos? Not very likely. Such reports would be highly restricted."

"So what does that prove about the Big O that we don't know already?"

Wittekind's eyes smiled. "Nothing yet. But it means the officer of the wastebasket must have had a connection with the intelligence headquarters. He must have known somebody there. And not just somebody, but most probably the 03 officer who prepared those reports."

"Meaning the Big O."

"Right. And if he knew the Big O well enough to receive those reports, he surely would have been witness to the role the Big O played in these so-called counter-partisan activities. If only we can get this officer of the wastebasket to talk when we face him with your friend Marina's documents."

"That isn't the only if. How do we face him when we don't even know where he is? Or even if he's alive?"

"If he's alive we will find him," Wittekind said. "I will find him. And together we will make him talk."

"I like your optimism, Wittekind. It's charming in someone your age. But even if the officer of the wastebasket is alive and we do find him, is it likely that he will squeal on a fellow Wehrmacht officer? I'll give you odds against that."

"You challenge me? We'll see. I take pleasure in being challenged. Especially when it involves digging out Wehrmacht officers who've been in hiding from the war."

"Well, I'm ready to go along with you if only on the chance that we can get some news out of him about Marina's blond soldier. Remember, you and I made a deal on that score. And I made a deal with Marina."

Wittekind ran his finger under the length of his damp neckerchief. "Of course we made a deal. And I never go back on deals, Ripaldo. Not since you Americans taught me that deals are one thing in life that must be considered entirely sacred. More sacred than sexual and political fidelity, isn't it so, my friend?"

Wittekind had less trouble tracking down the turncoat Wehrmacht officer than even he had anticipated. For a start, the committee's researchers had already done the basic work of scouring German and Austrian sources for the names of those officers who had served in Yugoslavia and Greece during the German occupation of those countries, and they had come up with a fairly comprehensive roster drawn mostly from a file of Wehrmacht organizational charts. Wittekind had dug out one of these labeled "Gruppe Ic/AO" of Army Group E and dated in early December 1943, which included the Big O and another officer under the heading 03, and he now came up with a second chart dated some two months later that outlined the quartermaster unit—including a subdivision for medical supplies—at the headquarters housed in the American School grounds below Arsakli. The officer listed as being in charge of that unit was one Oberleutnant Hertzel.

Through his contacts in the old-boy Wehrmacht network, Wittekind managed to dig up a first name and a current address for former Oberleutnant Wolfgang Hertzel. He also learned that after the war Hertzel had been for a time the manager of a modest shoe store in Vienna, quite low-key, but had then moved on up to become part owner of a high-price clothing store and had retired some ten years previously. He had two married daughters, one living in Graz and the other in Klagenfurt. Hertzel himself now lived alone in a second-floor apartment off Mariahilfer Strasse not far from the Auer Welsbach Park. On the way there, Wittekind and Ripaldo decided to drop their taxi at the park and walk the rest of the way so that they had some time to plan strategy before going up to interview the old gentleman.

"Of course you have a point," Wittekind said. "The local political situation has made people somewhat sensitive these days. And anyone who served as a Wehrmacht officer in the Balkans may have some problems speaking about that war. So we have to be rather careful."

"Well, I'm perfectly willing to let you do all the talking," Ripaldo said. "My school German isn't great anyway. So I'll settle for watching his face to see if I can tell when he's lying and when he's telling the truth."

"No, I think you should do some of the talking. At least you can pretend to be a naive American. Which allows you to ask certain direct questions when diplomacy doesn't work."

"Like what questions?"

"Like how did the gentleman happen to come by those documents. And how well did he know his fellow Wehrmacht officer who became our distinguished statesman. And then move on ahead from there."

"Well if it comes to pretending naivete, why not go to the heart of the matter," Ripaldo said. "Why not ask him if he can tell us who the O3 officer was who ordered the Hortiáti massacre?"

Wittekind gazed at Ripaldo with a little smile. Then his lips puckered up to the size of a quarter.

"That is not being naive, my friend. That is being dumb. A subject like that has to be approached delicately when one is dealing with a Nazi of his rank."

"Even a deserter? Somebody who came over to our side? My side?"

"Yes, but remember the year he did that and how much he would already have on his conscience by that time."

"Except that he wouldn't have been directly involved in massacres. He was at the wrong headquarters."

"Yes, but he must have broken bread with those who were at that headquarters or else how did he come by those documents? They must have been part of the same Wehrmacht men's club in one of those villas your friend the cafe owner spoke about."

Ripaldo stopped to check the street name. "Well, I hope he turns out to have a conscience, but I wouldn't count on it."

"Not your kind of conscience, Ripaldo. His Wehrmacht conscience. Wrong orders given, wrong orders carried out, the mess certain undisciplined officers made, and so forth."

"What makes you think he won't take the same line as all the others on that score? Orders are orders, and whatever the orders, he had to follow them. Just like the Big O."

"We'll see," Wittekind said. "Maybe you're right about deserters. Anyway those who have betrayed their country for reasons of conscience. They sometimes come away with a respect for the truth—or at least a terrible fear of betraying their betrayal. And I know what I'm talking about."

Hertzel turned out to be a man well into his eighties, hooknosed as Marina Angeloúdis had described him, with only a fringe of curly white hair left at the nape of his neck. But his eyebrows were still dark and seemed to rise as they came close to each other, so that his face had a look of perpetual pained astonishment, as though he had just received a knife point between his shoulder blades. He spoke gently, courteously, especially to Wittekind, who seemed to charm him right at the start by the mere sound of his name. And when Wittekind explained that he and his American companion were engaged in gathering an oral history of certain forgotten regions of the Second World War, specifically the history of the Wehrmacht in Greece, Hertzel appeared entirely at ease as he began to reminisce about his early years in the Wehrmacht, when it had to be considered a distinguished beginning for some-body from his relatively humble background. Wittekind sat close to him, bending forward in his chair, trying to sustain an image of unwavering interest in the old gentleman's soft-spoken nostalgia about the training in techniques of accounting and management that had allowed him to rise from the status of an ordinary field officer with something less than the appropriate social background to the position of senior quartermaster at the headquarters of Army Group E.

"I won't pretend I was one of those who longed to be at the front," Hertzel said, smiling quickly. "I was very content to be what I was where I was at that point in the war. You understand? And the experience provided me with surprising benefits for the work I did when it was all over."

"And I imagine there was more opportunity for comraderie that far from the front," Wittekind said. "The kind of fellowship that we officers knew at the start of our country's mission, when every-thing seemed possible."

"Of course we had to work hard even in that relatively remote region," Hertzel said. "Don't think for a moment that our life was easy. But naturally there were moments for relaxation."

"At the officers club, I imagine."

"Yes, at the officers club. And sometimes even in the city."

"Ah," Wittekind said. "It is curious, but during my limited ser-vice I still managed to make some excellent friends. Some I've kept in touch with all these years. And I imagine it must have been the same for you."

Ripaldo was sitting opposite Wittekind, Hertzel between them, but Hertzel had turned himself at an angle to face Wittekind, so that Ripaldo found it hard to hear, let alone fathom, what the old boy was saying in an accent that made Ripaldo's rusty German seem rustier yet. He decided he'd better get what was being said into his machine now that Wittekind appeared to be easing his way toward the crucial questions. As soon as Ripaldo clicked in the cassette, Hertzel wheeled on him.

"What is that? Is it what I think it is?"

"It's just a tape recorder," Wittekind said gently. "That is how we gather our interviews. It saves the awkwardness of having to take notes and it saves mistakes."

"Well, put it away," Hertzel said. "This minute."

Ripaldo put it back in his jacket pocket.

"No," Hertzel said. "Better put it here on the table in front of us so that I can be sure you haven't turned it on in secret."

Ripaldo laid the recorder out on the coffee table. Hertzel stared at it as though it was a loaded pistol and said not a word. Wittekind tried to draw him out again by chattering away about Wehrmacht friends of his who had remained faithful over the years despite certain political differences, one or two that the gentleman may have run into himself, but Hertzel had clammed up. It looked to Ripaldo as though the interview with Oberleutnant Hertzel was over before there'd been any chance of mentioning the Big O, let alone Marina and her wartime lover. He caught Wittekind's eye.

"Maybe Mr. Hertzel would prefer to answer our questions on his own and at his leisure," Ripaldo said in English. "As we were able to arrange in the case of Marina Angeloúdis."

Wittekind studied Ripaldo, then leaned forward in his chair again and set the smile on his face. He told Hertzel what his American colleague had suggested and worked patiently to convince the gentleman that nothing he might care to say would be used without his permission, he would not be pressed to answer anything he didn't want to answer, in fact, if he preferred he could be brought a list of questions to answer as he chose. These he could respond to on his own by talking into the tape recorder whenever it suited him, ignoring any he cared to ignore, revising what he had to say as he went along if he found that necessary. Hertzel took up the tape recorder and turned it over and back twice, then set it down. Wittekind picked it up again and moved in close to show Hertzel how it worked, went through the routine a second and third time, then handed it over to the Oberleutnant so that he could have a go at it, taking as much time as he needed.

Hertzel, muttering to himself, finally got it right. He put the thing down and watched it as though it was about to leap back at him, then pushed it aside to make room for the tray with coffee and cakes that his housekeeper brought in. While the coffee was served up, the talk turned to local Vienna politics, Wittekind pretending to agree fully with whatever ironic nuance the old boy offered about the state of affairs in Austria, and Hertzel now leaning forward so that Ripaldo had a full view of his back.

It took Wittekind and Ripaldo the best part of a morning to phrase a list of questions so that they seemed reasonable, diplomatic, but still to the point. Wittekind went back on his own to deliver the list, then waited through the weekend before checking back by phone to see how Oberleutnant Hertzel was getting along. By the end of the week the tape recorder and cassettes were back in Ripaldo's hands along with Wittekind's rough translation of what the committee's staff had managed to transcribe for him. Ripaldo, feeling rather left out of things, decided that the least he could do to earn his pay was edit the translation into more appropriate English.

Deposition: Oberleutnant Wolfgang Hertzel

Ha. I was quite ready to throw this dreadful machine into the wastebasket until I learned after some practice how it allows one to say things twice and three times and even erase whatever one has said and return to the beginning as though nothing had been spoken in the first place. How pleasing it would be if life itself were like that. Oh to have been able to erase so much that I have said after I said it. And think how gratifying it would be to have the means of shutting off some of the things other people say in the middle of their saying it simply by pressing a button. We have lost all respect for silence. Also all respect for changing one's mind. In any case, I think I am now in complete control of this stupid but wonderful machine. I will not let it record anything I do not want it to record, and I am quite prepared to erase the whole idiotic cassette—as I believe it's called—if I find myself becoming soft in the head or saying more than I should.

What I would like to say right at the start is that I am actually grateful to you gentlemen for giving me an opportunity to speak forthrightly about the Wehrmacht. My experience of the Wehrmacht. Though of course I speak within the restrictions about public disclosure that Count Wittekind has promised to respect. I can assure you in this connection that I personally have nothing to hide. Not any longer. And I am no longer interested in hiding others. At the same time I refuse to be treacherous simply to make myself look better than those who have chosen not to speak. There has been enough treachery of that kind. And there have been enough ridiculous stories, implausible stories, about what went on during the war that interests you. Accusations that cannot possibly be substantiated. On the other hand, there have also been lies, deceptions, long-held secrets about crimes committed that are scandalous in men who pretend to honor. Or used to when it was convenient.

Enough of that. You will think me a bitter old man who simply wishes to justify himself before the final silence relieves him of the chance. Think what you must. I propose to be as honest as my nature allows in answering as many as I can of the questions you've given me, though I assure you I will not pretend to answer all. I am not omniscient, gentlemen. Merely too clever for my own good. Now that I have had some practice, I think I can say that I have overcome whatever inhibition speaking into this infernal machine may have imposed on me when I first tried it out. It will speak the truth of things as they happened. In any case, about the past, the long lost past, the disastrous past, I always speak the truth these days. And I always remember precisely. Within the limits of my fading memory, of course.

First, let me state emphatically that I was not on intimate terms with the operations of the Ic/AO intelligence unit at the headquarters in the Greek village of Arsakli, though, on the other hand, I was not exactly a stranger to that unit and the people in it. The headquarters I worked for were below Arsakli, in what was once an American boarding school of some kind. My official duties had nothing to do with intelligence or combat operations but only with supply. I was head of the section at my headquarters that managed the ordering and distributing of all daily essentials in our region—food, clothing, medical supplies, what have you, but no arms or ammunition. That came under the ordnance section. I had no responsibility for intelligence or ordnance or anything else outside my duties as supply officer.

This does not mean that I knew nothing about intelligence activities. I received certain reports, like other senior officers, reports gathered by intelligence that were meant to inform section heads about enemy operations that might threaten us and about which we should exercise vigilance. But to know is not to do. An important distinction that I'm sure you gentleman understand. What I had to do was of small significance within the grand scheme of operations in our region of that war. I was little more than the manager of a hotel. Perhaps of several hotels would be more accurate, but all of them belonging to the second or third category, with a very mixed clientele and a staff made up largely of village idiots.

Of course, as I've suggested, I knew several of the intelligence officers who worked in Arsakli, why should I deny it? We often met at the officer's club in our region. And we sometimes shared transportation for brief trips into the city of Salonika to make use of the recreation facilities there, limited as they were. I see no reason not to admit that I was aware of what those officers and their staffs were concerned about at various times, what those officers had most on their minds. It is only natural to talk about such things among one's equals. Even if our specific duties were quite different and even if some of the things we talked about were meant to be secret. And there were times when things happened that became general knowledge among the officers in our headquarters because they were too disgusting or too absurd to stay hidden long. So I cannot pretend ignorance about some of the matters that your questions refer to. Why, in any case, should I want to pretend? Now, here, so many years after a war that even the defeated barely remember?

For example, about the O3 officer of Ic/AO who interests you, I can say that I knew the distinguished gentlemen slightly in those days, that is, long before he became distinguished, and I did not much like what I knew. Perhaps I am prejudiced. At my age I have a right to be prejudiced. This man, this officer, had his nose up in the air, which—if you'll excuse me—was quite a way up in view of how tall he was and how large his nose. He seemed to me a professor type. Too sure of himself, too insistent on his own opinions when he had opinions and the courage to express them. An Austrian who lived still in the time of our emperor, with a superior attitude toward other people not his own. This would include, I suppose, those of us who were Austrians belonging to the bourgeoisie. Not that he was anything but a bourgeois himself. As I recall, his grandfather was a cobbler and his father an obscure civil servant with an East European name that he was obliged to change in order to get ahead in life. But, as I said, I hardly knew the gentleman. And I must admit that others in our group appeared to respect him more than would be normal for an officer as young as he was at the time—twenty-three, twenty-four, how old? He had some learning, he was taller than most, and he appeared to have connections.

One of these who showed particular respect for him was a junior officer who worked under the O3 officer in question and who was, for a short while, a friend of mine. Which is of course no strong argument for taking his opinion into account, a thing I leave to you. This man—I will mention no names in this public way, as we have agreed. If necessary I can supply his name privately, though it is of no consequence now. The man is dead. Long ago worms feasted on the good sentiments in his brain and the gentle marrow in his bones. Few meals could have been so sweet. At least in the Wehrmacht. Not so, Count Wittekind?

In any case, this junior officer had the duty of helping with the daily reports on partisan activities that were presented by the O3 officer to the Ic section head, and from there to the Ia group in charge of operations, and from there, I suppose, farther up the chain of command. He was a specialist in Greek affairs because he had been a teacher at the German School in Salonika and knew the language and something about the people who used it. In fact, he taught me and others some Greek words, enough to allow us to get by when ordering things at the coffee houses or in dealing with our often delinquent Greek staff. For my purpose here, let me call him Leutnant Fried.

Leutnant Fried thought that the O3 officer who interests you was a superior diplomatic type with a broad knowledge, especially a knowledge of foreign languages. A man easy to work with, not one to cross others, and very careful about the positions he took. Which were always unquestionably within the official framework—call it the Nazi framework if you will. But let me also say there were others who had the impression that this officer was not a faithful Nazi in all respects. My own opinion is that he was a man who expressed himself in firm agreement with whomever he happened to be talking to. This meant that one could never be absolutely sure of where he stood on anything.

You ask, for example, how he stood on the Jewish question, what he knew or did not know about the deportation of the Jews from Salonika in the spring of 1943. You ask even more bluntly what I knew. I will answer just as bluntly. I cannot be sure what that officer knew, but in my case I can say for certain that I knew nothing at the time, because I was assigned to Athens until the summer of that year. But Fried knew. And if he knew, so must all the others have known in the region of Arsakli. That is the blunt truth, for what it is worth. The village in question is after all only three or four kilometers outside the city, in the hills above it. An operation of that magnitude—only a faithful liar could claim to have been ignorant of what was going on in the city week after week.

Beyond the question of who may have known what, I was not in a position then or now to verify your apparent suspicion that the deportations from Salonika and other places in Greece were actually ordered by the Ic section of Army Group E in Arsakli. But I must say that it seems to me unlikely. Such things were a matter for the SS to carry out through our local security police known as the SD, not through the Wehrmacht. Though of course the Wehrmacht may have helped in the execution of an order that came from elsewhere. So please don't misunderstand me. I don't defend the Wehrmacht unconditionally. I simply speak the truth as I perceive it. The Wehrmacht has enough sins to take with it into history without adding more at this time that cannot be proved beyond doubt.

The point I want to make is that my friend Fried knew perfectly well what was going on in the city of Salonika during that period, and he did not keep quiet about it. He told me of seeing a thing that appeared to haunt him because I heard the same story from him several times. He was returning from the north on the train into the city when he was passed by a freight train going out the other way. Some of the cars were regular cars that had windows, and he saw frightened faces pressed against those windows. He said he realized from those faces that this must mean the deportation of the Jews had begun. Now, you are free to draw your own conclusions. If that is what he realized at that time, he must have known in advance from somewhere that a deportation of Jews out of Salonika had been ordered. And as I indicated, he worked under the O3 in Ic/AO. But does that mean that the order came from there or merely passed through that office? Again, you will have to draw your own conclusions. I cannot even say for certain who the O3 officer was at the time since I had not yet left Athens for the north. I have my suspicions, but what value is that in the face of historical fact?

Of course one didn't raise a question during those days about who might have known or not known about operations of this kind. It was not professional to raise such questions. And this Fried was a sensitive man. It was only a few months after I arrived at our headquarters outside Salonika that Fried was granted a transfer from Arsakli to the front lines. He had requested the transfer himself. This was the result of his being asked at one point to deal with the personal effects of some Italian soldiers who had surrendered to us in Greece after the Italian collapse and who had suddenly disappeared. Fried became convinced that the Italians had not run away of their own accord. Where was there to run to in those days? He came to believe that the final connection of the Italians to our common cause had been terminated irreversibly by some of the more fanatical among us. Wehrmacht or otherwise.

Fried found this unacceptable. He told me that he had gone to the Chief of Staff to ask exactly what he was meant to do with these effects and papers belonging to our former allies that had reached him in rucksacks. He was instructed to send them to the exiled Italian government in Munich. This was supposed to be a joke, but

Fried didn't laugh. He told me he didn't even smile. And the next day he asked to be transferred to the front. The excuse he gave his superiors was that he had become bored with administrative work and wanted to join the fighting forces. Of course he couldn't give his actual reason, that would have been too dangerous. So his transfer was arranged on grounds of patriotism. It wasn't until long after the war was over that I learned that this—what shall I call him?—this honorable Wehrmacht officer had been killed in the retreat from the Eastern front.

It was not a good war, that war, whatever people on the other side may say about it. It was in any case not good for us Austrians and Germans quite aside from our defeat. Of course when one is in the war, one doesn't realize where one has come until it's too late. This Fried, as I've named him, was maybe wiser than most of us, but what good did it do him? What difference did it finally make to him or to anybody else that he knew what he knew and acted as he did? It didn't save any Jewish lives or any Italian lives or even his own life. Yet what he did was necessary. I will tell you why. That war was the great corrupter, the true enemy. It made one do one's job, whatever that was, as best one could from day to day because that is what one was trained to do for the sake of the Reich and its struggle with its enemies. Whether this was giving out shoes in the supply section, or preparing intelligence reports for those higher up whom one saw rarely, or shooting partisans in the hills. And if one's duty was to kill an ally or a villager, one followed orders and did one's duty. There was no room for personal honor in this war, and the war itself was not a thing to be questioned. At least not until it was too late for most of us. My friend Leutnant Fried was the exception that proves my point. As I was myself.

I will have to speak personally now. In any case I cannot really speak for anyone but myself. Who can? If those who seem to interest you most are unwilling to speak for themselves, you will never find out what they did or did not do during that war under the category of individual responsibility. Whatever they did was a matter of following orders, that is what you will hear. Everybody followed orders, from your young lieutenant to General Lohr. Even Himmler and Goering faithfully followed orders from the Fuhrer, who in turn faithfully followed orders from the Devil. And the purpose of these orders was to feed the monster called war until it swallowed enough lives to satisfy its greed and corrupted the rest it allowed to survive. The only acts of conscience—not counting those by a few holy Wehrmacht types like Fried—were those that would have to be called acts of betrayal. Going against orders. Or giving up. And even now, how many can you find who will admit to that?

I will admit to that. I will not be crude enough to play the game that some play now, saying they never really believed in Hitler and the Nazi party. They were just soldiers doing their duty, hating Hitler in their hearts, and other such easy rationalizations. We were all Germans, or Austrians who wanted to be Germans. We all believed in our great Germanic race. And for a while, Hitler and his party were the heroes of our race. When it was convenient and we were on the path to victory, Hitler, our fellow Austrian, was Germany for us. We loved him as we loved our united country. And when it became convenient to forget that we had loved him, or even why we had loved him, we did that as well. I refuse to rationalize. I will simply tell you why my personal betrayal became necessary.

It is not arrogance for me to say that I was a good officer, perhaps an exceptional officer, for most of the war. I can attest that my reputation was untarnished in any way under the military code of conduct. I provided whatever was needed almost always on schedule, I kept immaculate accounts, I treated my staff with authority but courtesy, I did not express eccentric opinions. I imagine it was for this reason that I was trusted by most others and was allowed to enter the discussion when I would meet informally with those who served at the intelligence headquarters in Arsakli. Sometimes I even received information that would have normally been considered outside my province. And I suppose my being in charge of distributing the limited delicacies that we were allowed to indulge in as officers may have influenced some of those who regarded me as acceptably within the inner circle. Not that I issued favors. Don't misunderstand me. It was simply necessary at times to make choices between equal possibilities for distribution, and one could say that being subject to the usual prejudices and loyalties, I chose as my impulse dictated when there were no more serious grounds for choice. How others may have seen it is another matter. In a bad war, one finds enemies on all sides.

In any case, I had been at my post in the supply group below Arsakli for several seasons when information came my way that changed the war for me. It was in the spring of 1944, when it was becoming clear to all of us who were willing to see beyond the daily ration of propaganda we were fed that things were not going well for our side. But, as I have suggested, the war creates its own inevitable rhythm. We continued our work from day to day as though nothing had changed nor was going to change until the final victory that was still promised us by some of our leaders. And to do this, we had to convince ourselves that the war must go on as usual. In fact, not simply as usual, but with more and more severe measures as our situation became more and more impossible. So it was not defeatism or even clear foresight that changed the war for me, and certainly not moral heroism in the manner of Fried. Yet I suppose, in the last analysis, a question of ethics was involved.

During the late spring of that year I received what for me was alarming information. Let me see if I can reconstruct the background. A group of British commandos in uniform, conducting a landing operation on an island not far from Rhodes, had been captured by our regular forces in that area, and after apparently unsuccessful interrogation in Rhodes, were transferred to the Ic section of Army Group E in Arsakli. The Ic section, after further interrogation, handed these commandos over to the SD security police for what was officially designated as special treatment—that is, they were murdered.

This information came to me late one evening, at a villa below Arsakli which was among the preferred places for officers to gather after hours, and it came when all of us there had taken in too much wine—a growing tendency in those days but especially so for one officer with a face like a sinking sun and a tongue that sometimes grew so thick and independent as to become ungovernable. This officer worked in the Ic section, and he too will remain nameless, though I think it matters little because he was among those few who disappeared into the mountains that summer of 1944 and never reappeared, as far as I know. Let us call him Major Hillmann for convenience. What this Hillmann told us that evening was largely in coded language, which all of us understood perfectly well but which was never translated into real language during the war, even in official documents.

The thing that appears to have unnerved Major Hillmann enough to make his thick tongue move more freely than usual that evening was the performance of the leader of the captured British commandos, whose name was something like Bliss—I don't remember exactly. This Captain Bliss was incorruptible. He refused to answer any questions our people put to him on Rhodes and he also refused to answer any questions when he reached Arsakli, only his name and identification number, nothing else. An honorable British soldier. Which of course made him intolerable to the Ic interrogators.

So measures had to be taken. And these in turn became intolerable to Major Hillmann. When one of us asked what measures had been necessary, the Major looked away. Then he shrugged. Then he made a gesture with his hand that every German schoolboy would understand meant that a stick had been used, though no doubt a stick somewhat thicker than what we were familiar with in the schoolhouse. And after this stick? The Major simply lowered his eyes. And where was this Captain Bliss now? Sent to the SD for special treatment, the Major said, in keeping with the Fuhrer's order. Had Captain Bliss given information in the end? Yes, the Major said, he had given full information.

Nobody that I knew in those days had ever seen the Fuhrer's order, but all of us had heard in the usual way that there was a secret order about the treatment of commando prisoners. It had been issued much earlier in the war in an attempt to meet the threat of these efficient allied soldiers, and it was an order guarded carefully by the Ic/AO group because it meant that these particular soldiers, though in uniform, were not to be considered subject to the Geneva convention or the normal Wehrmacht code of conduct in war. Still, it wasn't until that evening that I understood the full implications of this order when carried out to the letter, not only how illegal it was, but how dishonorable —in the end, how cowardly. Special treatment meant that soldiers, sometimes the best soldiers, who were captured in battle conditions could be tortured to get information, and whether the information was forth-coming or not, they would be handed over to the SD not to be transferred in the usual way to prison camps but to be killed and disposed of secretly. As happened to Captain Bliss and, as I later discovered, to the nine men under his command—British, Greek, Australian, the nationality made no difference.

One follows orders. That is the rhythm that propels the monster called war. And the virtue of orders in wartime is that they can remain abstract enough to hide their essence behind dishonest lan-guage. The cold reality comes with the act of fulfilling orders faith-fully, to the letter, to the limit. What changed my war that evening was not only this business about special treatment by the SD, this murdering of commando prisoners simply because they are the enemy's dedicated elite, but a thing that Major Hillmann said in his drunkenness, almost under his breath, before we had to help him out of the villa so that he wouldn't embarrass us by falling over and smashing himself. He said that he had finally been sent by the Ic command to tell this Captain Bliss that he could rest at ease, his interrogation was finished. He hadn't seen the British officer since the day before, and now he found him sitting on the floor of his cell with his head tilted back against the wall. The man had no face. His face had become mush. Hillmann said it was a face that could no longer answer him even if there was anything it had want-ed to say.

The change that came over me that evening did not lead to any immediate action, any plot—except that Major Hillmann must have sensed enough sympathy in me to choose me as his undeclared confidant in the weeks following. I went on with my duties as before, what else could I do? But inside me the war was dead. I had no conviction left, no belief in possibilities, no capacity to envi-sion honor emerging from our side of the war. The only emotion I could feel was the dread that comes with knowing you are serv-ing an evil thing that you cannot control. One might say enough had happened in the war long before that time to have brought on this dread—one might choose to mention Stalingrad, for example—but it was this incident with Captain Bliss, or whatever his name was, that was the trigger for me, a matter so close at hand, inescapable, inexorable. I was in this state through the rest of the spring of 1944 and most of the summer—and it did not really help my morale to receive occasional copies of documents by way of this Major Hillmann, documents concerning one or another commando raid that he hoped would bring me into some sort of collusion with his disgust about what was going on over his head in the Ic section. The last document from him crossed my desk in July a few days before his defection, an act that further unsettled me even if it did not really surprise me. But soon after this, something else happened that led me to see a possible way out for myself as well. One of my staff, a non-commissioned officer serving as an orderly in our medical supply room, was caught in a compromising situation with one of the enemy. An enemy woman, that is.

I assume from several of your questions that you have some knowledge of this episode, presumably from the woman you call Marina. I never actually knew her name. In any case, what you know will have come only from her limited point of view. Let me tell you what I knew that she couldn't possibly have seen, at least not in the same way. This young non-commissioned officer, a corporal, was rather remarkable in view of the education that those of us who belonged to the Hitler Youth movement brought to the war. His training seemed to have come from another country, almost from another worldly order, because there was very little nationalism in the man and no ideology as far as I could tell. I thought at first that he was simply stupid, because he never expressed opinions. And when others turned passionate about this or that issue, or released their hatred for this or that race, he simply went about his business as though deaf and dumb. But he wasn't stupid. His mind, his sensibility if you prefer, appeared to work on a different level, as though his place belonged among things that feel the life around them as it comes, not only without the gift of language but without the normal human responses of pride and anger. It was quite infuriating. Especially since I was powerless to rouse the expected emotion in him even when I found the need to criticize him for some trivial failing in his work. You could say he was the gentlest of men, but you could also say that his capacity to feel as ordinary people do had been wounded in some crucial way. In any case, I found him insufferable.

Of course the corporal's work, while serving the same monster

I was serving, gave him less cause for inner conflict than it gave me. He didn't have to worry about who was responsible for issuing this or that order and how to maintain discipline when the situation looked increasingly desperate. His business as a medical orderly was to deal with others as their need required without question of rank or authority or function, as though the war and its purposes were irrelevant. He could do his work as though it was God's work. And I suppose that made me envious too. I had some foul men on my staff over the years, the slippery kind, or the arrogant kind, or those with unexplainable malice, but none of them bothered me the way this man did. I now suspect that his way of accepting his own nature and its place in the world around him tormented me because I could never do the same. Not in those days.

In any case, I found myself watching him like a preying animal to see if I could catch him out, not to do him serious damage but simply to find cause to make him hate me enough to show it openly—that is, to make him as human as I was. I had little luck in this. Then a thing happened that put him in my power. He was a person with no private life, as far as I could tell, ready to be called at any hour to open up the medical supply room and provide what medicine was needed or treat some minor injury. He had his hours of duty like everyone else, but he was always available in the off hours and never went into the city or even into the villages outside our barbed wire enclosure. That is, until his behavior suddenly changed during the summer of 1944.

There were two occasions—I believe it was in July of that year—when I sent one of my staff to bring the corporal to the medical supply room after his duty hours to help with some minor emergency. The corporal was nowhere to be found. I thought this peculiar, because on both occasions it was too early in the evening for a noncommissioned officer to be off somewhere on a recreational excursion—at least this noncommissioned officer. That was not Corporal Schonfeld's style. You ask for his full name. Corporal Martin Schonfeld is his full name. No need to hide it in his case. This one was also an Austrian like myself and like the distinguished gentleman who so interests you, but unlike us and most others, an innocent, a human being who seemed incapable of subterfuge, except—and here is the point—except when human enough to fall in love.

It took me a while to discover that weak spot in his innocence. Once I found out that he was often unavailable during the off hours in the evening, I made an effort to fill in the pattern of his going and coming, sometimes myself passing by the medical supply room after normal duty hours, sometimes having a member of my staff try to track him down at his barracks. He was nowhere to be seen so long as the sun was up, but he would always return to his barracks after dark. Of course this was not necessarily suspicious in itself—he could have been walking, or exercising, off somewhere reading, as was an early obsession of his—but those I sent looking for him never spotted him doing any of these things. He would simply disappear completely for an hour or two, maybe longer.

I would like to say that my discovery of what he was up to came by accident, but that would be only partly true. It was a combination of coincidence and vigilance. Had I not been aware of approaching dusk and also conscious of Corporal Schonfeld's twilight absences, I doubt that I would have taken any special notice of the figure moving quickly, almost stealthily, behind a row of yellow brush along the outer periphery of the courtyard that separated our supply facilities from the main road, even though the figure was moving in a direction that led away from the barracks across the road and toward nowhere in particular. I left my point of observation instantly, but by the time I crossed the courtyard, there was no sign of the man. And though I proceeded casually in the direction he had taken, that took me to nothing more than a barren field beyond the last buildings in our enclosure.

I solved the mystery the following afternoon by concealing myself across the road from that field. Undignified in a Wehrmacht officer? Of course, Count Wittekind. But at the time this officer considered himself no longer a member of the Wehrmacht but simply a soldier in a lost war, an evil war. In any case, I will not deny that there was a certain gratification in catching my man. Aha, I said under my breath as I spotted him coming in my direction on the clear side of the brush lining the road. I watched him cross over to the barren field and move quickly through the undergrowth there only to disappear out of my sight.

I followed his path down the road until the brush concealing me was about to give out so that I had to stop. And what I then saw made a shiver run through me. A woman, really a girl, came out of the trees on the far side of the field and ran across it to come up against the sliding door of a shed that marked the outer edge of our compound. The door opened to show a slit of darkness, and then the woman eased into it to disappear.

I don't think it very useful for me to tell you gentlemen the rest. But I will. I came to that spot the next afternoon, and some afternoons after that. I would wait for Corporal Schonfeld to appear, watch him make his way to that doorway, watch his woman come out of the woods and cross to enter the darkness that hid her lover. And I would stay. I was never crude enough to approach the doorway, to listen to what was going on in there. It was enough for me to squat at a distance where the brush would conceal me from the road and let my imagination invent what it pleased. In short, instead of reporting what I had seen more than once as I had every right and obligation to do, I let myself share in his pleasure by way of fantasy. At least for a while. And by the time I tired of that, I felt too complicit in his fraternization with the enemy, too besmirched by what I myself had done, to turn the man in.

Do you understand now what I mean about the subtle ways that war corrupts? It wasn't simply that I made the decision not to report him to my superiors but that I felt a certain liberation by not doing so. We were both on the outside now. And yet I couldn't tell him that, couldn't bring myself to warn him that what he was doing was profoundly dangerous. I merely watched him from a greater distance, silently, perhaps jealously. I had moved in a matter of days from gratification over discovering his weakness to sharing in it and then to shielding it, but without the courage to let the man know that this was what I was doing. And of course the consequence was that he eventually got himself into serious trouble.

It was about three weeks after my last encounter with his—with our—secret fraternizing that I received a call from the Ic headquarters in Arsakli telling me that a corporal on my staff was being held for questioning because soldiers guarding one of the pillboxes on the ridge above the village had spotted him wandering alone through the countryside—in uniform. They had apprehended him, and he had not given a satisfactory explanation of why he was that far off limits. All he would say was that he was on a personal mission. The Ic headquarters wanted to know what I could tell them about the man and this odd behavior of his. They said they had him in custody and would keep him there until I appeared to identify him and assist them in preparing their report.

That gave me my opening to reveal what I knew, but I didn't take it. Instead, on my way up the hill to the Ic headquarters, I made up a story. What I told them was that Corporal Schonfeld was indeed on a mission, one that I had sent him on, which was what he meant by personal. I said that I had told him not to speak of it to anyone, and he was simply too innocent, no, too stupid to realize that "anyone" did not include guards on duty and intelligence officers. The fact was, I said, that Corporal Schonfeld was investigating a theft of medicines from our supply room that we suspected had been committed by one of the cleaning women working in that building. I had sent him off to find out where the woman lived so that we could make a surprise raid on her living quarters in the hope of finding the missing medicines where we believed she must have hidden them away for distribution or sale to her fellow villagers. I pretended to be irritated that this prospect of catching her with the evidence was now much diminished. Obviously these guards having marched my corporal back to Ic headquarters after they intercepted him would be the talk of the village that evening and the next. Surely our little plot was now out, I said, and surely there would no longer be any chance of pinning down the culprit and recovering what we had lost from our supply room.

Someone has said that the best strategy for defending against accusation, whether just or not, is to accuse your accusers. Ha. At least at this moment it worked for me. This was perhaps because most of the younger officers in Ic headquarters were in any case too demoralized by the turn the war had taken to concern themselves with making a strong case against one of their own, even if only a corporal. In fact, there were only two officers at the Ic headquarters in Arsaklí that day, and neither of them was the gentleman who interests you because he—will you believe this, Count Wittekind?—was said to be back in Austria on leave in order to get married and have a short honeymoon. Fiddling his lady back home, so to speak, while his war burned on hopelessly in the field of battle. In any case, I took Corporal Schonfeld back to our headquarters with me, still without speaking to him about either his conduct or mine, and the next day I arranged his transfer to the medical unit in a village with a long name that I can't remember. This village was also on the lower slopes of Mt. Hortiáti but far enough from Arsaklí to keep him out of trouble. That is what I hoped.

Why did I hope this? Clearly I wanted him out of my life. I suppose because I was tired of him and his failed innocence, as I was tired of the war that had corrupted both him and me. And with his going, I made up my mind to leave the war behind me too. I had no definite plan at that time. I simply made the thought of escape my waking preoccupation, and I became vigilant about possibilities. One possibility was to find some local person I felt I could trust to give me help with turning myself safely over to one or another of the enemy's resistance groups, as I assumed had happened with others in our region who successfully disappeared without trace. But the only local people with whom I came into direct contact were a few merchants we used in our business, those whom one might call agents for dealing with the villagers in the purchase of foodstuffs and other commodities. No one of these seemed to me trustworthy in the sense I had in mind. Since their function was to deal with their enemy, even if their first motive was to take their fee from him and cheat him a bit in the exchange, how could one trust them to deal honorably with someone deserting that enemy? Where was the profit in it for them?

I had not yet worked my way through this dilemma when a local person of the kind I thought I needed suddenly stepped into the path of my meditation. It was the woman you know, the girl I had seen coming out of the woods more than once to meet her lover in the darkness we shared for a while. One afternoon I went back to my private office after hours to complete an inventory, and as I entered the doorway from the outer office where the clerks work, I found the girl dusting my desk—only dusting it in a way that told me she was testing the drawers to see if she could find one open. I had never seen her in there before and never that close, but it was unmistakably Corporal Schonfeld's girl. "Aha," I said to myself "what have we got here? This lovely dark companion of our twilight fraternizing is clearly up to no good." And almost at the same time, I blessed her corrupt young soul.

I stood in the doorway. My first impulse was to tease her a bit, play with her fear of me so that I had time to indulge myself in her physical presence, set that against what I had seen of her in my imagination. Something of that must have shown in my face because she wouldn't look at me, and the thrill of my cruelty didn't last long once she turned back to her pretense of dusting. "What are you up to there?" I finally said to her in German. She either didn't understand or pretended not to. Of course I had no way of knowing what language she and her lover had used if they had used any language at all, so I decided to assume that her German was primitive at best. It had now occurred to me that this enemy, given her attachment to my blond Corporal, might possibly view my predicament with some sympathy, might even find a way to help me out of it if I could only gain her trust. But how could I do that, especially without a common language? She went on with her work as though I wasn't watching her, and when she picked up her trash bag and crossed to leave, I prevented her from going out by barring the door with my arm.

It was a crude gesture, but what else could I do? I was desperate not to lose the possibility she'd laid before me by trying to steal from my desk. The closeness of her, even for that second, was profoundly disturbing. I watched her back off against the wall, obviously still terrified of me. And then I tried to calm her and make her understand what I had in mind by going through a little play I invented on the spot—this another crude gesture in its way. I picked up my wastebasket and brought it to her to try and show her that she should pay attention to what was in it when she next cleaned my office. Since the wastebasket was empty, she seemed to take this as merely a bit of malicious bullying on my part. So I went to my desk and went through my papers until I came up with a document that would be of little consequence to anybody if it happened to fall into the wrong hands, though it could have meant something to her had she been clever enough to decipher it. I'm quite sure she wasn't. It was a chart of the dates that the water source in our region needed to be treated for purification, with the quantities of chemical that my office had to supply for the purpose.

It was of course too much to hope that she would understand from this chart that it was her lover who was now responsible for receiving the chemicals in question and assisting in their disposition by way of the medical group in his new village across the valley from hers. What I hoped she might understand was that I was prepared to offer her more valuable documents in due course if she could show me that I could trust her and that what I offered her in good faith might help me reach those of her people who could effect my escape. It was a dangerous game, but I felt I no longer had any choice but to play boldly, win or lose.

She played boldly too, at least at the start. I left my wastebasket full the next day, and she must have understood enough of what I intended from the previous day's bit of theater to return to my office and empty the wastebasket. That surely took some courage in view of the fear she had barely been able to control after I discovered what she was doing at my desk. It boded well. And she was rewarded by some documents of true value this time. And the next time. As I remember, one of these was in fact the report you mention regarding a commando raid that came to me by way of Major Hillmann, the one bearing the initial of the gentleman who is your primary concern—though my memory of this is not entirely reliable. The point is that these documents demonstrated my seriousness of purpose whether or not they proved useful to the enemy in other ways.

Of course I had no idea what she made of them herself or what she chose to do with them. And I felt it might prove dangerous for both of us to be seen together under circumstances that would allow me to learn about that directly, even if we could find enough common language. So I simply played my side of our game and waited out of sight. Nothing happened. And this finally unnerved me. I am generally a man of calm temperament, not easily unraveled by circumstances beyond my control, but I was in an unusual state of crisis. And this led me to make a mistake. Instead of more documents, I sent her money. German money. I didn't mean it as a bribe, or even as a gift for her, I only hoped that it might ease her way with those I needed to reach. But when the money came back into my wastebasket the next day between the covers of a magazine that I had used as an envelope for sending it, I knew that the girl had misunderstood my intention. I think now that it must have been the same pride that had allowed her to face me down in my office despite her fear of me, but whatever it was, it now worked to make me unsure of her. Was she, after all, working for or against my hope?

I waited a few more days, increasingly desperate, and then I sent the woman the only photograph I had of my two young girls, golden children in those days, blonde as her lover. I hoped in this way to stir the mother's milk in her, so to speak—if she had any that hadn't yet curdled. Nothing but further silence came of this. I decided not to wait any longer. There was one other possibility, an even more desperate one, that I turned to now, quite recklessly when I think back on it.

The only local person I had come to know in something more than a routine professional capacity was a landowner in the village of Arsakli who had vineyards somewhere and a storehouse on the edge of the village where he kept his wine barrels and those of others in the region who used him as their agent. He was a man of some means in the village, a man of some authority, and he appeared to be afraid of no one—neither his fellow villagers, whom he no doubt cheated on occasion, nor us Germans, whom he cheated regularly but always within reason. He had kept on my good side by bringing out a bottle of his oldest brandy whenever I visited his storehouse to select wine for our month's quota, and more than once he insisted on bringing me a platter of roast lamb from the spit he had set up in the yard outside for some local gathering of friends or relatives that he was hosting. The lamb proved to be exquisite.

I don't know what it was that made me trust this man. We spoke only those few trivial words of his language that I could speak or understand, and I knew nothing about his politics, nothing about his actual feelings toward me. I simply liked his face: a crinkled map of ruined blood vessels and deep worry lines, softened by cheeks that became light bulbs when he smiled. And I liked his heavy, guttural laugh, full of old sin. Still, I suppose I went to him in the end because there was nowhere else for me to go. It seemed to me now that it was either turn my fate over to him or go into the long night on my own. The one thing I was no longer willing to do was serve the monster that was corrupting me and everyone else it had allowed to survive.

I decided I would take with me only what I could fit into my satchel. This included a few personal things but mostly a selection of reports and other documents from my drawer, a stack of papers that I didn't bother to consider carefully but chose because they looked official enough to impress those I hoped to reach. While I was gathering these things from my desk, I noticed that the same magazine I'd used as an envelope for the photograph I'd sent out into the darkness was lying in the bottom of my wastebasket. So. Corporal Schonfeld's girl had something to tell me after all. What I found inside the magazine was the photograph of my two blonde girls, and attached to that, a curious drawing I finally decided was a map. There was also a drawing of a clock set at seven above a sun that was placed below a line I took to be a horizon. The time was clear enough, the place—after further close study of the map—was the woodshed at the outer edge of our headquarters where she used to join her lover. The girl's message was inescapable. I was to meet her there.

Just how was I to respond to this? Meet her in that dark place that had served her and her lover as their house of illicit pleasure— my pleasure too, if you will? And for what purpose? It could hardly be for the same purpose. Or could it? I have to admit that the thought tempted me more than it should have, but I dismissed it in the end. It was more likely that she simply wanted to tell me, in whatever language she could find, to give up what she now must have seen as an unacceptable obsession on my part, a dangerous obsession, which I had been pressing on her since I first caught her trying to steal papers from my desk. Or maybe it was something more sinister, a trap to get rid of me. She would expose me, bring others there to discover me, free herself from a game that she neither understood nor cared to play any longer and in this way get her revenge for my having tormented her. Maybe she even understood now that I had been the one who had sent her lover away. Who knows where her mind had moved since Corporal Schonfeld disappeared from her life so suddenly and finally.

I decided in the end that even if I granted her the benefit of the doubt, I had best put my fate elsewhere. I went to the woodshed the next day, but I went at noon rather than at the time her clock had told me to. I wanted to leave our courier there, our magazine, with nothing between its covers, this to show her that I was releasing her from any need to communicate with me further, setting her free at the same time that I hoped to set myself free. I felt stupid doing this. What, after all, was the point? But entering that place transformed me, led me in another direction. There was the sweet smell of thyme in there, and resin, and dry grass. I sat down with the door partially open and breathed the air, looking out at the empty field beyond the doorway that framed the hot August light. And a moment came that I can describe only as a moment of mystery, quite unnerving. I felt the ghostly presence of those lovers there as though their image had actually appeared in the dark corner where the winter's wood was still piled, standing naked beside each other with only their hands touching, and the feeling that gave me had no trace of lust in it but was one of immense sadness, of irredeemable loss. I couldn't sit there any longer. I left the magazine on the ground beside me and rose quickly to go out, but as I crossed that empty field, I found myself gathering a few wild flowers to take back and lay on top of the magazine before I hurried off to finish my escape.

Did she understand this gesture? How could she possibly? In any case, it allowed me to dismiss her from my mind. I picked up my satchel from my office and told the clerk on duty that I was going to Arsakli on business. Luck was with me, because I found my friend the wine merchant alone in his warehouse, taking an inventory of what little retsina wine he had left before the new vintage came in. He was of course surprised to see me there without warning, but he made me sit down and have a brandy that was more welcome than one would have thought in the heat of the day. The man was clearly in a mood to spend the rest of the afternoon moving toward oblivion, bubbling away with one story after another that he seemed to think I understood perfectly, though he was quite happy to let loose his guttural laugh for both of us when I showed no sign of grasping whatever joke was there—that is, until I couldn't stand the pressure of his joviality any longer and abruptly opened my satchel to spread my papers before him.

It was as though I had pierced his plump cheeks with a skewer. He stared at the documents, leafed through them, then studied me, then studied the documents, his eyes small, deadly sober. The surprising thing is that I didn't have to say a word. He leafed through the documents again one by one, slowly, as though deciphering ancient epitaphs, and then, without looking at me, gathered them up and put them back in the satchel. I thought he was going to hand the thing back to me. Instead he picked up the brandy bottle and filled my glass, then tucked the satchel under his arm and walked out of the warehouse.

What was I to do now? I had no choice but to wait there and see whether my act of betrayal merely produced another such act or served to save my skin. I didn't brood over the question. It wasn't that I'd become such a fatalist as to dismiss concern about things over which I had no control. I was in fact quite frightened. But at the same time, I felt I had finally made a decision to act in a way that was—how shall I put it?—unequivocal. This decision was without ambivalence, without pros or cons, a choice to put my life on the front line for a thing that I felt essential to my soul: the end of my servitude to our monstrous war. And frightened as I was, my ear tuned sharply to every new sound that came into that room, there was also a sense of liberation that kept me calm at my center.

The rest can be told briefly. Some three hours must have gone by before the wine merchant returned with two companions, one of whom—an elderly man—spoke a horrible chopped up version of German that he must have learned from an illiterate foot soldier in a previous war. In any case we had enough language between us to establish that I wanted to give myself over to the enemy, though I was certain by that time that my documents had already made the point. The wine merchant presented us with a round of brandy while we remained standing in the center of the room, and then I was given a change of clothes—quite indescribable, I assure you, a haven for lice—and a cap that must have been used at some time as a makeshift pail for goat milk. The wine merchant inherited my spotless uniform, and that pleased him greatly. As we went out, he gave me a half-bottle of brandy, fresh from the barrel, to ease my journey into the unknown.

My escape to the middle finger of the Chalkidiki peninsula and from there by caique to Egypt is of no consequence now. At that stage of the war it was not especially difficult because the route had been established long since for helping British soldiers to escape and others with reason to be helped, though there were moments of danger along the way. I was treated well by the peasants who were my guides and my hosts, and I became intimately familiar with a curious liquor that came from local vineyards, what seemed to me pure alcohol that had merely passed a night or two breathing the same air as the grapes that were meant to give it flavor. Though I was dressed as somebody I could never have imagined to be a person I knew, I felt that my dress set me free, and I gradually came to celebrate this feeling. A peasant no longer at war who could belong to any country he chose. Even the British who interrogated me once I reached the Egyptian coast appeared to be members of a race I could now recognize as related to my own. I spent more than one evening with the officer I saw the most of during that time arguing over the meaning of Sophocles' play "Antigone," which suddenly made much more sense to me than it had in my school days. In any case, it certainly made more sense to me than it did to my British colleague, and I finally gave up trying to educate him in the subtleties of personal rebellion, a thing as foreign to him as the smell of my cap.

But I begin to ramble. Let me finish this account of my Wehrmacht days in Northern Greece by answering the question that you have starred. I know nothing about a massacre in the village named after the mountain that lay in the shape of a pregnant woman behind our headquarters near Arsaklí. You say this massacre occurred in early September. I was in Egypt at that time. As a prisoner of war, I was given no news of that kind or anything having to do with our forces in Greece except the expected news that the German army had begun its retreat everywhere in that region. And after the war was over there was too much to discover about ourselves, with too little room left to learn about massacres on Mt. Hortiáti when there were so many larger crimes in Poland and elsewhere that the monster we helped to create had committed in the name of our race. Regarding this Hortiáti business, I suggest you ask the distinguished gentleman you came to see me about in the first place. I'm sure he was in the Ic headquarters at the time, in charge of anti-partisan intelligence. Unless, of course, that episode came during the period of his honeymoon leave in Austria. In any case, that is undoubtedly what he will decide to tell you.

And there is another person who would surely know what happened on Mt. Hortiáti: Corporal Schonfeld. He was closer to that village than we were at the end, and his duties in the place I had him transferred to included attending to the purification of the water that had its source somewhere near the village that interests you. If Corporal Schonfeld is still alive—and I'm fairly certain you can find that out from the same people who sent you to me—he should be able to give you a more or less first-hand account of what actually happened in that village and who on our side was thought to be responsible for it. Not that I am in a position to guarantee that he will speak to you. By now you must realize that the evil which was spread by that war had many heads but few of them are the kind that talk. And let me say something else. There are certain kinds of evil that are so grand as to be obvious, whether you call that evil natural or unnatural. We had many examples of that during the war, and not only in Austria and Germany. But the evil that corrupts most in ordinary men is complicity with evil, and the final corruption is to hide the truth of that complicity from yourself. I leave it there.

FOUR

On his Grand Tour, Ripaldo had come to Salzburg straight from northern Greece and Yugoslavia, so that the rhythm of the landscape heading north was from dry yellow fields and bald mountains with much dust in the air to forested plains and green valleys between mountains that still had snow in their crevices, high and close enough, he remembered, to hold in all the sweet odors of such rich planting. At that time, shortly after Tito opened his southern border, he had thought it possible for an American to study Europe without feeling naive or backward—to take what value was left in the old regime after the war and make it his own without being intimidated by it. Salzburg had been full of student tourists that summer, more Americans than British or French or Italians, most with enough money to satisfy their hunger first for the music and old-world landscape that had brought them there, and then for each other.

Ripaldo had settled into the back room of a boarding house with no place to sit other than the bed or the chair at its foot but with a window that gave on the full spread of the old city, from the banks of the river to the castle on the Monchsberg. The bed filled the room, especially after he began to share it with a blonde heiress from California. It had been his first long vacation after his G. I. Bill money ran out, and he knew it would be his last without some kind of deadline hanging over his head. So along with all the other new barbarians, he and his companion, though a bit older than most, had drunk life to the lees in that place, and as the summer flowed on and they'd tired of too much baroque culture, they'd taken to the high mountains for some clean air and open spaces, only a degree more aware than their younger compatriots that they would never again be so young and careless and indifferent to anything but themselves.

What had totally escaped the new barbarians in their happy innocence, Ripaldo saw now, was the fact that their post-war invasion of Austria and Germany remained outside history. Those arriving for that all-out pleasure had little sense of the skeletons that lay buried under their European playground, and those who had done the burying were not in a mood to talk. Austria was waiting for its future in the movies, for the sound of music and lighthearted children prancing over its green hills in dirndls and lederhosen. What had happened there before and during the war, what had grown in that soil so recently to spread its poison wherever the Grand Tour might take a tourist, seemed no longer on anybody's mind. The war was over. History was dead. The future was open country.

The mission that now brought Ripaldo back to Salzburg after so many years worked against his nostalgia. The excitement, the anticipation, especially on coming out of the last tunnel when the view opened out on the Hohensalzburg fortress, lasted less than half the distance into the city center. What took its place was a sinister feeling. All that high gothic and baroque charm now seemed to him a cover for what the Fuhrer had brought to his fatherland out of his Realschule schooling in Linz and his grubby political education in Vienna. And that black shadow over the fortress now crossed the living image of the Big O, educated under Hitler's tutelage, with his apprenticeship in the National Socialists' Studentenbund and the riding club for Nazi storm troopers that he joined while preparing for a public career at some elite academy in Vienna.

And then Arsakli. Ripaldo could just see that tall, long-nosed Wehrmacht lieutenant sitting there in the officer's club below the village dreaming of a future that in fact had turned out better than anything even the Big O, in his youthful arrogance, could have plausibly imagined. And now, as his country appeared ready to raise him yet again to the mountain top, rumor had it that Salzburg was getting set to receive him later in the month as their honored guest at the opening of the annual Jederman morality play in the forecourt of the local cathedral. Suddenly the city seemed to Ripaldo to be hiding its dark side under a lush cover just as it had way back then, and what the young poet of Ripaldo's political awakening had said about the local high country in her poem to Daddy was right after all: the snows of the Tyrol were not very pure or true.

Ripaldo's coming to Salzburg on his own had been at Wittekind's insistence. They'd met again at the Schwartzenberg the previous week to go over the edited text of the Hertzel deposition and to work out what to do next. The heat wave was gone, but Wittekind suggested that it might be best in any case for them to sit inside at a discreet table because he could no longer be sure that he wasn't under surveillance of some kind. There had been recent indications of official displeasure, he said, probably a delayed after-math of his interview with the Big O, and certain members of his committee had begun to feel under pressure. Phone calls had been made by some of their government contacts, not direct threats so much as pointed inquiries about exactly what the committee was up to. They'd learned that there was concern in high places, any-way within the Big O's party, and some of the usual sources had begun to clam up. Wittekind wasn't worried personally, he said, but he felt he'd better begin to keep a low profile for the time being so that he didn't end up losing what contacts he still had with his old Wehrmacht network and others who were of his reformed per-suasion but less willing to take chances.

"That's discouraging," Ripaldo said. "And I'm discouraged enough already."

"Don't be. It's no big deal. Not yet, at least. I just have to be more careful."

"It isn't only that. I begin to feel that we're losing our man. I mean, for all his talk, this Hertzel doesn't really help us pin things down. He ends up not knowing much more than we do ourselves."

"Not so," Wittekind said. "For one thing, he knows that Corporal Schonfeld was alive after the Hortiáti massacre."

"I don't see how you get that from the deposition. All he says is that if Corporal Schonfeld is still alive, he should be able to give us a first-hand account of what happened there. Pure supposition."

"Ah ha. But the man is subtle. He tells us what he wants us to know without actually telling us. When he says if still alive, he means if still alive now, so many years later. He must know the Corporal was still alive back then or he wouldn't speak about first-hand accounts."

"But how could Hertzel have known that for sure since he was on his way to Egypt at the time?"

Wittekind tweaked his goatee. "Either he is stretching the truth about his travels, or he learned about the Corporal and what happened at Hortiáti some years after it happened. My guess is that he learned about it from Schonfeld himself."

"What makes you think so?"

"A hunch. An old Wehrmacht hunch. For a start, my guess is that someone so obsessed with a soldier he thought a much better man than he was would have looked him up at some point after the war was over. If only to put his demon to rest, as your friend Marina would say."

"What makes that a Wehrmacht hunch, Wittekind? It sounds pagan Greek to me."

"The Wehrmacht part. Ah. The Wehrmacht part is what I believe to be Hertzel's hope that we catch the Big O. He doesn't like the man at all, that is obvious, but he also doesn't want to seem the one responsible for spearing him."

"Possible. You know the mentality better than I do. So, old boy, how do we check out your hunch?"

"We don't, Ripaldo. You do. I'm afraid at this point you'll have to do it on your own."

"I wouldn't know where to begin," Ripaldo said. "Even if I felt comfortable working in German on my own."

"Your German is fine. I'll take some time off and give you a refresher course if you insist. And then I'll show you where to begin."

"I can't say I like the idea," Ripaldo said. "I really can't."

"You have to like it, Ripaldo. You have to find this Corporal. It may be our last hope."

Wittekind went on to argue that there was no longer any question in his mind but that Corporal Schonfeld's duty with the group assigned to purify the water below Hortiáti village meant that he was either with others at that ambush or close enough to those who were to be able to offer the committee the equivalent of eye-witness testimony. And not only about what actually happened at the aqueduct that day but about who was in command of the massacre that followed. At the very least he would be able to verify what Wehrmacht officers were in the area at the time and how much they were thought to have been in collusion with what had happened. That in turn could provide valuable new leads.

"All right," Ripaldo said. "We go for the Corporal. I go. But you'll have to put me on the right track."

"Hertzel will do that for us," Wittekind said. "You let me handle that part of it. And from now on we talk only in German. Austrian German, O.K., my friend?"

Wittekind did not have as much success with Hertzel as he had hoped. He reported back to Ripaldo that during another generally amicable visit, the old Wehrmacht supply officer hadn't exactly stonewalled on the question of Corporal Schonfeld's whereabouts, but, courteous as he remained in manner, he nevertheless hadn't come entirely clean. Hertzel did admit to having made one attempt to trace the Corporal some years after the war was over by way of others who had served on his staff in Greece, but all he had managed to learn was that the Corporal had in fact survived the retreat and had returned to Austria at the war's end to settle in Salzburg. He had seen no reason to pursue the matter further, he said, certainly no reason to travel there merely to satisfy his curiosity. An address? Yes, he had an address, but it was so old that he doubted it would be of use now. In any case, he offered to dig it up and pass it on to the Count by phone the following day, and that he did. Wittekind ended up convinced by Hertzel's vagueness that the Oberleutnant had in fact gone to Salzburg at some point and had either been repulsed by Schonfeld or had stood in the street gazing at the Corporal's residence from a distance without the courage to follow through on his intention—incurable voyeur to the end.

"So," Wittekind said. "We know that the Corporal is alive and we have an address. The rest, my friend, is up to you. Please don't let me down."

On his first morning in Salzburg Ripaldo discovered that the address Wittekind had squeezed out of Hertzel was an address that no longer existed because the relevant building—in fact, the whole block of buildings—had been torn down to make room for a modern hotel and parking lot at some point after the post-war tourist invasion began to define the new face of the city. Ripaldo also discovered that Wittekind had so stirred up his juices by the challenge he'd laid down that, far from taking this development as argument for returning to Vienna empty-handed, he now felt a surge of new energy come into his mission. He told himself that he may have lost the advantage of a specific address, but he still had a name, a place, and a likely profession to work with—at least he assumed that Corporal Schonfeld had used his army training as a medical orderly, and his apparent commitment in that direction, to find himself an equivalent civilian job. His search now focused on hospitals and clinics. These proved numerous enough to discourage the retired reporter in him but not the budding detective, though he decided he'd better follow his reporter's impulse to start at the top rather than the bottom and head for the largest hospital in the area.

The register at St. Johann's hospital told Ripaldo that Martin Schonfeld had indeed been on their books for a number of years but had not been active for at least five. He learned the reason for that farther along on the Mullner Hauptstrasse from one Fraulein Lotte Kistner, a senior nurse at St. Johann's hospital, where she and Martin Schonfeld had worked together for some years before they began to share an apartment not far from the Augustiner monastery. It was Fraulein Kistner who answered the door to Martin Schonfeld's apartment at the address that had appeared in the hospital's records. Ripaldo explained to the lady that he was an American historian writing a book on the German occupation of Northern Greece in World War II and had reason to believe that former Corporal Martin Schonfeld could give him some useful information.

Fraulein Kistner was a woman that Ripaldo judged to be somewhere in her mid-fifties, but she had the kind of glowing skin and slender figure that belonged to a woman ten years younger than that. He found her so attractive that he had trouble keeping his eyes steadily on her until she started speaking: dark-haired, high cheekbones, large eyes wide apart and the lids slightly tilted either by nature or expert makeup so that she had an almost oriental look. But when she spoke, her heavy Austrian intonation forced him to watch her plum-colored lips with less pleasure than they deserved. He learned that the address was correct, Martin Schonfeld used to live there but he was not there now. Where might he be now? Fraulein Kistner answered with the name of a place that Ripaldo came to see was a local cemetery, since, as the lady went on to explain, Martin Schonfeld had died five years previously of heart disease. When Ripaldo simply stood there gazing at her, Fraulein Kistner finally moved aside and motioned him to come in, then led him into the living room.

"Now," she said. "Forgive a question before you ask another of me. You are an American but you speak German. Your parents are German?"

"My parents are Italian," Ripaldo said. "I learned German in college. And I've spent some time here. Many years ago. I've forgotten much of what I knew, but I'm picking it up again."

"And yet you are writing a history of the German army during World War II? Excuse me, but that seems to me a rather unusual subject for an American of Italian background who hasn't lived here recently."

"Not exactly a history of the German army. Of the war. In part. In the countries I know something about. Greece and places north."

Ripaldo was still having trouble looking at her.

"Well, I'm afraid I can't help you with that," Fraulein Kistner said. "I know very little about Greece and places north."

"I understand," Ripaldo said. "I wouldn't expect you to. I was just hoping I might learn something from Corporal Schonfeld. From his direct experience of the war."

"Well, it's too late for that now," Fraulein Kistner said. "May I offer you coffee? You look so disappointed, I feel I should offer you something."

Ripaldo stood up to go. "I really don't want to put you to any more trouble."

"Please sit down," Fraulein Kistner said. "Not finding Corporal Schonfeld, as you call him, seems to have quite upset you."

"Well, as I said, we were counting on him, I was counting on him, for some important information. But there's no point in bothering you about that now."

Fraulein Kistner stood there studying Ripaldo. "I wish I could help you. But though I lived with Martin for some years, one thing he never discussed with me was his war."

"And I suppose he never discussed it with others. I mean, within your hearing."

"What others would you have in mind, Mr. Ripaldo? Is that the way it's pronounced? Ripaldo?"

She gave it a strong, rolling "R" and an Italian hover on the "pal."

"Right. Close enough. What I meant was anybody who might know anything about the time the Corporal spent in Greece. In Northern Greece. Some fellow soldier. Since you don't know anything yourself."

Fraulein Kistner was still studying him. "I didn't say I don't know anything. I said I never heard anything from Martin himself."

"Forgive me," Ripaldo said. "I don't quite understand what you're saying. Are you saying that you do know something about his war experience in Greece?"

Fraulein Kistner turned away. "I'll get some coffee. You'll have to excuse me, but I work a long day at the hospital and all I can give you quickly is what I have left over from this morning. You make yourself comfortable. And please, for your own health, stop taking life so seriously."

Ripaldo was tempted to get up and go while Fraulein Kistner was out of the room. He felt thoroughly awkward now, a complete stranger to this woman who had no idea how much he already knew about the man she'd apparently lived with intimately, a foreigner who had misrepresented his motives and had intruded on her privacy to ask questions that she must surely think were out of place and anyway now beside the point. At the same time, he had come out of their conversation with the distinct impression that the woman knew more than she was letting on about Corporal Schonfeld's war and was half ready to tell him what it was. He decided to sit tight and make up a more appealing excuse for his interest in Schonfeld's past. When Fraulein Kistner came back with a tray bearing two mugs of coffee and sat opposite him to offer milk and sugar, he explained to her as best he could that the book he was writing was meant to portray a side of the German occupation of Greece that was not generally known in his country, and this included not only forgotten examples of what one might call cruel behavior by the occupying army but also unrecorded examples of generosity and even heroism on the part of individual soldiers in that army. The latter concern was what brought Corporal Schonfeld squarely into the picture, Ripaldo said, as he'd discovered during a recent trip to Northern Greece, where the Corporal was still remembered for the help he had given to certain villagers during the occupation and where his reputation for kindness remained alive even after all these years. What would be very useful for his purposes, Ripaldo said, would be any information she might have about his service in Greece during those years: letters he may have written, the names of fellow soldiers and officers he may have known, reminiscences about events he may have shared with her or others, anything that might provide the details to fill in what was clearly a heroic period in his life.

"I don't know how heroic it was," Fraulein Kistner said. "All I know is that it was a period of his life that obsessed him."

"And how do you know that?" Ripaldo asked, almost too softly.

"Because he never spoke to me about it," Fraulein Kistner said. "As I told you."

"But I have the impression that nevertheless you know something about that period of his life."

Fraulein Kistner set her cup down and got up to walk to the window on the far side of the room. She stood there for a moment, then turned to gaze at Ripaldo with her hands crossed under her breasts.

"You are a clever man. Maybe a bit too clever. What is it that you really want to know?"

Ripaldo couldn't meet her eyes again, but now it wasn't because she was stunning to look at, though the figure of her standing there in her black dress with a deep diamond shape of bright skin below her throat was enough to take his breath away. This Lotte Kistner had caught on to his charade so sharply and quickly that he couldn't find a way to block out what she'd seen and lead her on further. He decided that the only possible way was to tell her the truth. He stood up and went over to take her hand and guide her back to the chair across from his, then sat down and told her about Hortiáti village, and the Corporal's presumed knowledge of the massacre there in 1944, and the connection between that and the so-called anti-partisan activities of a young Wehrmacht lieutenant in Ic/AO who had become an international celebrity and a well-documented fabricator now running for high office but with a still incomplete if greatly suspicious wartime record—all that had brought Ripaldo to Salzburg from Vienna and the dryer regions to the south. When he was done, Fraulein Kistner stood up again and went back to her window.

"It must not have been easy for you to be so honest with me," she said without turning. "You have no way of knowing how I might feel about your burning interest in our country's distinguished elder statesman and his alleged war crimes. I am an Austrian, after all. And loyal to my country."

"I felt I had to take the chance," Ripaldo said.

That made her turn to gaze at him. "It means that much to you, does it? To your American sense of injustice, or moral outrage, or whatever it is? After so many years?"

"I guess you could say that," Ripaldo said.

Fraulein Kistner was still gazing at him. Then she turned and walked out of the room. Ripaldo sat there wondering what he should do next. Get up and go quietly? Wait for her to come back, thank her for her trouble, and then go quietly? Follow her out of the room and invite her to dinner on the off chance that a little more persuasion might get something valuable out of her—and in any case give him that much more time, intimate time, to study her eyes? He stood up and went to the window. It was raining lightly, and the clouds, broken but heavy and dark, had moved in against the Monchsberg castle, covering it mostly with gloom yet opening to allow a shaft of light against one of the outer towers. It struck him that it looked almost plausible in that fractured light, real enough to be home to more than just the evil ghosts of this sinister century. He suddenly felt a light touch on his shoulder. As he turned, Fraulein Kistner handed him a notebook of the kind he once saw a group of pre-war kids in Greece use to beat each other over head as they emerged from a German school that was said to have the aura of an asylum for the criminally insane. He opened the mauve cover, but there was nothing in it to identify the handwriting, which was clean and precise enough to seem a draftsman's sample.

"Martin's war journal," Fraulein Kistner said. "Make of it what you wish."

She motioned Ripaldo to sit down again, and when he did, still focusing on the first page, she went out and eventually came back with a plate of cakes. Ripaldo read on.

1944

March 21. I begin this journal, dear Lotte, on the first day of spring, a bleak day for us in Northern Greece but maybe no better for you at home. In our dormitory and mess hall we hear daily of new bombings of cities in Germany—Berlin, Leipzig, Frankfurt am Main—in return for our bombing of England. We also hear that the Russians have reached the borders of Romania and that our enemies in Italy have established a dangerous beachhead not far from Rome. It will not be long before this wretched war is over. One sign of how serious our situation has become is this morning's announcement that we can no longer expect regular mail deliveries in either direction. And along with that comes a ridiculous warning that even so we must be especially careful from now on about what we write our loved ones and others at home. In any case, it seems foolish to think that the letters I would want to write you would get past the censor even if they proved lucky enough to travel safely north as far as Austria. At the same time, I can't bear to speak through a veil, to hide the truth in what I write so as to make sure that it passes through the hands of those in control of the disaster ahead of us. That is why I have chosen this way, writing you when I can in this notebook, without any assurance that you will ever see what I have written but with some hope that I will survive to hand you what I record here when the right time comes.

The truth, dear Lotte, is that we have lost our soul. I don't know how to explain this so you understand that I'm no longer speaking simply as an Austrian soldier or even as a citizen of the new Germany that swallowed our country, but as an ordinary man of flesh and blood. I turned twenty-three last month, which is young enough, but you are so much younger, even if only five—now six—years separate us, that I feel I must protect you. Or maybe it is that I've become so old in this war that I see myself now more as a father to you than the substitute older brother I've tried to be, in any case a friend who feels as close to you as I might to a brother or sister by blood had I one, and more concerned for your well-being than my own. I suppose I've felt that way almost from the day your family moved in next to mine so many years ago. This closeness makes me want to shield you from things that a seventeen-year-old girl has no business turning over in her mind when spring has begun to show us that at least the world beyond our control has turned green again. But at the same time, I realize that you should see things as they really are for your own protection.

When I say we've lost our soul I don't mean we've simply lost our direction in this war and with it everything that we were led to believe was our purpose. I mean we've gone over to the side of the devil. And when I say that, I'm not talking in the language of religion, which in any case has never been my language, though, as you know, for a while I studied our great philosophers in preparation for the university and was once moved by them. I speak about something quite down to earth: in our arrogance we have thought ourselves better than all others on this planet, and believing that, we have made enemies of all others, including our own allies and those who live among us who belong to another race.

I can be specific now that I am sure nobody will read what I say here until I pass this journal on to you in person someday, assuming I make my way home again. The allies I have in mind are the Italians and what we did to them after their surrender last September. Nothing of this is official. For obvious reasons, there are no records in the files of what we did. But the stories came to us in the mess hall from eyewitnesses when our Army Group in southern Greece was dissolved after the Italian capitulation and some of the officers and staff from that group, including one Austrian lieutenant and several Austrian noncommissioned officers, were transferred to the intelligence section of Army Group E here in a village next door to us called Arsaklí.

It was of course the noncommissioned officers who talked. And this is what we learned. The Italians were supposed to turn over their arms to our people and prepare themselves to be transported back to Italy. Some of those who were slow to turn over their arms were simply shot where they stood. The rest were then told to give up everything they owned to be stacked in piles, including the uniforms they were wearing, which meant that they were made to stand naked through the night and the next day until it became simpler to give them back a uniform—anybody's uniform—rather than attempt to find another kind of clothing for them to wear. They looked ridiculous after that, we were told, comic figures, ill-fitted and now bowed down with humiliation, no longer soldiers worthy of the name. And then they were sent to the cattle cars, fifty or sixty to a car, for transportation not to Italy as they had been told but first to Vienna and then to camps for forced labor, I suppose in Germany, Poland, God knows where. And to keep them healthy during this journey into the unfamiliar northern autumn, pieces of bread made up mostly of wooden shavings were thrown into the cars for those strong and hungry enough to fight over them.

This for our former allies. I don't want to tell you what other stories we hear about the treatment of our enemies in this region—and I don't mean the resistance fighters, who are armed themselves, I mean ordinary people. If I were to speak about what some of our group have seen with their own eyes in the city that curves around the bay below our headquarters, you would think that this war has damaged my brain, my sense of what is possible and impossible. At this time last year, as spring was beginning to show on our mountainside, hundreds and hundreds—no, more than that—many thousands of those living in this city, of both sexes and of all ages, each wearing a yellow star on their clothing to separate them from their neighbors, were rounded up by some of our group and sent to a special district to wait for transport somewhere to the north. I don't know how long they stayed there or when they left the city. We heard only broken accounts of this operation, and nothing that was official. And we don't know where these people were sent. The only certain thing is that, given their race, they were not sent to

Austria or Germany. One has to wonder if they will ever come back to their city from wherever our leaders have decided they must go.

And now, this spring, it becomes our turn to wait for transport to another country, the closest to the north. The difference, of course, is that we will decide when we leave, and we will know where we are going—at least on this earth. The only uncertainty is how long we will have to wait to pay for what we have done.

I am truly sorry, dear Lotte, that this season brings me thoughts of this kind for what should be thoughts to please you. I would much rather tell you about the beauty of this place and the change in the fields that we have begun to see out of our dormitory window, the tall grass speckled now with red poppies and the daisies spread over the hillside behind us where sheep once grazed. It's almost enough to make one think that peace has returned to this land that we have desecrated for three years now. But peace has not returned. And it will not return until the devil in us has been defeated and the price has been paid for our arrogance. What, my dear Lotte, will the cost be for you and me, who were too young and ignorant to know what was waiting for us when it all began and who would not have wanted any of this had we known?

April 15. It has been a busy time since I put this journal away, thinking I would add to it at least once a week. Since I last wrote, I've been transferred to new duties. Though I am still on call during certain periods to serve as an orderly whenever the need might arise, I've also been put in charge of a dispensary where medicines and other personal items are available and where people come for first aid during the working day. The hours are long, but they are set, which allows me regular periods of free time, and I promise, dear Lotte, to spend more of that time writing you in the only safe way I can until writing is no longer necessary. I am also pleased to have duties that are beneficial not only for our own people but also for the Greek staff who work in this place. That gives me a good feeling even if it doesn't really help to make up for what we have done to this country—what we are still doing with increased severity as the enemy moves closer and closer to pushing us back home.

The one problem I have in my new position is the officer in charge of the unit I now belong to. He is a curious-looking man, with a beak of a nose and a way of holding his head high as though there is a ruler in the back of his jacket to keep his spine absolutely straight. He is not exactly vicious or even mean in the manner of other officers I've known, but he is very difficult, very particular to have a continual accounting of every item I make use of in my dispensary, from the simplest bandage to the expensive medicines that I would in any case never use without further instructions. I feel that he is always watching me, like a school teacher during an endless examination. And he has a way of dropping by the dispensary unannounced, I suppose to make sure that I'm not drinking from a bottle of rubbing alcohol for my pleasure or stealing cotton to stuff my ears against his quiet but always slightly critical voice. "Is it necessary to keep so many bottles next to the sink?" he will say. "Surely one bottle at a time is enough for one injury at a time, don't you think?" Or he will open one of the cupboards and ask why so many packages of gauze are in there, piled on top of each other. "What if someone were to topple these over so that they spilled onto the floor? Please, wouldn't that be dangerously unhygienic considering the condition of your floor?" What can one say to that? I never say anything, but it does not sit well in my stomach.

My free time is another matter. I have found an escape from Oberleutnant Hertzel—that is his name—and every other connection to the regulated life inside the barbed wire enclosure that is my home here. My escape is to the basement of a building that used to be a place where classes were held at the American school that provides us with most of our work and living quarters. The basement is full of school desks and other old furniture piled almost to the ceiling, but there are also stacks of books in another corner, books of all kinds, some in Greek and the others in English and therefore just as unreadable. I cannot take pleasure in what used to be my first love until the war killed my hope of studying philosophy at the university. But among these generally unreadable books there are some that have to do with chemistry and physics and, best of all, biology, because one of those has a section on anatomy. They are full of drawings and therefore not impossible for me to understand, especially since I have a good background in some of the subjects from our school in Graz and a bit more from my army training. I feel I've become a student again in this curious way. I spend hours in that room studying graphs and pictures, and when I think I've worked out their meaning, I sometimes memorize them.

Now I will tell you a secret. All this studying in my free time is not just to escape from the unpleasant normal routine in this place, though there is much of that in it. I've been thinking about the future—and I must hope that there will be a future that will allow me to go home whole. My secret is that I've decided to become a doctor. I don't know how I will accomplish this when I still can't be sure that I will find the means to begin an ordinary university course, but I am determined to find a way. I have always been a good student. Maybe there will be a scholarship for which I can qualify. Maybe veterans of this war will get special dispensation when our government changes, as it surely must. Nobody can tell what lies ahead for our country, what kind of country it will be and who will be its leaders. But I need this bit of hope. And, my dear Lotte, I want you to hold it for me as our secret until the right time comes so that it's not exposed to those who may ridicule the thought or do what they can to destroy it. If I am certain of anything in this corrupt world, it is that you will do neither.

April 29. Again, dear friend, I have taken too long to return to you and this journal, but my days have not been easy and my nights have often shown me the wrong kind of dreams. It was less than a week after I last wrote you that I was discovered in my private library retreat and very nearly brought before our military court here for doing nothing but reading to myself. My locker was searched on the suspicion that I had stolen books, and when they found no books there and nothing on my person, they had to withdraw the charge of theft. And since nobody had posted that basement as off limits, they couldn't charge me officially with being someplace I shouldn't have been. But they didn't like it. I don't know who betrayed me. Somebody must have seen me go down there and stay a long while. I suspect it was Oberleutnant Hertzel, since he appears to be so concerned about what I do and don't do in my place of work, but I have no proof of that. And I must admit that he argued for leniency when I was brought before the major who handles such matters at our headquarters. The only thing they could accuse me of was reading books that had not been approved by our command, but since the books were not in my language, even that accusation did not go into my file. I refused to tell them what I was actually doing among those books except to say that I was looking at pictures. In the end I was warned to spend less time by myself if I wanted to stay out of trouble and to join in the activities of others of my rank.

I have no intention of doing that. The others of my rank are men I do not know well and who do not know me. We have little in common. They gamble with cards and gossip and tell ridiculous stories, mostly old stories from the days before the war and what terrible things they did to their teachers and to each other in school, rarely anything about the life around them and what they have done since coming to this country. And their trips into the village or the city have one purpose only, which is to drink enough wine to return to the dormitory in a stupor, a thing I really can't blame them for in view of what daylight brings them. I don't know how many times I've been called to clean up after one or another of them and do what I can to relieve the pain that goes with vomiting away a night on the town and rising early to pretend that one is fit for a normal day of work. So I prefer to spend my free time alone, even if I can no longer use that time to read in my awkward way.

What I've been doing instead is taking long walks inside our enclosure. With spring in full blossom there is much to interest me, much to learn about what lives among the trees, some ordinary animals and birds but some quite strange, and many wild flowers that have begun to appear along the old road to this school and in the open fields within our enclosure. I recognize only a few of the flowers because this climate is very different from ours, especially different from the climate in the mountains around Innsbruck where my father comes from and where we used to spend our summers. I gather up whatever new wild flower appears—yellow, purple, pink, sweet-stemmed or prickly—and I put them between the leaves of another notebook I keep next to this one in a secret place I've made in the matting that covers the springs of my bed. I hope the flowers will keep long enough that way so that you and I can spend some time trying to learn their names when the war's end gives us the chance.

I found something else of value during my evening walks. At the far end of the buildings that hold our offices, on the edge of an open field that has been left unattended, there is a shed that seems to be out of use now, a place where wood is stored in the winter. It has a sliding door on one side, but no windows, and one reaches it by way of an old broken road that doesn't lead anywhere at that end of our enclosure. This makes it a very private place. I can sit in there with the door open to give me light, and I can look out across the open field in front of me and the forest below that and feel almost unburdened, almost as though the field and forest belong to an untrampled land in another country that is mine as much as anybody else's.

That's where I will go to write you next time. It's a place where I can clear my mind enough to imagine what you may be doing as I write, even what you might want to say were you able to answer me. This is a game, of course, no true substitute for a letter in your handwriting with your quiet, unclouded way of telling me what is on your mind and how you spend your hours and days. I will have to imagine that, make it all up. What else can I do, dear Lotte, now that I miss your voice more and more in this unnatural silence that has come between us?

May 9. I hope it will not always be something distressing that brings me back to this journal, however late, but the truth is that you are the only person I can speak to about those things that touch me closely, whether with pleasure or pain. A curious thing happened two days ago that still has me worried. A villager from this region was struck by one of our military vehicles while he was leading his donkey cart to the market place in the village of Arsaklí above our headquarters. The villager was brought to our dormitory, which is near the main road, and I was summoned to provide first aid. I arrived there just as an officer and three soldiers from the vehicle in question had laid the villager out on a bed. The man was truly a mess, covered with what turned out to be squashed tomatoes from his cart. His exposed flesh was badly scraped here and there, and he was shouting and moaning as though calling on death to release him from his unbearable life. We got enough of his clothes off to discover that he had a broken arm at the elbow and a broken ankle.

We don't have a hospital at our headquarters. I'm the only hospital, and a very poor one, I must admit, since my equipment is only my own hands and what little I can carry in them when I'm called on suddenly like that. In any case, I arrived at this man's temporary bed with no choice but to do what I did. I bandaged him as best I could and put splints on his ankle and arm as I've been trained to do, hoping that this would serve to get him without further damage or pain to the military hospital on the outskirts of the city. I believe that I did what I had to do efficiently though no doubt imperfectly. And I heard nothing more about it until the next day, when Oberleutnant Hertzel called me into his office. He spoke calmly, with a little smile that I've come to distrust, or anyway to take as a warning.

"So. I understand that you have now become a doctor. Do I understand correctly?"

"No, Herr Oberleutnant," I said. "I have no such pretension."

"But you seem to be able to set arms and legs. So I've been told. And that is almost miraculous if you are not a doctor."

"Forgive me, Herr Oberleutnant. If you have in mind yesterday's accident, I merely applied bandages and splints."

"Is that so?" said Oberleutnant Hertzel. "The report that came to me indicated that the doctors at our military hospital found the bones already set. I suppose what you mean to tell me is that the doctors were lying."

"No, Herr Oberleutnant, I don't mean to tell you that. It's true that I tried as best I could to have the bones in place before I applied the splints but I certainly did not pretend to set them as a doctor might."

"Well then, it must indeed be a kind of miracle. Unless someone has taught you to do that."

"No, Herr Oberleutnant," I said. "Nobody has taught me to set bones. What I have learned outside my training I have had to learn by myself."

"So. Perhaps we should call you a self-taught doctor. Would that be more accurate?"

"No, Herr Oberleutnant."

"Then let me give you a warning, Corporal Schonfeld. Playing the doctor one time is sufficient. Playing the doctor another time could be dangerous, both for you and for the patient. From now on, when you are called in to help with serious injuries, you are not to do anything so difficult and complicated as you did yesterday until a doctor has been sent for to supervise the case. Especially when it involves one of our own but even when it involves a villager. Is that clear?"

"Yes, Herr Oberleutnant, that is clear."

"Now, so that you won't think I'm being merely harsh with you, I must tell you why this rule has to be absolute. Obviously in the case of our own men, we want only the best medical assistance at all times, but also in the case of villagers, of the enemy if you will, we do not want to leave ourselves open to the charge of mistreating the local population by making medical mistakes. Especially when there has been an accident that was our fault. Do you understand my position?"

"I understand. I did not mean to do more than my duty."

"The point is," Oberleutnant Hertzel said, "one must know the limits of one's duty. Do you understand the point, Corporal Schonfeld?"

I said I understood the point, but I didn't really. How is one supposed to treat an injured person under such restrictions? If I'm called in to help someone with broken bones, what am I meant to do, wrap the poor creature in a blanket and put him in the back of a truck to take him moaning to a hospital so many kilometers from here—who knows how many—over a mud and gravel road that doesn't deserve the name, so that the poor man's bones can break through the skin on the way there and present themselves naked to some doctor at the end of this cruel trip? And what if someone comes to me with an open wound that is bleeding freely? Am I to let that person, enemy or friend, bleed to death while I run off to find a car that will take me wherever I have to go in order to bring a doctor back with me to supervise the cleaning of a corpse? It's too ridiculous. I refuse to understand his point.

Please forgive me for ranting like this, for boring you with my small worries. I suppose it's a sign of where we have arrived in our miserable enclosure on the underside of the continent so far from you. Everyone here is nervous and irritable these days. I suppose I even have to forgive Oberleutnant Hertzel for thinking up these petty regulations that are supposed to keep us from mistreating our enemies during the odd moments when we are not trying to blast them off the face of the earth. What else does the man have to believe in if it isn't his faith in order, and what else does he have to satisfy his sense of station beyond his power to make others follow procedures that he considers correct? There is nothing else left to guide his days, no purpose in the war, no prospect of advancement, no future for his kind of—what shall I call it?—his kind of mindless devotion. How could he avoid becoming twisted?

I mean to say that all of us have known something of what he has had to give up since we left the days when we were made to think ourselves the beautiful children, the best in the world. All those speeches, all the cheering, the singing together, the marching and drilling and gymnastics, everything in our school that taught us the wrong daily lessons while the great philosophers and poets we studied were supposed to be teaching us something else. At least I still have my work to believe in. What does Oberleutnant Hertzel still have?

I don't know how much of this will make sense to you because I don't know what they may be teaching you during wartime in our school or who your teachers are—surely few of the men who taught me can still be there now. But whoever they are, men, women, old or young, let me warn you, dear Lotte: do not listen to those who speak of our race as the pure race and the people of our Reich as the best people. There is no such thing as a pure race and a best people. Those who say these things are either blind or stupid or evil but in any case dangerous. They do not teach the truth. We Austrians, we Germans, are nothing more than what we are, and until we find our soul again, those of us who have lost it in this satanic war, we will remain the lowest of the low. That is the truth.

You may be too young to know this for yourself, and that is only just, because it's not really your war, and when it's over, you have every reason to begin your life without our burden. But do not let your teachers corrupt you before that day arrives. Believe what I say, dear Lotte, and be vigilant.

May 22. I have something to tell you that I hesitate to write down even in this secret way. But writing you like this, telling you my most personal thoughts, seems to be the one thing that keeps me sane while an unspoken insanity surrounds me everywhere. And what happened to me yesterday is a thing I can't hold back from an honest account of my days here. In any case, I will write what I feel I have to in this journal and decide later when the right time has come to show you what I have written—if that time is ever given me.

Let me also say that I have to trust you not to be angry with me or at all upset about what I am going to tell you. Nothing that may happen to me here will change the special place you have in my life, I promise you that. We are brother and sister in the only way that matters, the true way that has nothing to do with blood, and we will always be that close for whatever life is given us together. That is a thing you must believe.

Yesterday I met a woman, a woman who has moved me as no other has during my years away from home in this war. She is a Greek woman, somewhat younger than me but not much, one of those from the village of Arsakli who work at our headquarters. This is how I met her. Yesterday noon, while I was rearranging one of my wall cabinets a third or fourth time to please Oberleutnant Hertzel, a group of the village women who work for us came chattering down the corridor to my dispensary to deliver one of their group, clearly the youngest, who had somehow cut the middle fingers of her left hand almost to the bone. Of course I had no way of finding out exactly how this had happened since I wasn't able to understand what the women were saying, even if I could have quieted them down enough to get them to talk one at a time. The injured woman was the only one who was really calm, and this despite her pain. That was the first thing that impressed me. I threw off the dirty dish towel that somebody had used to bind her hand, and in place of that I wound gauze tightly around her fingers to stop the flow of blood. Not a murmur came out of her. While she sat there quietly, entirely in control of herself, I managed somehow to make the other women see that she would be all right and that it would be best if they were to wait for her in the corridor so that she was not disturbed by their sighing and exclaiming and so that I had some peace to work in. The second thing that impressed me about the girl was the way she looked at me the minute we were by ourselves.

These are things that I would find difficulty talking about to anyone, but I have to believe that I can say them to you or I will be left completely alone. We have always told each other the truth. And though we haven't spoken often about the intimate things that happen between men and women, I know that you are no longer so innocent as to come to these things the way you might have as a child. You are not a child now, and I am not a child, and if we are to be to each other as we have always been, I cannot keep from you the intimate thoughts and feelings that sometimes reach the center of my being.

This young woman looked at me in a way that was direct and unashamed, as though I was neither a stranger to her nor an enemy, as though she had enough pride and courage to face me, a German soldier, as she might any other man—any other man who touched the woman in her. It was not exactly a lover's look, but there was something of that in it. At the same time, it made me feel that some of the pride in it was meant to show me how unworthy I was to meet her look with the same honesty. In any case, I didn't. I gave all my attention to the injured hand as I removed the bloodied gauze, then held the fingers tightly so that the cuts stayed closed when the bleeding started again. I looked up to see that the woman had her eyes shut now. I asked her in German—how else could I ask her?—whether I was hurting her too much. She didn't answer me. Instead, she opened her eyes and touched my face with her fingertips, and her look now had a sweet sadness in it that I found more unbearable than the bit of pride I'd seen there earlier.

I finished treating the hand when the bleeding stopped, cleaning the wounds gently with hydrogen peroxide and binding the fingers again and then the whole hand with new gauze. She was very brave. And to show her that I understood that, I brought the bandaged hand to my lips quickly when I was finished and stood up to see her out. She didn't move from her chair. She sat there looking at me as she had at first. I smiled and gestured toward the door with my hand, and that made her stand up. Then I realized that I couldn't just send her off like that without telling her to come back in the evening so that I could check on her wounds to make sure there was no infection and change the bandage, especially now that I had taken charge of her injury in defiance of Oberleutnant Hertzel's new regulation, ordinary though the injury was. But how was I to tell her what I wanted? I had no way of talking to her, though I tried my best in German, rather stupidly. And then I found the way. I took a piece of paper from my desk and drew a picture of a clock, setting the hands at seven.

I have to say, dear Lotte, that there is something else about this woman that is striking: she is unusually bright compared to most of the village women who work for us. As soon as I had drawn the clock, she not only understood the drawing, but in a manner of speaking corrected it. That is to say, she took my pencil and drew a horizontal line under my clock and then a circle above her line with an arrow beside it pointing up and another pointing down. It took me longer to understand her drawing than it had taken her to understand mine, but I finally recognized her circle as a sun and her arrows as a way of showing me that I had not told her whether I meant seven in the morning or seven in the evening. I circled the arrow pointing down. As she hurried out, it came to me that we had discovered a way to talk to each other, but why that thought both pleased me and frightened me didn't bear further thinking, at least not at that moment.

When she returned exactly at seven yesterday evening, there was only another cleaning woman in the building as far as I knew, on the floor above, but I made a point of keeping the door to the dispensary open. I was nervous, not so much about her being there as my patient, which I probably could have explained away as a necessary emergency even to Oberleutnant Hertzel, but about what had been going through my mind since she'd turned to leave the dispensary that morning more abruptly than she'd needed to. Suppose I was making more of what had happened between the two of us than what was truly there. What did I know about the customs in her country, the significance—or lack of it—that went into talking with the eyes? Maybe even her touching my face as she had was simply a way of thanking me for my worry about her when we had no other language in common.

I decided I had to be very careful. But when she came into the dispensary that evening and sat down, I had more time than I needed to see how beautiful she was. Not as beautiful as you will be at her age, maybe as you are already—it's been so long since I've seen you, dear Lotte—but with eyes that reminded me of yours. In any case, I was no longer sure as she sat there that I could be careful enough.

I wish there weren't more to tell you, but I'm afraid that is not so. I worked on her hand with full concentration and as skillfully as I could, removing the old gauze with its dried blood and bathing her wounded fingers until they were absolutely clean so that I could touch them quickly with iodine and bind them up again. Her bravery astounded me, not a sound, though she held her breath when I applied the iodine. I studied her, then let go of her wounded hand, then took up her free hand—I don't know why, I can't explain it—and put it to my face, and when she didn't take it back, I moved it so her fingers brushed against my lips. When I let the hand go, I knew that I had now crossed over to the enemy, and it was clear from her look that I was welcome there.

We are to meet this evening at the place only you know about. I drew her a map to show her where. We meet at seven again. If she comes to me.

June 8. I wonder if you will have heard all the news that has come through to us this past week on the wireless. Are they telling you that Rome has now fallen to the enemy after being evacuated by the Fuhrer to protect it from the peril of destruction and that the Americans and British and their allies have landed in Normandy in great numbers and are trying to press ahead along a broad front that we are said to be defending heroically? If they are keeping this news from you, or if they are painting it over so that it isn't recognizable for the catastrophe it shows, what difference does it make for me to tell you in this way what most of us here suspect the truth to be? By the time I decide that the right moment has come to let you read this, if I am given the chance to decide, it will all be long over. There will not even be the excuse of setting the record straight. Nobody will want to know the record by then, and if we are lucky, our national memory will be dead.

I've found a way to put the catastrophe behind me where I can't see it most of the time because my mind is elsewhere: in a sweet darkness where no shadow can reach. I live in that darkness when the sun begins to get low, and when it sets, I live in the recollection of where I've been until the sun comes up again. Marina is her name. She came to me in the evening of the day I last wrote to you in this journal, and she has come every evening since, except on Sundays, which is her day at home. We meet each other in the shed without windows, where the only light that touches us comes from the cracks between the wall-boards. The language we have is the language of our eyes and hands and the rhythm of what we make each other feel. Nothing enters our privacy from beyond that partial light, and the only words we can use to speak the pleasure we know is to say each other's name. How long, dear Lotte, can this purity of feeling last? And what is it in me that makes me ask you, my spiritual sister, the innocent one, a thing you cannot possibly tell me?

June 30. There is no point in berating myself for taking more than three weeks to return to this journal and our one-way correspondence, which I believe more and more will remain hidden forever in this notebook. Writing here in any case does not ease your days. They must now seem intolerable to you, even if you're safely out of range of the bombers that are destroying Berlin, as we have now begun to destroy London with our Fuhrer's sinister rocket bombs. Some here have actually been celebrating the news of this desperate secret weapon of ours, which we are told arrives with a terrifying buzzing until the last silent minute that lets the victim know about the fate that is directly overhead. How could our greatest scientists conceive of such a weapon? And can there possibly be worse to come? Surely there isn't time. We must hope so if we are to save ourselves from still another curse to haunt our history.

I've been worried about you in the most important part of my thinking mind since I last wrote, but the truth is that most of my days have been strangely peaceful. No, more than that, almost outside time, certainly so in the final hours before the sun goes down. You will have understood what has come into my life during those hours from what I've already told you, but that isn't all I mean. I am almost at peace about the war in the sense that it can no longer touch me personally with those emotions that we were trained to feel about the Reich and its noble ambitions, along with the hatred we were meant to hold for those who would rise against us. I see no enemies any longer. My enemy has become what I am. And I would die for that enemy now, just as I would die for you, my dearest friend.

What I am trying to say to you—please, beyond any cause for jealousy—is that I have come to see my blood and yours as the same blood that flows in the veins of those we were taught to hate. Marina is now me, as I am now Marina. Even though she is a woman, I cannot think of her as different from me in any way that touches the center of my being any more than I can think of you that way. In this sense we are all one. We feel the life around us with the same intensity, and there is no room for hatred in that feeling. You and I know that from the time we had together before the war and things we have said to each other. Marina and I know that from what we have discovered in the darkness.

The only thing that separates us now is language, and we have begun to find a way to conquer that. Occasionally we leave our door ajar just enough to give us the light we need to see each other clearly. That allows us to name in each other's language everything we can see of each other and the space around us. And outside that, we have begun to learn what little is needed to make a phrase that follows from naming the things we can see. It is a slow beginning, but, my God, what new pleasure there is in it, at least for me. One can live only so long without language, dear Lotte, language that can be trusted, and this simple new language begins to make up for what yours and mine has lost.

July 15. With the coming of summer heat, our once dark woodshed has become a lighted schoolroom. For some days now we have had to open our sliding door to let in air, because our room becomes a furnace by late afternoon, and this square of light has provided us with the means to learn so much that was incomplete or quite beyond us in our earlier darkness. We now teach each other as children new to speaking might, from the sounds that go with pictures. Marina has learned the names of many things in my language, things I draw for her on a pad and then say for her again and again in German until she has their sound as best she can. And then she teaches me the sound in Greek. We've even begun to find the words that build a passage to and away from the things I draw, so that we now have the beginnings of a conversation. Of course we can't say much that we would like to, much that really has to be said, but this richer feast of words has brought each of us back to the world outside our woodshed without our having to give up the private safety of it.

That's a good thing, because I begin to see some restlessness in Marina. She's the one who always moves to open the sliding door farther even after our lessons are over and the heat has begun to fade with the setting sun. She will sit down in front of the opening to look out on our same unchanging garden of weeds, signaling me to sit beside her, as though that dry patch of bristly land leads to an endless green valley. It leads only to danger, as she well knows, though when I try to get her to sit a bit farther back so that there's no possible chance of anyone sighting us from the road, she holds me where she's chosen to sit with her arm tucked in mine and her head on my shoulder, the way she might if we were a new couple showing ourselves to our neighbors from our front doorstep. It's touching, I admit, but it's also quite unwise, and I allow it only because I can't find a means of explaining why I think it isn't right for us to sit like that even for a moment.

I wonder if there will ever be enough language between us for me to say those other things that have to be said, for a start, what little the future holds for us. Even though I've managed to put the war behind me, as it seems Marina has too, the war is not going to let go of us so easily. I know what will happen when the retreat begins, but does she? And does she know how soon it will come? One sign that it must be near is the fact that no one talks openly about the possibility any longer, at least not in front of me or those of my rank. And another sign is the fact that Oberleutnant Hertzel has begun to treat me like any other soldier rather than like his mischievous dog. He even came to the dispensary the other day to ask me if there was anything I needed, not in the way of medical supplies but for my personal use. And when I said there was nothing, he reached in his pocket and handed me a bottle of cologne water. I was amazed, embarrassed. He just smiled, then reached out and patted my cheek. I wonder if he thinks that I'm just waiting for peace to arrive so that I can find myself in a position to do him some harm and that the time has now come for him to be decent to me. He doesn't know me at all if he thinks that. I have to say that this isn't what I sensed behind his smile, but I can't find words to tell you exactly what I did sense.

I'm tired, dear Lotte. I can't think clearly any longer. But please know that you remain close by me always, no matter how long it has been since we last saw each other and even if my mind is often elsewhere these days.

July 28: We've had our first quarrel, not a lover's quarrel, something more serious. I suppose that comes in part from learning each other's language too quickly and imperfectly. We've now said more than we should have, and we've understood too little. But I'm afraid the difficulty goes deeper than language.

Since I last wrote here, dear Lotte, we've had a heat wave of a kind you and I have never known even in the plains south of Graz, and this provided an excuse for Marina to draw me outside. That has been her wish for some days now, not just sitting together to study the barren garden beyond our open doorway but, as soon as the dusk thickened, to sit out far enough to catch something of the evening breeze. When the heat refused to die even after the sun disappeared, I couldn't really argue against that. But the heat wave ended as abruptly as it came some time ago, and Marina still drew me out to watch the dying light uncover the first stars. Of course one could say that's simply what lovers might choose to do, but please, not these two, not in this wounded country.

A few evenings ago I learned that she now considers our woodshed a kind of prison and has for some time. She doesn't blame me for that, she blames the heat and the pressure of time and I can't be sure what else that keeps her from blaming this war and the fate that has brought the two of us to know each other at a time when we have to remain in hiding from our own shadows. I've tried to make her understand that we should be grateful for the hours we've been given and not hope for something more, certainly not for anything as grand as the freedom to breathe openly, not now, not any day that we can see ahead. But how do you say that without the right language to a woman who cannot sit still to hear your worn-out caution, even if she could understand it, when freedom to do and feel as her pride allows is what you have helped her to learn as you were learning it yourself? What I discovered two evenings ago is that her pride now wants her to sit with me under the night sky.

At first she said this not in so many words but with a gesture. We were sitting inside our doorway later than usual, hardly any light left outside, and she spread her arms as though to take in the full expanse of the heavens and its early stars, and then she brought her arms in to close around her breasts as though to complete an embrace. She glanced at me, then went back to gazing up at the sky. And when she spoke in her broken mixture of my language and hers, her eyes not on me but on the fading seam of light at the horizon, she made me understand that what she wanted was for the two of us to escape from our barbed wire enclosure long enough to see the hills behind her village and watch the night come on from there, where space had no margins.

I ruined that thought for her by taking it lightly at first, and then, when I saw how serious she was, by trying to explain to her that the idea was simply impossible, especially now that people at our headquarters were watching each other carefully, nervously. There had been several defections to the enemy, I told her, including an officer who had been in charge of important military documents, and everybody in the mess hall was talking about that these days, talking too much, stiffening their own attitude toward the war in public so as to put off any suspicion. The climate was very confused, I said, very dangerous. And the more I talked about this climate, the closer she came to tears, until I finally realized that she either had no idea what I was talking about or understood all too well. So I shut up. After all, who was this enemy I spoke of if it didn't include her and her people? And who were these defectors and these others so full of suspicion if they didn't include me? And why was I bringing this war climate back to put so much distance and confusion between us when both of us had risked so much already to meet our need for each other?

These thoughts didn't come to me quite so clearly at that moment, because I was too threatened by her new pride and by what I took to be her childish failure to see things as they were. They settled in me late during the solitary hour that I spent in our woodshed last evening, after I finally decided that Marina wouldn't be coming to me as usual. I knew then that what I had said must have disturbed her deeply, must have wounded her in her heart, because she wasn't the kind to make me suffer simply to force her argument. And I also knew by the end of that waiting alone that whatever her pride required, it was likely to get, because I couldn't bear to wound her again—this though it pained me to think of risking what little time we had left by choosing to act recklessly. What finally tormented me most was not being able to tell her that.

She gave me my chance this evening well before the sun went down. When I reached the woodshed, she was already there, leaning against the pile of logs left over from the winter. She had never before arrived ahead of me. She said that she'd come to give me a map she'd made, a map of her village and the place she wanted the two of us to meet tomorrow night when darkness came. I glanced at the map, then put it away in my shirt pocket and made her sit down beside me so that I could try to explain to her more simply than I had the last time about the danger to both of us in meeting outside our barbed wire enclosure. I spoke softly, caressing her as I spoke. But if she was listening, she gave me no sign of it, and when I was finished, she took the map out of my shirt pocket and showed me the large X she'd drawn to mark the new meeting place she had in mind in a field beyond the village of Arsakli. I couldn't really study the map just then, though it seemed clear enough— clear enough to put the fear of death in me. That must have shown in my face, because as I put it away again, Marina turned to kiss my cheeks with tender force. But when I tried to hold her to me, she broke free and was gone through the door without another word.

Do you understand what she's done, dear Lotte? She's left me no room for further talk, no room for choosing between this and that. How else am I to take her going off as she did? If I want to see her again, I must go to her in the way she's designed, follow her map into some new darkness that is surely more dangerous than the one we've known. Does she realize what she's done? Is this some sort of test to see how much I'm willing to risk for her? Why does this thing matter so much to her just as our time together is running out?

August 2. The worst has happened. Tomorrow I must pack my things to move elsewhere. I went to Marina as she wanted, but only two nights ago. I didn't manage to find a way of escaping this enclosure until the third day after she'd left me alone to study the map she'd drawn. During those days the mood here was impossible. There had been another defection to the enemy, a non-commissioned officer this time, and all trips outside our headquarters were forbidden to those under the rank of lieutenant. I was trapped for two days, with no way of letting Marina know because she didn't return to our woodshed during those days, as I knew she wouldn't. By the third evening I was frantic because I saw things ending without my even having a moment to take my leave of her in the right way. There was no assurance that I'd find her if I followed her map to the X she'd drawn beyond her village, but I had to take the chance. I knew now that if I didn't make the attempt to see her again, I wouldn't be able to sleep or even think on the right side of reason, and that could be even more dangerous for both her safety and mine.

After I went off duty that evening I stayed in full uniform and put my first aid kit in order. I took it up and walked as fast as I could to the guardhouse on the upper side of our enclosure so that I would seem to be out of breath, and I told the guard on duty there that I'd been called out on an emergency to treat a soldier who had passed out at the intelligence headquarters in Arsakli. Why wasn't I going there by armored car? he asked. I stared at him. What armored car? I said. The armored cars are all out on patrol, for reasons I'm sure I don't have to tell you, not while this new emergency is going on. He studied me, uncertain, then waved me on with his rifle.

I was honestly out of breath by the time I reached Arsakli. I kept to the main road, which went through the outer edge of the village, clear of the main square and the school house that served as our intelligence headquarters. Marina's map was not exact, but there was only one path beyond the village that stayed close to the main road for a while, and this path took me through a meadow between hills to a sheepfold that clearly hadn't been used for some years because there were large gaps in it here and there and other parts seemed to have taken root in the ground. Marina was inside, hunched like a frightened animal under a section that had a low roof of crossed branches and straw for a floor. She didn't move when she saw me, only her eyes moved. I crawled in beside her under the roof and held her to me. She was trembling. I told her there was no reason to be afraid, but the lie in that showed because even the thick shirt of my uniform was soaked through with sweat. I got up to check the path I'd taken to make sure I hadn't been followed, then I sat down and held Marina's hand in both of mine. She was still tense. When I got up again a minute later to check the path a second time, we both realized that there could be no peace in that place.

Marina was gentle with me. We spoke very little. I told her I couldn't come there again, things were getting worse for us each day and we were now under severe restrictions. She said she understood, I didn't have to come again, we would meet where we always had. I tried to tell her that even that might be too difficult now, but she held my head against her and wouldn't let me talk. When she released me, she saw that I was weeping, so she held me again until I stopped. We sat and watched the darkness come on, holding hands as though in the cinema, without talking even in our awkward way. When the early stars had come out clearly and I rose to leave, Marina cleaned the straw off my uniform bit by bit, taking more time than she needed. She told me I should go on ahead of her, it would be safer that way. Then she said "tomorrow?" in German. I studied her without answering, then kissed her, then said "tomorrow" in Greek. As I put my cap on and stood there with my first aid kit in one hand, she did a strange thing. She took my free hand and guided it to make the sign of the cross on her chest in the way of her religion, then did the same thing on my chest, and at the end kissed my hand. Then she stepped back as though signaling me to go.

I hurried off across the open meadow to the path that led to the main road on the far side of a low mound bordering that stretch of pasture land. I'd barely started downhill among the first houses along the main road when I spotted two of our men with rifles slung over their shoulders coming down the slope of the hill on the upper edge of the village. They were coming in my direction but from a considerable distance, and since I had no special reason to believe they were coming to meet me, I kept my pace fast but even. They caught up with me as I reached the turning for the village square, and they ordered me to halt. I knew then that I must have been their target all along, but I couldn't be sure why.

What happened after that, dear Lotte, is difficult to explain. When they questioned me about where I'd been and where I was going, I refused to tell them more than enough to identify who I was. What could I tell them about where I'd been? What sort of lie would have made any sense to them? So I was marched to the school house on the square and was brought before one of the officers on duty there, a young officer who was tall and thin-faced, with a quiet manner that I didn't trust at all and that really put the fear of God in me. More questions, one after the other. What was I doing wandering through the countryside carrying a first aid kit? On whose orders? Did I know that I could have been shot without question by those on guard in our pillbox above the village? Who was I taking my medicines to at that hour anyway? Members of the resistance in the hills? Villagers serving the enemy?

I stood there without answering. As the officer stared at me with what seemed to me the controlled smile of a maniac, I suddenly thought of Oberleutnant Hertzel and his special smile when he'd handed me his gift of cologne water. I saw no way out now but to hope that Oberleutnant Hertzel might have enough pity in him to save my skin. It was a desperate hope, but I found myself telling this stiff young officer with the quiet voice that I was on a personal mission under orders from the head of my unit and that I was not in a position to answer his questions without the permission of Oberleutnant Hertzel.

I won't describe the look on this young officer's pinched face, but if he said anything, it was under his breath. I was marched off to an empty back room that had only a table and three chairs in it, a room that I assumed was used for interrogations. I sat there alone for over two hours, but no one interrogated me. Not even Oberleutnant Hertzel after he was escorted into the room to bring me suddenly to attention. He simply stared at me, then shook his head, then ordered me to march ahead of him out of the school house and across to the main road that led down the hill to our barbed wire enclosure. He said nothing to me on the way. As we approached the enclosure he came up beside me and marched in step with me right past the saluting guard, but when we were well inside and on the way to my dormitory barracks, he dismissed me curtly. "Tomorrow," he said, "you will come to my office as soon as you are free from your morning duties. If you don't come then, you can consider yourself dead."

I went to his office. What else could I do? Did he think I had wings to fly out of our enclosure and glide across the bay of the city below so that I might soar to my freedom over the high mountains between you and me? He was sitting behind his desk waiting for me with the old familiar smile that meant some new test for my patience. "So," he said. "You've decided to travel the countryside in search of animals or villagers or who knows what else to cure with first aid, is that your personal mission these days?" I didn't reply. "Women villagers, maybe? Young wives or unmarried girls who need help to rid themselves of unborn children, is that it?" I still said nothing. "Well, whatever it is, Corporal Schonfeld, those personal duties are now over. From no on you will work under the direction of a medical staff that can keep a better eye on you than I can." He reached across the desk to hand me a sheet of paper, and from that I learned about my new assignment.

I am now to work with a group that is part of the large military unit stationed in a village at the other end of the road that goes along the foot of the mountain behind us, more than ten kilometers from here, a place with a name—Asvestohóri—almost too difficult to pronounce. My group is assigned the task of distributing medical supplies to our troops there and also the task of supervising the municipal water service that is supposed to keep our water pure in this region. It looks like boring work on the whole, in any case work that will mean I am always watched by somebody in a new kind of prison so far from here that I might as well be in another country. I'm sure Oberleutnant Hertzel expects me to be grateful for what he has done. The truth is, I can't help hating him and his war more than ever. Right now, dear Lotte, I am very much alone.

August 25. I've really had very little chance to pick up this note-book in the three weeks that I've been on duty outside the village of Asvestohóri, where my new unit is stationed. Except for part of one day a week, the work here is endless, with only the occasional hour or two of free time, usually after the night has blackened our barracks. Those of us who have been transferred from other units are put to work at the most menial assignments outside our official duties, as though we are new recruits meant to earn our right to belong to the society of our veteran companions, some of whom have been in this war for a much shorter time than I have. Even among those who have been transferred here there is an order of priority, with the newest arrivals of the same rank assigned the meanest work. Only soldiers of the rank of private—sometimes no more than children—work under me. And the work I supervise is the most humiliating kind, sometimes the garbage area in the kitchen, sometimes the toilet area, hardly more than a series of filthy tiled holes in the ground. I will spare you further details. My official duties are a relief: two periods a day in the medical supply room arranging bottles and packages, and one or more trips a week into the countryside to help with purifying our water supply.

These trips have the feel of a brief escape from prison. We are given the whole of a morning to complete our work, because the officer in charge of our group is himself in no hurry to return to our unit in Asvestohóri. He likes to linger over a coffee and a cognac in the village of Hortiáti in the foothills of the same moun-tain that used to rise behind us above Arsaklí, only here to the southeast rather than the northeast. After we have added our chemicals to the water supply, the two of us from the lower ranks are assigned to the local first aid station for an hour or so of treat-ing the villagers for minor injuries. Then, while our leader sips his second cognac, we are allowed to wander in the village as we please for a while or walk the fields below the village in the neighborhood of the water source, our official excuse for being in the open coun-tryside so pleasurably long. I mostly walk the fields. There is a high point above the ruined aqueduct that marks our source, and from this high point I can see across the valley to the meadow where I left Marina that evening almost a month ago and beyond that place to the first houses in Arsaklí. That high point is where I take my rest, for as long as I can bear it.

My several trips into the countryside have also given me a chance to talk a little with the men of the municipal water service in a mix of my broken Greek and their broken German, men of some education, it seems, who are meant to escort and supervise in this operation. I've learned more than I choose to tell the others from these bits and pieces of conversation during those moments when we stop briefly to escape the sun under a tree or in the shade of our armored car. It is clear that some of these Greeks not only fear that Germany has lost the war but that we will be leaving the country soon and they will be in danger for having worked at our side, the enemy's side. I try to convince them that surely their work as water purifiers will be considered by the local people to have been necessary work, but either my primitive Greek is inadequate or their cynicism is too deep to allow simple words to penetrate their gloom.

I don't argue with them about the question of when we will be leaving. Every single day rumors pass through our unit that our army's departure has already been decreed, and no one doubts any longer that this is so. There are rumors that Paris has fallen to the French, that the Bulgarians have withdrawn from the war so that our northeastern flank is now exposed, that there is total mobilization at home. This tells us how desperate the situation must be since there is surely no one left to mobilize other than children and old men. The only question now is when we will be leaving Greece: this month, the next, in any case certainly before Christmas.

Is it too much to hope that I may be in Graz by then, dear Lotte? Dare I hope that? I'm not sentimental about Christmas, not any more, but I remember that you are. Forgive me if I recall how much you cried when you were eight and they denied you the role of the Virgin Mary in your school play because you were considered too small to hold the infant Christ in your arms. And so instead you became a pouting angel at the back of the set with one wing broken and a look in your eyes that would have turned any watching shepherd into stone. Then, when you finally got the role three years later, you still cried about it, though that was because you couldn't stop worrying about whether you were good enough for the part. The sadness that this brought into your sweet face made you a perfect grieving Mary even if it was at your child's birth rather than his death.

Do you mind if I'm playful about these things that mattered so much to you then? And does your belief matter that much to you still? I wish I could talk to you about it as I once could, but I'm afraid I'm no use to you in that way any longer. If there is a God, He is not with us here. Our God has forsaken us or was never with us from the start. In either case, we are now alone in a wilderness of our own making.

September 4. I must write about what has happened. I think it's the only way I can hold myself together, keep my mind from going out of control. I have more time now than I could want, because things have fallen apart here, and for the moment I seem to have been forgotten. I sit by myself hour after hour waiting for some new assignment, but none has come. My old assignment, the best part of it, vanished last Saturday, our usual day for purifying the water below the village of Hortiáti. There was an ambush, and Naegele was killed. Naegele is the Sergeant who has been with our medical group far longer than any of us and who would always go with me into the village to treat those villagers who wait for us each week outside the first aid station. He had been doing that for months, more than a year, and the villagers had come to think of him as some kind of healing saint even if he was a German soldier. They would kneel before him sometimes, cross themselves, much to his embarrassment. He was not much older than me, but the war had turned his blond hair mostly white. Everyone in that village must have known Naegele by now. I can't believe any one of them would have lain in wait to kill him, though I've come to believe anything is possible in this war. The one certain thing about what happened is that Naegele is now dead, and because of that, the village of Hortiáti is burned to the ground.

I can't help but think that this was my fault. I was assigned to drive the car. When the ambush wounded our officer, Leutnant Ebert, who was riding in the back seat, Naegele opened the front door to see what was going on and was shot in the face. I pulled him back inside and drove off first in the direction we were headed, toward the aqueduct, then realized my mistake and swung around to head back the way we'd come. The shooting was going on, but it must have been aimed at the car on the far side of the road belonging to the municipal water service. Leutnant Ebert was moaning in the back seat, so I knew he was still alive, but I could tell that Naegele was dead beside me even though I couldn't bring myself to look at what was left of his face.

I drove on like a maniac until I came to the place where the road splits. I took the left branch heading toward Arsaklí and our old headquarters, then decided that was too far to go with a wounded man and backed out to head toward Asvestohóri. I stopped to look at Naegele, then took off my shirt to cover his head, and when I looked in back I saw that Leutnant Ebert had his eyes closed and was white, but he was still breathing, and there was no blood near his mouth. I decided to keep going. As we arrived at the outskirts of Asvestohóri, Leutnant Ebert came to suddenly and asked where we were. I told him, then asked him if we should stop to work on his wound. He said it could wait, it was only his arm, grazed by a bullet. When we reached the guard house, he was out of the car and past the guard before I could get out to help him. He picked up the phone in the guard house, I suppose to sound the alarm. I called one of the guards over to help me carry Naegele into the shade.

I know now that I should have kept going on the road to Arsaklí as I started to. It would have taken us much longer to get help, yes, but that might have been long enough to save the villagers in Hortiáti. That is what Naegele would have done. Instead I took the short route for the benefit of Leutnant Ebert. And that hardly gave the villagers, in any case too few of them, enough time to escape into the mountains before he sounded his alarm. He must have got through to Arsaklí by phone from the guard house, got through to the intelligence headquarters responsible for counter resistance operations, because the retaliation started almost immediately. The trucks in our compound had begun to fill up with men before we'd managed to wrap Naegele in a blanket and carry him inside the mess hall. And by the time we did, the famous Sergeant Schubert had arrived outside our compound with his specialists from the Partisan Pursuit Unit and their Greek informers. We all knew something terrible was going to happen. There were too many trucks and armored cars lined up for a simple counter-ambush operation. And it happened, within the hour. And while it happened, all I could do was sit on the floor beside Naegele's body and hold my head and try to understand why he was the one who'd been killed rather than Leutnant Ebert or me. Naegele would have shot Leutnant Ebert before he would have let him do harm to that village so late in this war we've lost.

They took me there yesterday. An investigation team, two officers and their aides, arrived from the intelligence unit in Arsaklí to interview Leutnant Ebert. Since he wasn't thought healthy enough to ride in a car, I became the only witness who could show them where the ambush had taken place. One of the officers from Arsaklí was the same thin-faced Nazi with the quiet voice who had questioned me last month at the intelligence headquarters in the school house, but he pretended not to recognize me and I saw no reason to recognize him. The other officer, even taller and large-nosed, I'd never seen before.

I showed them where we'd been ambushed. That should have been enough, but they made me stay with them through their tour of the village beyond. There was little left that one would call a village—a few houses more or less untouched, most of them blackened shells, some ashes only. There was total silence in that place. The bodies of those who had been shot in the streets were mostly gone. We barely stopped to look at those still left. The smell of charcoal and burned flesh was everywhere, but especially on one street near the center of the village. Nobody asked why and nobody took notes. The team turned back before we'd reached the upper edge of the village. They said there was nothing more to be seen that hadn't been seen already, but the real reason was that one of the aides had become sick from the smell, and there was talk of possible infection in the air. Also, we were being watched from the hills. One of the officers, the one I didn't know, said he was certain he'd heard the sound of a shepherd's flute on the mountainside above the village and this made him realize suddenly that we were completely exposed. He'd taken it for a signal. I'd heard it too, and I'd thought it a sound that could chill the gods.

FIVE

There was no answer at Fraulein Lotte Kistner's apartment when Ripaldo went back there to return Martin Schonfeld's journal less than a week after she'd let him borrow it so that he could share it with Count Wittekind, his "interpreter." She'd told Ripaldo that, within reason, he and his interpreter could keep it as long as necessary for their purposes, but under no circumstances were they to copy it. In his hurry to have a thorough look through it in private the day she'd given it to him, Ripaldo had left her apartment without asking for her phone number or what time of day might be the most convenient for him to bring it back. Late afternoon had seemed right because that was when she'd been there the first time, but he realized now that a head nurse was likely to be on call at odd hours and he should have checked out her schedule at the hospital on his way there. He decided to have a coffee across the street from her place, and maybe a glass of wine after that, and if she hadn't appeared by then, he'd make a move to track her down at work. Anyway, this would give him a chance to think over exactly how he was going to say to her what he had to say now that Wittekind had come to Salzburg for the weekend at his urging and the two of them had been through Corporal Schonfeld's journal together to make sure they agreed on its implications.

One thing they'd agreed on was that it was now virtually a sure thing that the unusually tall, large-nosed Wehrmacht lieutenant who had walked at Corporal Schonfeld's side through the burned village of Hortiáti was the youthful 03 intelligence officer from

Arsakli become international hypocrite. But the problem remained of verifying this beyond doubt and demonstrating his precise connection to the massacre itself. Another thing they'd agreed on was that it seemed very odd that a man of Corporal Schonfeld's sensibilities regarding war crimes in general and this one in particular had not come forward at any point before his death to confront this large-nosed officer and any other officer who may have been directly involved in an act that struck the Corporal as so horrendous that at the time he had trouble staying this side of sanity. Ripaldo hoped that Fraulein Kistner might cast some light on that mystery. He also hoped that she might be able to explain why the Corporal appeared to have drifted into obscurity after leaving Greece and had never returned to look up Marina Angeloúdis, as her account of their last days together held that he'd promised to do.

That was a subject on which he and Wittekind did not see eye to eye. It had come up while they were in Wittekind's hotel room as the weekend was running out, Ripaldo sitting on the bed with Schonfeld's journal in his lap and Wittekind sprawled on the floor gazing up at the ceiling with an unopened bottle of scotch beside him. The talk about the journal seemed to have dried up when Wittekind suddenly raised his head and then sat up.

"One thing I have to say, Ripaldo. I really cannot see that your interest in why Schonfeld quite reasonably decided not to return to his wartime mistress in the country he once occupied as an enemy has anything to do with our purposes at this point."

"I promised Marina I'd find out what I could. That's how we got her documents, remember? I have to keep that promise."

"Well, you've found out that he left Greece alive and that he's now dead. Isn't that enough? What more can Fraulein Kistner tell you?"

"Why he disappeared so completely back then. It doesn't make sense to me. Not after reading this journal."

"What doesn't make sense to me is why his Greek lady friend was so ready to believe he was dead. Why she still believes it."

"I think I've figured that out," Ripaldo said. "Whether she realized it or not, when she made him leave their enclosure that time she was testing him to see if he would risk everything for her. The way that red-faced German soldier in her village finally risked everything for the baker's daughter. And though her Corporal went far in that direction, he ended up not going far enough. So of course she would prefer to think that he died at the aqueduct."

"That's one way of looking at it," Wittekind said. "Anyway from her point of view. But as I read the Corporal's journal, what I see most clearly is that from his point of view the person he was really in love with all that time was not your Greek friend Marina but your Austrian friend Lotte Kistner. Though for a time he obviously thought he was in love with Marina."

"That's exactly the point," Ripaldo said. "Was he fooling himself or Marina or both? It makes you wonder just how reliable his testimony is."

"It's as reliable as it seems," Wittekind said. "What are you, some kind of undercover literary critic?"

He stood up suddenly and went into the bathroom with the bottle of scotch in one hand.

"The point is," Ripaldo said to the bathroom door, "Marina's deposition says he promised to come back and find her after the war, and Schonfeld's journal says nothing of the kind. And I happen to think she's the one who's telling the truth."

Wittekind came out of the bathroom with two glasses and handed Ripaldo one.

"Both may be telling the truth," he said. "Hold your glass."

Ripaldo took the glass. "Both?"

Wittekind filled Ripaldo's glass half way. "He may well have told her what she says he told her and then changed his mind after the massacre. Couldn't bear to face her again. Couldn't bear to face the country. Who knows? In any case, let me ask you just one question. Whatever he said to her, is it possible that he would tell his young friend Lotte about a promise of that kind made to another woman? His journal was written to Lotte, for Lotte. Not so?"

"Right. O.K. So what do you suggest I tell Marina when I get back to her as I promised? That in some complicated way Schonfeld was really in love with another woman all along? A seventeen-year-old Austrian girl back home roaming the green hills in a dirndl while she was risking her life to meet her lover in a sheepfold beyond Arsakli?"

"What you tell your friend Marina is up to you," Wittekind said. "I'm just trying to suggest that Schonfeld's position may have been desperate, which makes it something other than simply unreasonable or cruel."

"And what about the Big O? I suppose you think I ought to let Schonfeld off the hook on that too. He's dead now, so the cruel past that he knew more about than anybody else is dead with him, right?"

"I didn't say so. Relax, Ripaldo. The Big O is another matter. We can't afford to let anyone off the hook where he's concerned. But unfortunately your friend Lotte Kistner was not a witness to who was actually working for the Ic/AO group in Arsaklí on September 2, 1944. And without a living witness, I'm afraid we end up back where we started from with regard to that particular massacre."

"But suppose she knows of somebody who was assigned there at the time. Somebody Schonfeld may have kept in touch with who's still alive."

"Now you're talking," Wittekind said. "That's the kind of thing we've got to hope for. So what I suggest is that you arrange another interview as soon as possible with the sweet Fraulein Kistner."

"I had that in mind," Ripaldo said.

"I thought you might. Now that we seem to have put the Corporal and his journal to rest, I can see you on your way to taking up with the beautiful Fraulein where Schonfeld left off."

"Get lost," Ripaldo said.

"I see what I see," Wittekind said, studying his glass.

"Forget it," Ripaldo said. "Fraulein Kistner is not the kind to give you or me a second look."

"Me, of course not. You in your American innocence, maybe. In any case, you have my blessing."

Wittekind raised his glass in a salute.

"Get lost," Ripaldo said.

After Wittekind returned to Vienna, Ripaldo began to wonder if he and his friend were still on the same track in all ways or if Wittekind had begun to reveal a less than objective impulse to defend, anyway to protect, those Austrian compatriots of his generation who had emerged from the war as critical of the Wehrmacht mentality as he was himself—and Ripaldo had Corporal Schonfeld and his journal specifically in mind. But as he sat with a glass of wine waiting for Lotte Kistner to show up at her apartment, he found himself leafing through Schonfeld's mauve notebook without reading a word of it, glancing at page after page of the Corporal's clean script as though scanning an illuminated text, and this caused him to set it aside with the feeling that, far from being a document for objective analysis, it was so personal that it had best remain closed to all eyes other than those it had been addressed to. He then decided that he had to go along with what he'd seen as Wittekind's impulse, at least to the extent of dealing with Fraulein Kistner's sensibilities as gently as he could, ready to back off the minute it seemed he was violating her privacy or threatening whatever tender sentiments she might still be carrying for her dead Corporal and the life they'd had together.

Fraulein Kistner came around the corner during Ripaldo's second glass of wine. He watched her head across the street toward her doorway, still in her nurse's uniform, walking firmly but with just enough swing in her stride to suggest that she knew she was off duty and was ready to be. She seemed taller than he remembered, and her waist was broader in that uniform, but she carried her head in a way that told him she had a fair idea of how good-looking she was whatever the style of dress. Ripaldo got up to follow her, then thought it best to let her get herself changed and settled in before he gave her doorbell another ring.

When she answered the doorbell, she was wearing a red skirt and a white blouse with a broad collar. She'd left the top button open in the blouse so that the pale hollow of her throat showed and the full rise of her neck. She studied Ripaldo for a second, but not with a look that told him she was surprised to see him. And she remembered his name.

"So, Mr. Ripaldo," she said, with a quick smile. "You've had your fill of 1944 and Martin's war?"

Ripaldo handed her the notebook. "Not entirely," he said. "May I come in for a minute?"

"Of course."

They went into her living room. She motioned Ripaldo to the

couch and sat in an easy chair opposite, her long legs crossed and slightly tilted away from him. She waited for him to say something.

"Look," Ripaldo said. "I'd like to ask you a few more questions, but I don't want to pry into your private life in any way that is embarrassing to you, so please let me know if I'm going too far."

"How can I let you know until you begin to pry?" Fraulein Kistner said. "And why does it have to be prying?"

"I meant when I pry. If I pry. Speaking in German makes it difficult to say what I mean."

"Your speaking is clear," Fraulein Kistner said. "It's your intention that is sometimes difficult to understand. I prefer you to be completely honest with me. As you finally were the last time we met."

"Good," Ripaldo said. "I'll try to be completely honest again. What I'd like to know first of all, Fraulein Kistner, this for my own personal reasons, is why Corporal Schonfeld never got in touch with the woman he left behind in Greece, the woman in his journal called Marina. Never saw her again, never wrote to her, nothing. I know this from her own testimony. She still believes Corporal Schonfeld was killed in the war."

Fraulein Kistner uncrossed her legs and leaned forward. "May I ask something of you first? You can call me Fraulein Kistner if you insist, though I prefer Lotte, but please don't call Martin 'Corporal Schonfeld' in a tone of voice that comes from films about how terrible the Nazis were during the war."

"I'm sorry. Good. Lotte and Martin. And I'm Jackson from now on. That's my first name. And I'll do what I can not to show how terrible I think the Nazis were during the war, though I have to say that's not always easy."

Lotte sat back. "Of course it isn't easy. Now. To answer your question. I don't know why Martin never returned to Greece or never wrote to his friend from the village there. As I told you, we never spoke about his time in that country."

"But he gave you his journal to read. Which means he wanted you to know about what happened there. Not only about the woman, but the burning of the village and the rest that happened."

"Yes. But he didn't give it to me right away, as the journal said he planned to do. He only gave it to me when he knew it wouldn't make any difference."

"Why was that?"

"You mean why didn't it make any difference? Because by then I'd accepted Martin for what he was. We were lovers by then."

"I thought it might have come to that," Ripaldo said.

"Did you?" Lotte said. "But did you also think it might come to our being lovers who never made love? At least almost never?"

Ripaldo looked away from her. "No. I can't say I did."

Lotte stood up. "Well, that is what it came to. And that is why I'm not entirely at ease talking about that country and what happened there. I mean, in view of what it did to Martin."

"Forgive me, but it wasn't the country that did it. And I don't think Martin would have thought it was."

Lotte went over to look out of the window. "Whatever he might have thought, he came back from that country a deeply wounded man. Deeply wounded in his spirit. A man who would never really be young again. He spent the rest of his life taking care of the sick yet couldn't find a way of curing himself."

"But you said you became lovers."

Lotte was still looking out of the window. "For a while. But it was never right. And yet I could never do anything but love him. Which wounded me as well."

Ripaldo sat there running his finger absently along the binding of Martin's notebook on the coffee table in front of him. He finally pushed the notebook aside.

"You're still young," he said to Lotte's back. "Still attractive to men."

"Do you think so? That's kind of you. Martin's been dead five years now, so I've had a few years to practice being more or less young again."

"So maybe it's time to just forget about Martin."

Lotte showed him half a smile. "You're the one who's having trouble forgetting. You can't seem to understand that for us the war was over a long time ago. The price has been paid."

"Not by everyone. Martin was a decent man. An honest man. Others have proven less honest, and you know who I mean."

"Others are survivors. What's the good of being honest when it ends up taking the life out of you?"

"What's the good of surviving if it means selling your soul?"

Lotte came back and sat in her chair. She leaned forward as she had before, her eyes squarely on Ripaldo.

"I'm going to tell you something. You clearly think Martin was somehow heroic back then—wasn't that what you said the last time we met? Heroic for helping others, including many villagers, and so forth. And I suppose one could say he was noble for seeing the truth of things and for telling the truth about what he saw. Maybe all that is correct from your point of view. But whatever Martin himself may have thought was correct while he was Corporal Schonfeld, and for some years afterwards, was completely gone by the time he became too sick to work in the hospital any longer and had to depend on me."

"You took care of him at home?"

"For more than two years. And during that time he told me openly what I'd suspected almost from the day he came back to me in 1944, which was that no day had gone by without his feeling guilty for having survived the war. And that, he said, was a thing that was unforgivable."

"Martin said that?"

"Yes. And, as you see, I lied to you. That one time he did in fact speak to me about the war. But what he came to see came too late to matter for either of us."

"So you think he ended up on the side of the survivors, is that it?" Ripaldo said.

"He ended up on the side of those who believed in life at any cost," Lotte said. "Even if it came too late for him."

"Well at least he ended up still telling the truth as he saw it," Ripaldo said. "Which doesn't quite put him in the same camp as your distinguished Austrian statesman."

Lotte studied him. "Since it seems you can't forgive us for the sins of our fathers, I'll tell you something else that may surprise you. A man came to see Martin during his last days, a Wehrmacht officer who had served in Greece with the distinguished statesman, as you call him.

"What sort of Wehrmacht officer?"

"Just an officer. He was part of a group that was apparently trying to deal with certain rumors about the distinguished gentleman's alleged war crimes that at the time had begun to float in the air and in the newspapers, and he had come to speak to Martin in that connection, Martin refused to see the officer except to tell him to go away."

"Did he say why?"

"I don't know what he said to the officer, but to me he said he'd had his war and the so-called distinguished statesman had had his, and as far as Martin was concerned, for both of them the war was over."

"So that was that?"

"That was that."

"The Wehrmacht officer went away and you never saw him again?"

"Never."

"But you have his name? And maybe an address?"

Lotte sat back in her chair. She gazed at Ripaldo, shaking her head. "So, Mr. Jackson Ripaldo. You're as obsessed as Martin used to be. Just as fanatic in your way. Only you haven't learned when it's time to give up as he did, have you?"

"Not yet," Ripaldo said. "Maybe that's because I'm not lucky enough to have had the same teacher. But I can assure you I'm not giving up while that great Nazi hypocrite is still out there pretending to be as clean as your Tyrolean snow."

"Do you think saying that about me as a teacher will get you what you want?" Lotte said.

"No. I was just being completely honest. Isn't that what we agreed to be?"

"So now you appeal to my conscience, is that it?"

"If you prefer to put it that way."

"Well, I will not tell you this former officer's address because I don't know it. And I will not tell you his name, because you know it already."

Lotte stood up and waited. When Ripaldo didn't say anything, she kneeled to hand him Schonfeld's journal from the coffee table.

"If you're clever, you'll find it in here. But you'll have to do so on your own, because I don't want to be responsible for giving you more than Martin himself would have. So take the journal away again, Mr. Jackson Ripaldo, and clever or not, please bring it back to me next week or at the latest the week after. You may possibly find me in a better mood then, especially if you no longer have a need to ask me questions that seem to embarrass you more than they do me."

The Wehrmacht officer's name was Max Ebert, and he lived in Klosterneuberg on the Danube outside Vienna. Ripaldo found his full name and address through Wittekind's old-boy network less than a week after the two of them agreed that, of the Wehrmacht officers actually named in Martin Schonfeld's journal, Oberleutnant Hertzel and Leutnant Ebert, the latter was surely the one that Lotte Kistner's had meant to identify by her parting clue. Both Ripaldo and Wittekind found it hard to believe that Hertzel would have given them an old address for Schonfeld had he visited the Schonfeld-Kistner apartment in Salzburg as recently as Lotte's revelation suggested, and they also found it hard to believe that this onetime turncoat, who clearly had little use for the former 03 intelligence officer in Arsakli now become international celebrity, would have been part of any group trying to defuse early rumors about the alleged wartime crimes of that particular Wehrmacht lieutenant. Hertzel had seemed inclined toward the opposite.

Max Ebert was another matter. The portrait in Schonfeld's journal suggested that he was the type who might well have come out of hiding to join others who belonged to a club of former Wehrmacht officers out to protect their own. And, as Wittekind pointed out, what could prove highly significant for his committee's purposes was that the journal not only identified Ebert as the other survivor of the ambush below Hortiáti village but seemed to pinpoint him as the officer who, by way of a call to intelligence headquarters at Arsakli, had sounded the alarm that brought on a quick reprisal. Only he and Schonfeld knew about that call, and only Ebert knew who had responded to it at the other end of the line. So, Wittekind said, this man's testimony could prove crucial to their mission. But he and Ripaldo agreed that there was a potential problem: if Ebert had finally come out of hiding to track down Schonfeld in connection with new rumors regarding war crimes in the Balkans, was it to persuade the Corporal to bear true witness to what had happened after the ambush below the village of

Hortiáti or to cover up what the two of them knew that nobody else could know? And whatever Ebert's motive for visiting Schonfeld's sick bed several years back, would he be willing to tell the full truth now? Wittekind thought it unlikely, but both he and Ripaldo thought it essential that they try to find out.

When Wittekind phoned Ripaldo in Salzburg to report back to him on what he and his Vienna committee had managed to dig up about Max Ebert, he began by describing the man as though for a WANTED ad: early seventies, medium height, walks stiffly upright as though suffering from hemorrhoids, face owl-shaped and blotched by too much sun or too much drink, small beak of a nose that fits with the bird-like tuft of hair rising on the front of his otherwise bald crown, unarmed except for the occasional riding crop or walking stick. Wittekind said that his reputation in the Vienna circle of former Wehrmacht officers, which he'd moved in and out of over the years, was that of a politician with rigid convictions. He'd actually made his living before retirement as a life-insurance salesman, but he'd also been involved in right-wing politics for a while and had run unsuccessfully for Burgermeister of his home town.

At the point of Ebert's retirement, the research on him became thin. Wittekind said that few people had seen him in recent years. And rumor had it that the man had turned bitter even against his former political allies—and that included some of the Big O's current entourage—because of what he considered unprincipled revisionism. Except for the occasional encounter with a diehard Wehrmacht elite in his region, the man's uncompromising political stance had apparently caused him to retreat into a wilderness of lost possibilities. At least one member of Wittekind's committee felt that there were some grounds for believing that if Ebert had once been in sympathy with the predicament of the distinguished former Wehrmacht officer who had tried to conceal his wartime service in Yugoslavia and Greece, he was now indifferent to him or maybe even hostile. In any case, Wittekind felt that it would have to be Ripaldo who smoked the man out because Wittekind was certain that he himself would now be thoroughly suspect within the small circle that Ebert still belonged to, and if his name were to surface at any time, it might kill whatever prospects there were of getting Ebert to become the essential witness they needed. This meant that Ripaldo would have to work his way into Ebert's confidence on his own.

"So just how do you suggest I go about that?" Ripaldo said.
"I mean given that the man is clearly a reactionary son of a bitch."

"You will find a way. As you did with your friend Fraulein Kistner."

"It's hardly the same situation."

"Just be charming," Wittekind said. "Be American. A little naive but with a very big heart and very open. You know. And when he is no longer guarding himself, thrust boldly into his old-world conscience."

"Thanks, buddy. Thanks a lot."

"Think of the Aegean, Ripaldo. Think of our trip to the Turkish coast. A great new world of adventure waits for you if you succeed in this."

Ripaldo decided that the best way to get through to former Leutnant Max Ebert was not to follow Wittekind's stated advice but rather Wittekind's established strategy: speak to Wehrmacht types with a forked tongue and cover your intentions. One of the desk clerks at his Salzburg hotel proved amicable enough to help him work out a text in German that he sent off to Ebert's Klosterneuberg address as a letter telegram. It explained that a mutual friend who had served with him in the Balkans had passed his name on as somebody an American could trust to tell the true story of the Wehrmacht's role in Greece during 1944 for a book on that period that was meant to set the historical record straight from the perspective of the occupier as much as the occupied, and in this connection Ripaldo hoped Herr Ebert would be gracious enough to meet with him in Klosterneuberg wherever it might be convenient if Ripaldo were to stop there on his way to Vienna at any time during the week ahead. Reply prepaid. The reply reached Ripaldo's Salzburg hotel the following afternoon: "Expect to meet you briefly Cafe Veit, Niedermarkt 13, Klosterneuberg, Wednesday, 16:30 sharp. Ebert."

Reading that, Ripaldo clicked his heals—*Jawohl*, Herr Leutnant—then gave the message his middle finger. And when he reached Klosterneuberg on Wednesday with plenty of time to kill, he thought he might treat himself to a long walk around town, anyway long enough to let the former Wehrmacht lieutenant sit by himself in his cafe a while to brood a bit over buried history and who this American might be who wanted to dig it up again. But by 16:15 Ripaldo found himself checking his map to pinpoint the cafe address, and nervous now about giving Ebert an excuse for walking out on him, he decided to wait across the street from the cafe so that he could watch the man go in ahead of him and then time his late arrival with his eye on the door to make sure he didn't lose his prey.

Despite Wittekind's description, the persistent image Ripaldo had of Leutnant Ebert came from Schonfeld's journal, several generations out of date. When a rotund old man with a bald head stepped out of a taxi in front of the cafe, what finally convinced Ripaldo that this must be his man was the way he held himself as he stood at the cafe door: chin high, thick neck stiff, the tilt of his head authoritative, self-assured, that of someone still in command of an imaginary platoon on a forgotten battlefield. And the same tilt was there when Ripaldo decided the time had come to walk up to the man's table inside the cafe.

"Ripaldo, is it?" Ebert said in English. "Have I pronounced the name correctly? And I gather you speak German. Yes? Well, we will speak in English, I need it for the practice, but in either language you are late, Ripaldo. More than ten minutes late."

"Actually, my watch says just ten minutes," Ripaldo said. "But maybe it's a little slow. Or maybe yours is a little fast. May I sit down?"

"Of course," Ebert said, gesturing toward the chair opposite him. "But I think I must say my watch is never fast, as I am never late. It is a matter of principle with me. You're American, I understand? A historian."

"Not exactly. To be perfectly honest, I'm a journalist. That is, a retired journalist on special assignment. I suppose you can say that sort of thing is a matter of principle with me, as you put it."

"Excuse me, what sort of thing?"

"Trying to tell the truth about who I am."

Herr Ebert was studying Ripaldo with a stiff little smile of mixed curiosity and distaste, as though he saw him standing there wearing only a G-string and a headdress of bright feathers.

"Is that so? Very commendable. Very American. Please do sit down. So, exactly who is this mutual friend—is that what you said?—who sent you to talk to me about the Wehrmacht?"

Ripaldo sat down. "I suppose in all honestly I'd have to say Corporal Martin Schonfeld."

Max Ebert's face turned sober. Then he looked away from Ripaldo and took up the menu to stare at it.

"Corporal Schonfeld, as you call him, is dead."

Ripaldo leaned back in his chair. "He is indeed dead. That is a fact. But the truth is, a bit of him still lives on. I think I should tell you that he kept a journal about the period of his service with the Wehrmacht in Northern Greece. That is where I found your name."

Ebert put the menu down. "And besides my name, what is it in this journal, Mr. Ripaldo, that interests you so much that you went to the difficulty of coming all the way here to talk to me about a war and a place that I have forgotten about almost completely after all these years?"

Ripaldo thought a moment. "I guess I'd better be absolutely straight with you, Herr Ebert. One thing that interests me very much is the Hortiáti massacre."

"The what?"

"The burning of the village of Hortiáti in September, 1944."

Ebert took up the menu again. "I have no recollection of that village."

Ripaldo decided to look at his menu too. "I don't mean to press you," he said over the menu's rim. "But I'm sure if you give yourself a moment to think about it, you'll remember the village. It's the village where you were ambushed and shot in the arm."

Ebert remained focused on his menu. "Of course I remember the ambush. But I know nothing about the burning of this village. I saw nothing of that. Will you have coffee or tea or something more satisfying to the tongue, more fulfilling, Mr. Ripaldo? A brandy, maybe?"

"Coffee," Ripaldo said. "Milk but no sugar, if I may."

"And while we wait for someone to give us service, will you be good enough to tell me whether your interest in my past is professional or personal. That will help me decide if I have anything more to say to you this afternoon."

Ripaldo put his menu down. "I'm really not interested in your past, Herr Ebert. I'm only interested in getting at the historical truth. And I suppose as much for personal as for professional reasons. I used to spend time in that village in the days before it was burned to the ground, and I've just come back from a visit to the depressing new village that replaced the old one surrounded by green fields where you and Corporal Schonfeld and the other officer who was killed in the ambush used to spend time drinking wine or brandy or whatever it was."

Ebert was studying Ripaldo again. "I can assure you that I had nothing to do with the burning of that village. I was wounded at the time, as you seem to know already. And the reprisal was in any case not a Wehrmacht operation."

"According to Corporal Schonfeld, the reprisal was under the command of one Sergeant Schubert, who was in the Wehrmacht. And there is reason to believe that it was ordered by the O3 officer of the Ic/AO intelligence group in Arsakli."

"That, Mr. Ripaldo, is ridiculous. Who told you a thing like that? It was simply a routine operation."

Ripaldo put his menu down and pushed it to one side. "Excuse me, but that is exactly the horror of it, Herr Ebert. The retreat from Greece had already been determined by that time, and 146 villagers of all ages and both sexes were shot or burned to death in a routine operation."

"You misunderstand my meaning," Ebert said. "Routine in the sense of—what shall I say?—of an established procedure. To counter a guerrilla ambush in which one of our men was killed. An action conducted by special forces trained for that purpose."

"Well, whatever one might choose to call it in military language, killing 146 villagers in retaliation for one German soldier was an action that Corporal Schonfeld clearly considered cruel and stupid. Not to say criminal. A thing that shamed him."

Ebert turned and raised his hand to get the waitress's attention. She signalled that she would be there in a minute.

"In any case," Ebert said, "it was not a Wehrmacht operation. It was an action undertaken by the Partisan Pursuit Unit, and this included our Greek allies charged with security. That is the fact."

"But it seems from Corporal Schonfeld's journal that it was indeed a Wehrmacht operation since it was ordered by the O3 intelligence officer in Arsakli. Isn't that your understanding, Herr Ebert? That the order came from Arsakli?"

Ebert's ambivalent smile came back. "And what makes you so certain it was the O3 officer?"

"Because we believe we know from the Corporal's journal that this was the officer who was alerted about the ambush."

"Is that so? Then why have you bothered to come to see me?"

"For confirmation, Herr Ebert. Since it seems from the journal that you were the one who sounded the alarm."

Ebert dropped his smile, then sat back in his chair. "Forgive me, Mr. Ripaldo, but you are misinformed. I did no such thing."

"Well, I'm afraid that is not the impression of the one witness who survived the ambush. I mean, besides you yourself."

"But of course that witness is no longer a witness, isn't it so Mr. Ripaldo? Since that witness is dead."

"His journal is the witness."

Ebert stared at Ripaldo. "His journal? And what does his journal say, that I called intelligence headquarters in Arsakli?"

"I'm afraid that's what is says, Herr Ebert."

"And who does it say I called at intelligence headquarters in Arsakli? Since this journal seems able to listen in on private conversations?"

"We assume you called the O3 officer on duty there. Whose responsibility it was to deal with counter partisan operations. Including those that burned down a number of villages in the region."

Ebert leaned forward again. "We? We? Please. Who is this 'we' you speak of, Mr. Ripaldo?"

"I'm afraid I'm not at liberty to tell you that at this moment. That is, unless you're willing to confirm for us who the O3 officer was that day."

"Aha," Ebert said. "Now I begin to see. It is not me that you and your 'we' are interested in. It is what you Americans would call the public enemy number one, am I right?"

"May I take that for a confirmation? Since it seems we both

know who we're talking about?"

"I confirm nothing. If you want my opinion, my opinion is that an 03 intelligence officer would have no authority to order such an operation. Like the rest of us, he would only follow orders."

"Then may I ask one more thing? Why did you take the time to visit Corporal Schonfeld when the rumors first began to circulate about the distinguished gentleman in question? Wasn't it because you were afraid that Corporal Schonfeld might offer damaging testimony and you wanted to protect the gentleman from that?"

"Please, Mr. Ripaldo. Tell your 'we' that I know nothing and confirm nothing. I protect only myself. Though of course I refuse to belong to those who betray what they once believed when the political wind turns in another direction."

The waitress, uniform immaculate, had come up to stand at a discreet distance.

"It's not a question of betrayal," Ripaldo said, his voice low. "It's a question of honesty. Of integrity. Of—how can I put it?—of being responsible for what one has done and acknowledging the truth of one's past instead of living a lie."

"And what is the question of honesty when a journalist hunts another person's past while pretending to be a historian? As you have done this afternoon, Mr. Ripaldo?"

The waitress caught something in Ebert's tone and turned to move away. Ebert motioned her to come back.

"Please, bring this gentleman a coffee with milk. And for me, a glass of brandy."

Ebert turned back to smile benignly at Ripaldo. "Now, my friend, to speak of something more pleasant. Is Greece still so beautiful as I remember it? I can in all honesty say that next to my own country, it is the most beautiful country I have had the good luck to know."

When Ripaldo reached Vienna to report on the Ebert interview, he persuaded Wittekind over the phone that if total privacy was in order before they got into the details, they should meet near the giant Ferris Wheel in the Prater and take a long walk from there. Ripaldo said that in any case he wanted to check out that territory for a possible opening into a piece he planned to write at some point on the relative innocence of Harry Lime and the Third Man black marketeers of the late 1940s when compared to the city's still unregenerate Nazis who were now coming out of hiding with renewed arrogance, along with their skinhead heirs. After making sure they were not being followed, he and Wittekind had gone over most of the details of the Ebert encounter and were well into their stroll down the Hauptalle when the Ferris Wheel suddenly lit up, and with that, the subject of Ripaldo's project came up again. Wittekind told him, frankly, though the Harry Lime comparison had its value for nostalgia, the new danger his proposed article pointed to, however important, was already receiving considerable attention these days. A more subtle danger he might want to explore at the same time was the spiritual death that had spread among the local younger generation with the arrival of total satisfaction: enough money to buy just about anything the heart might desire, convenient transportation whether public or private, free and easy sex even if one chose to be careful, a job for everybody whether qualified or not, an obligatory window in every office to encourage daydreaming, more vacation time than anybody could reasonably tolerate, almost every need except relief from boredom and lethargy and lack of serious challenge gratified by some government program or regulation.

Wittekind had stopped in mid-path to climb up on his soap box. The bad politics of the right was of course ominous and unforgivable, he declaimed, but the supposedly good politics of the mushy center was equally insufferable. How, he asked his one-man audience, can a country, a way of life, survive without anything to challenge the individual citizen, without any cause for divine discontent? Of course, my friend, under such benign circumstances neo-Nazi skinheads will begin to creep up out of the sewers to enter the moral vacuum with their filthy ideology and evil-smelling racism.

"Don't tell me you're a crypto-reactionary," Ripaldo broke in to say. "I don't want to see you joining forces down the line with the likes of former Leutnant Ebert."

"No chance, my friend. Ebert, it appears, is nostalgic for fascist idiocy. I am nostalgic for the spirit's liberation. For the fruits of adventure. You won't ever find me sitting at Ebert's table."

"Well I didn't stay long myself. Two swallows of coffee and I was out of there."

"That was my fault," Wittekind said. "I should have gone with you whatever the risk of exposure. I apologize to you for that. I should have been there to throw the coffee in his face."

"No. I was at fault for letting him have the last word. But at least I got one thing out of him that we were looking for. The old boy clearly gave himself away when he recognized who it was we were after without my having spelled it out for him. And when he didn't deny having tried to get to Schonfeld."

"True. But unfortunately that doesn't provide us with the witness who can testify as to who was in Arsakli at the other end of the phone call Ebert made and who actually ordered the Hortiáti massacre."

"No, but it proves beyond doubt that our distinguished elder statesman knew exactly what was going on despite all his denials. Which at this point is good enough for me."

"But we still don't have a witness willing to challenge him," Wittekind said. "From what you told me, it seems Ebert would take the same line of defense as all the others. Nobody at his level knew anything about these terrible happenings, and in any case, everybody was following somebody else's orders."

"I'll be the witness," Ripaldo said.

Wittekind stopped to look at him. "You? I'm afraid your testimony doesn't really count for a thing since it's all second-hand. Just like mine."

"It will count with the Big O," Ripaldo said. "Now that I'm certain he knew and still knows what we know."

Wittekind was gazing at Ripaldo. Then he gave him a half-smile.

"I'm not sure what you have in mind," Wittekind said, "but I think you'd better forget it. They'll never let you get close to him when they find out who you are. Besides, he isn't in Vienna."

"Where is he?"

"Salzburg, I'm told. For the Everyman play. Then off on a trip to someplace in the Middle East. The only place abroad that still seems happy to receive him."

"Then back to Salzburg I go."

Wittekind shook his head. "You're mad, Ripaldo. You'll only get yourself into trouble. And you'll lose Fraulein Kistner as well."

"So be it. Besides, who are you to talk? You challenged the great hypocrite yourself. Challenged him openly. Liberated your spirit, so to speak."

Wittekind stood there studying him. "Of course do what you have to do, my friend. But don't say I didn't warn you."

Ripaldo didn't answer him. And when Wittekind tried to bring the subject up again during the walk back, Ripaldo just grinned at him and let the thing drop. He then got Wittekind to tell him about the latest developments in local politics and the prospects for this and that faction depending on how the election turned out. Wittekind ended his commentary by saying that, whatever the aftermath, the election itself was no longer much of an issue as far as he could see, since it had become clear in recent days that the distinguished gentleman with the international reputation was bound to win, if for no other reason than the fact that he had come under increasing attack in the foreign press. Apparently a false prophet dishonored abroad is a false prophet honored at home, Wittekind said, gazing up at the giant Ferris Wheel—unless, of course, there was some new revelation that the best of the local press could use to turn the election tide at the last minute. Ripaldo and Wittekind stood there smiling at each other, but neither seemed to have anything more to say. When they finally shook hands, a bit more formally than usual, Ripaldo said he'd be in touch again as soon as there was reason to be in touch, and then they went their separate ways.

Ripaldo returned to Salzburg with no specific plan in mind other than attending the opening-night performance of Hofmannsthal's Jedermann, what Wittekind had called the Everyman play. He was holding a priceless ticket that he'd managed to wangle with the help of his outdated press card and an old Wittekind contact at American Express in Vienna. He'd headed for American Express after stopping in at the government press office to check out Wittekind's tip about the Big O's whereabouts, and there he'd learned that His Honor was indeed still scheduled to visit the Salzburg Festival briefly and, along with other dignitaries, to attend the opening night of the new production of the annual Jedermann before returning to Vienna to prepare for a pre-election tour of several unspecified regions in the Middle East. At the National Tourist Office in Vienna, Ripaldo was told that the new production would of course take place as usual in front of the Salzburg cathedral as announced and would follow the traditional pattern established by Max Reinhardt in the original 1920 production, though certainly with a few innovations—in short, much the same production that had bored his restless blonde heiress from California to the edge of tears that summer of godless pleasure in the aftermath of World War II.

Back then Ripaldo had the advantage over his companion of having survived the boredom of reading the medieval morality play called The Summoning of Everyman in a college drama course, and he'd managed to keep awake during the Salzburg version by watching the shrewd way that Hofmannsthal introduced grotesques to liven up his stark medieval model—Mammon, Fat Cousin, Thin Cousin, Everyman's Mother, who else? But what he remembered most about that version was all the partying and singing and rhyming, all the romantic playfulness between Everyman and his much younger mistress that not only turned the garden of earthly delights Everyman hoped to build for her into a seductive image but made this hedonistic sinner suddenly more accessible, more desperately human, when the voice of Death arrived from some distant high point above the cathedral square to send terror through his gathered revellers and a shiver through at least one member of the play's audience that night.

On his way back to Salzburg the day before the opening, Ripaldo wondered if his progress over the years from a half-believing romantic with a lapsed Catholic upbringing to a skeptical relativist with only a fading nostalgia for his lost faith would allow any sort of sympathetic response to Jedermann and the hero's Lutheran journey to save his soul. He also wondered if he would be able to focus on the play at all when his mission had now become to focus on the figure of the distinguished international statesman who would be sitting somewhere down front from his own last-minute press seat much farther back. The thought had come to him, Hamlet-like, that he might find some small sign of self-recognition in the distinguished gentleman by watching his face as the sinner Everyman is summoned by Death to face his final reckoning. But that thought was killed by the cynical journalist in him: any official as long practiced in the art of deception as the Big O, no doubt including the putting on of an appropriate face to get through tedious social and cultural obligations, would probably offer nothing more than a stone smile to show what might be stirring in his soul.

Whether or not the play proved to be the thing, Ripaldo was now determined to go for a direct confrontation, a man-to-man confrontation, down to earth, in this world, and no chance for further evasion as he forced the man to look squarely at a truth that he'd managed to avoid all these years and would now surely find it impossible not to acknowledge. Exactly how he would stage that confrontation remained to be worked out, but it seemed to him that his best chance would be to wait for the right moment at the end of the Jedermann performance and then head down front as quickly as he could to face the man and let him know what was on his mind in language that the distinguished gentleman and those around him could no way misunderstand or dismiss. And the more who heard him the better.

When he reached Salzburg that afternoon, Ripaldo walked over to the Domplatz to check out the setting. The square was already closed off for the opening the following afternoon, but there was room at the back end to stand and get a full view of the cathedral's Renaissance facade, with its mix of pagan wreaths and pilasters as the embroidery for statues of saints and evangelists serving the crowning figure of Christ. Some workmen were putting the last trimmings on the high stage that jutted out from the top of the cathedral steps well into the square. It looked to Ripaldo as though the platform they'd built was much more ample than the one that had held Everyman's rich banquet table when he'd last studied that set so many years ago, and now it had a grand new backdrop of three bronze cathedral doors that his guidebook told him represented the virtues of faith, hope, and charity. The trap door in the middle of the stage that would open to receive Everyman's descent into his grave was more discreet now, without the open wings that back then had made it seem the way down to somebody's earthen cellar.

Ripaldo figured that this more elaborate and realistic set had come in with the television age, because he spotted a TV crew taking sightings at the far end of the square. But the seating arrangement, which is what really interested him, still consisted mostly of movable benches with plank backs placed side by side, though there were now many more rows of chairs down front obviously reserved for dignitaries, the press, and others willing to pay the price. There were a number of aisles that broke the wide layout of benches and chairs into accessible sections. Ripaldo couldn't get into the square at the right angle to check his seat exactly, but he'd been assured that it was an aisle seat, and though at the back of the reserved section, close enough to the center of the makeshift theater to give him an excellent view of the action and far enough forward to make hearing easy. He decided that this situated him well enough for his purpose since the action that most concerned him would be in the front row of chairs, and however far back his seat might be, the fact that it was on an aisle would allow him to get to the front row with a few quick moves. He left the square and went back to his hotel with nothing left to occupy him but the long wait ahead.

He had a bad night. Twice he woke with a vision of falling from a height to a stage and then limping off to come up against a wall offstage that had no route for escape. The second time that happened, he realized that his subconscious was reshaping his image into that of John Wilkes Booth trying to get out of the Ford Theater after shooting Abraham Lincoln. By the time he finally got to sleep, he was so exhausted by his restless churning that he didn't wake up until late morning. He spent the lunch hour persuading himself that the intrusion of Booth into his nighttime psyche was not merely irrational but grotesque, perverse. He was no self-righteous murderer, and the Big O was no Abraham Lincoln, even from an unrevised southern point of view. Whatever the point of view, there had been no honor in the kind of war the young Oberleutnant had fought, no recognition in defeat of the evil that had been done, no public cleansing at any time that might have earned him the right to lead his people toward renewal. The rhetoric his war had taught him was not that of a suffering soul but of an arch hypocrite. By the time Ripaldo's Kaffee mit Schlag arrived, he could feel his gorge swelling to challenge his fear so that he could barely get the coffee down.

He was relatively calm when he took his seat for the opening of Jedermann in the late afternoon. There was a delay in starting because the Big O and his entourage arrived fifteen minutes late. As they filed in, the distinguished statesman stood for a moment facing the audience—tall, still fairly lean, hair slicked back, only the missing curl in it and the gray at the temples and the deep crow's feet at his eyes telling of the half century that had gone by since the German retreat north from Salonika. Wittekind had shown Ripaldo a famous photograph from that period which had the youthful Oberleutnant standing casually at the side of General Lohr in Sarajevo some months before Lohr was hung as a war criminal and a few days after his Ic/AO section of army Group E had tried to incite the local population to murder by dropping leaflets that urged them to "kill the Jews and come over to us." Now, as the graying gentleman stood there tall in the front row, nodding in response to the applause from here and there, Ripaldo saw little chance that this figure of a man might be touched at his core by history that old—and certainly not by the irony of his coming there to honor a production that had originally come out of the rich imagination of a Jew who had escaped to America to avoid the Nazi occupation of Austria in 1938. The gentleman's stone smile was already in place, and it stayed in place, as far as Ripaldo could tell, right on through Everyman's entrance and the banquet that followed—though he couldn't see well enough to be sure, because his seat was too far back and in a line almost directly behind that of the distinguished late arrival and the bodyguards assigned to protect him.

Ripaldo had trouble concentrating on the play. He kept returning restlessly to focus on the back of the Big O's head. He told himself that he was getting too hungry for his moment, too eager to have the thing done and over, he had to relax, but telling himself that didn't seem to help. Nor did his attempt to clear his head by glancing sideways at those sitting near him, a mix of tourists and local enthusiasts, in any case total strangers. He felt completely on his own now, and there was little comfort in that. In fact, it pierced his courage and left him wondering if he was up to what he had in mind. Then, suddenly, he was brought back to the stage by the sound of bells, and distant voices calling Everyman, and the appearance of Death. It created nothing like the same effect that it had those many years ago, but that was because his mind had shifted abruptly elsewhere. There was one character on stage who now seemed familiar in a bizarre way. The actor playing Everyman's Thin Cousin, whether through makeup or naturally, appeared to be the twin of Oberleutnant Hertzel, though maybe twenty or thirty years younger: hooknosed, bald except for a fringe of curly brown hair, eyebrows rising to give his face a look of fixed astonishment.

Ripaldo was perfectly ready to believe that it was the heightened tension of the moment that had brought on this apparition, but what had brought it on didn't matter. Once seen, he couldn't get rid of it. Hertzel was there, on the stage, playing some kind of fool who was now refusing to join Everyman on his journey to a final judgment before the Lord God because he had a cramp in his toe. "Besides," he was now telling Everyman in rhyme, "it isn't customary to ask people to help you on a journey of that kind. You have plenty of servants you can use for that purpose. Your own relatives are too good for that." Hertzel's bitchy tone of voice, the touch of arrogance and snobbery, the rational coolness—it was all there.

Whatever Hertzel was doing in that play, he served to kill Ripaldo's restlessness. His mind drifted off to hear Hertzel's other voice telling of his days in the neighborhood of Arsakli, his obsession with Corporal Schonfeld and his curious courting of Marina, and the account of his escape. Hertzel's courage had been pierced toward the end too, but Ripaldo remembered him speaking with a certain elation about the moment when he'd been forced to make an unambiguous choice. How had he phrased it in his rather stiff way? Something about putting his life on the front line for a thing he felt essential to his soul. And what turned out to be essential was betraying his side to go over to the enemy so that he no longer had to serve the monster called war. However self-serving, that decision had liberated him, he'd said, had brought calm to his center. And that is where Ripaldo, implausibly, found the image of Hertzel pushing him now.

Good Deeds had just given Everyman her hand to help him into the opening in the stage that led to his grave when the distinguished statesman and two men on either side of him rose in their seats as though by a signal. They stood there watching Everyman sink out of sight, listening to Faith's epilogue, and when the angels began to sing from the cathedral facade, they started clapping before anybody else did. Ripaldo realized that the three of them were about to position themselves for getting out of the square before the audience engulfed them, so he made his move. When he reached the front row of seats, the Big O had already stepped into the aisle in front of the stage and was shaking hands with somebody down the line. He had his back turned to Ripaldo, and one of his bodyguards on the near side of him was leaning toward him to say something, probably urging him to get going. "Sir," Ripaldo yelled in English. "I want to tell you something. I want you to know that we're on to you." The bodyguard whirled to stare at Ripaldo. "We know about what you did in Arsaklí and we know about the Hortiáti massacre." Ripaldo saw the Big O turn his head to glance back at him. The man's face remained expressionless, but his eyes stayed fixed. Ripaldo raised his rolled program like a baton and pointed it at him. "We know exactly what you know," he yelled. "Everything. So you can't get away with lying any longer. Have you got the message?"

The near bodyguard came at Ripaldo in a rush. He heard a ripple of exclamation next to him and then the sound of the audience clapping farther back. The bodyguard had him on the ground now, and another arrived to hold him flat, smothering him with his weight. They turned him on his side. He felt his wrists wrenched behind him, and he felt one arm torn out of its socket at the shoulder. He passed out for a second, then came back as they stood him up and hurried him out along the front row of seats. He could hear the audience clapping full force now in waves. Then he went limp again.

They had his arms locked behind him by the time they put him in the back of the police car. The pain from his shoulder came wafting over him, but he was clear-headed now. He kept thinking: the man heard, he knows that I know the truth about him, I saw it in his eyes. There were three plainclothesmen in the car, one on either side of Ripaldo and one up front with the driver. Nobody said anything. Ripaldo realized that they must have frisked him at some point because the man up front was leafing through his passport. When they drove off he closed his eyes and let his head fall back. He heard himself say "the son of a bitch knows" under his breath, and then he passed out again.

They brought in a doctor at the police station to pop Ripaldo's shoulder back into its socket and to put his arm in a sling. He refused to take the pills they tried to give him, but when the doctor said it would be a good thing for him to lie down on the bench, he decided to take him up on that. At one point a plainclothesman and a police officer of some kind came in to question him. The plainclothesman did the talking. He wanted to know why Ripaldo had attacked one of Austria's most distinguished citizens and what organization he represented. Ripaldo told him he hadn't attacked anybody and he represented nobody but himself. The plainclothesman said things would go better for him if he cooperated, otherwise he could expect no mercy, even if he was an American, because whatever the custom might be in America, attacking a political figure was a very serious crime in Austria.

That made Ripaldo sit up. "I didn't attack him," he said. "I simply spoke to him. About things he already knows."

"We have witnesses," the plainclothesman said. "You were seen pointing a weapon."

"That's absolute nonsense," Ripaldo said. "There was no weapon. And whatever you may think of America, speaking the truth is not a serious crime in my country."

The plainclothesman came over to stand above him. "Next time you decide to attack an important political figure, you should choose a more private place. We don't know what you did with the weapon, but there were enough witnesses who saw you holding a gun or a large knife to hang you by the neck in any country."

"There was no weapon," Ripaldo said. "I simply told the man the truth. And your important political figure knows that to be so."

The man was studying Ripaldo. "I will let you think about what your chances are of proving that under the circumstances. Please take as much time as you need. We will talk again in the morning when you have had a quiet night to consider your situation."

"I request that you notify the American Embassy in Vienna."

"Of course. That has been done already."

"And I request a chance to call my lawyer in Vienna."

"Your lawyer? What lawyer?"

"My local contact then. A friend. Don't I have the right to make one phone call even? At least in America you have the right—"

"I will make the phone call," the plainclothesman said. "Give me the number. Here on my pad."

Ripaldo took the pad with his good arm and put it on his thigh. The plainclothesman held it there for him while he wrote out Count Wittekind's name and phone number in Vienna. When Ripaldo handed the plainclothesman the pencil and the pad, he thought to himself that there was about as much hope in that move as putting a bottle out to sea.

The plainclothesman touched the corner of the pad to his head. "Think," he said. "Think hard. We will be waiting."

Ripaldo spent a relatively comfortable night on a bunk in the police station after calling for the doctor to give him a pain killer. It had occurred to him that these people needed him alive and coherent, so it wasn't likely that the doctor would try to dope him seriously, and a truth serum would serve him at that point more than it would his enemies. But what had really made the night easy for him was a deep contentment that had come over him in the aftermath of his interview with the plainclothesman. However long it might take him to get out of there, he felt that he'd done the thing he had to do, borne witness, so to speak, and he was certain it had struck home. He had nothing more to base that on than what he'd seen in the Big O's eyes after he'd turned toward him, but what he'd seen appeared to him unmistakable. And even that look wasn't the only crucial thing any longer. Whatever the old Nazi may have allowed himself to take in, however much acknowledgment was there, Ripaldo had seen all he needed to see from that confrontation, and not only in the man he'd faced but in himself. So he slept easy.

Wittekind arrived a little before dusk the following day. Ripaldo had woken up to a continental breakfast and a mug of coffee brought in by a young policeman, but nobody else had approached him that morning, and when the same policeman brought him a lunch of schnitzel and potato salad and dark beer, he figured they must be trying to unnerve him with kindness. He took a long nap after lunch, and just as he was beginning to get a little stir crazy in that barren room without a window, the policeman appeared again with Wittekind, who stood there in the doorway shaking his head. Ripaldo was relieved to see the beginnings of a smile above his friend's goatee.

"So, dear Ripaldo," Wittekind said. "This is your day to be famous. The morning papers were full of the terrible things you've done."

"What terrible things?" Ripaldo said. "I deny everything."

"You deny that you interrupted the opening-day performance of Jedermann at its most moving moment? When the hero was sinking into his grave with the good deeds he'd done?"

"I couldn't help myself," Ripaldo said.

"And you deny that you threatened our honorable elder statesman by flashing what some say was a bread knife and others a silver gun and others a section of pipe with some kind of explosive in it? Pointing it at the distinguished gentleman and exclaiming that you were Hercules with enough strength to kill him and all those protecting him?"

"Hercules?"

"What is what one of the papers reports, Ripaldo. Two witnesses claim they distinctly heard the name Hercules, though neither claims to know English or Latin."

"They're crazy," Ripaldo said. "Everybody around here is crazy. To begin with, the only thing I pointed at the man was my rolled-up program, for Christ's sake. And all I actually did was yell at him."

"You yelled at our elder statesman? Insulted our honorable leader? What did you yell, Ripaldo?"

"All I yelled was that we were on to him. That we knew what he'd done in Arsaklí, and we knew that he knew about the Hortiáti massacre."

"Aha," Wittekind said. "So Arsaklí became Hercules to the ears of our faithful Austrian deaf and dumb. And I see that whatever strength you showed was not enough to keep you from breaking your arm."

"It isn't broken," Ripaldo said. "They just ripped it from its socket. And I wasn't even close to the man."

"Well, whatever you did, you are famous enough to be the talk of the American Embassy. They phoned me late this morning to say that I was now to take charge of you and bring you in for consultation as soon as possible."

Ripaldo motioned Wittekind in to sit down beside him on the bunk.

"How can I go in for consultation when these people are about to hang me for threatening to assassinate their beloved leader?"

"You can relax," Wittekind said. "The Big O has called off his dogs. His office let the Embassy know that he will not be pressing charges."

"He won't be?"

"They said serious as the episode was, they don't have enough proof that an actual serious crime was committed. Other than disturbing the peace in a public place. Which our honorable elder statesman is willing to forgive."

"Is that what he's willing to do? How decent of him. The man is all heart."

Wittekind was really smiling now. "You're not grateful, Ripaldo? When he's made you a free man? A famous free man?"

"The hypocrite. I know why he won't press charges. He knows that I know the truth about him."

"Well, you will have to explain that to your Embassy," Wittekind said. "They are treating this as a major diplomatic episode and they are truly upset."

"Big deal. They should be upset about the way I was roughed up. Who do they represent, anyway?"

Wittekind took out a cigarette and put it in his holder. "I think you had better try to cool it, as you Americans say. I have something else to tell you that makes the situation less simple than it may seem to you. The Big O's office was also in touch with our local committee."

Wittekind was studying his cigarette holder.

"About what?" he said.

"About you, for one thing. The distinguished gentleman must have heard enough from you to know just what we're trying to dig up about his past, and he must think others heard as well. In any case, his people did enough research overnight to trace you to me and the committee."

"I knew he'd heard," Ripaldo said. "I saw it in his eyes."

"The point is, my friend, he wants you discredited. He's now found somebody willing to testify that he was not in Arsaklí at the time of the Hortiáti massacre. Somebody who was the liaison between the secret police and the Ic/AO section at the time and had an office near our distinguished Oberleutnant. This man says that the Big O returned to Arsaklí from his honeymoon leave the day after the massacre."

"And the committee is ready to believe him?"

"Not necessarily. But the man says he has documents to prove his claim."

"Documents. What documents? And even if the Big O did return the day after the massacre, that doesn't exonerate him from having gone to that village to look the place over after it was burned and then lying all these years about where he was in Northern Greece and what he knew and didn't know."

Wittekind made a face. "I suppose he's ready to concede that his memory failed him badly in this particular instance. Though his witness told our people that he himself remembered the reprisal vividly, and he actually pronounced the name of the village as it is. He said the blood bath there had caused a great commotion at intelligence headquarters in Arsaklí. He said he and all the other officers there were very indignant about what had happened."

"Give me a break. The order for the massacre came from intelligence headquarters in Arsaklí."

"That," said Wittekind, "remains to be proven."

"I think we've got enough to prove it. Where else could it have come from? Besides, we've got Schonfeld's eyewitness journal with his account of Ebert's phone call."

"I'm afraid that will be considered rather speculative since it's only one man's hypothetical account. Though of course an order had to come from somewhere in the region. In any case, this new witness appears to take the Big O out of the picture for the time being."

"Not out of my picture, he doesn't," Ripaldo said. "I don't trust this witness any more than I do the Big O himself, whatever documents he may have. I say we really go after him now that we have him cornered. Make a public statement. Whatever."

Wittekind stood up to look for an ash tray. There was none, so he flicked his holder at the lunch plate on the floor.

"The trouble is," he said, "it doesn't look as though it's going to be 'we' any longer. Some members of the committee seem to feel that you've compromised yourself by what you did. They say now that you've shown your hand so openly, you can't pretend to be objective for purposes of our report."

"Goddam right I'm not objective. I—"

Wittekind touched Ripaldo's shoulder, the good one.

"Calm yourself, dear Ripaldo. All is not lost. Wittekind is still here to carry on the crusade."

"So I'm out of it. Is that what you're telling me?"

"Not yet. Not if you trust me. I promise to defend you before the committee and also to make our case against the Big O whatever the committee decides to do about you. Do you trust me to do that?"

"Sure. Of course. What else can I do?"

"You can have dinner with me and celebrate your new freedom. And I don't mean only getting out of this bloody non-smoker's cell."

Ripaldo didn't understand the full implications of that remark until the following day, after Wittekind headed back to Vienna to face his committee. The arrangement was that Ripaldo would follow him there after he'd taken care of some personal business in Salzburg—a matter, he told Wittekind, that he was sure required no explanation between friends—and as soon as Wittekind left for the airport, Ripaldo called Lotte Kistner for a date that evening to return Schonfeld's journal to her. When he suggested dinner, she suggested a glass of wine at the place across the street from her apartment. Ripaldo read natural reticence into this, not a clear brush off, since he figured that his recent notoriety could have easily provided her with an excuse not to see him privately at all. He decided that what he might do to overcome that reticence had to depend on the feel of things after the two of them got together.

Ripaldo then spent the morning climbing up to the

Hohensalzburg fortress and wandering through its medieval torture chamber and clangy state rooms because he thought that relatively isolated setting would give him the best chance of avoiding anybody in town who may not have appreciated his recent contribution to the opening-day performance of Jedermann. He ended up spending the lunch hour with a sausage and a roll at a lookout post that opened out on a broad spread of the city and the mountains around it. He found it hard to enjoy that rich landscape now. It felt increasingly alien. And while he was sitting out there he decided that he wasn't going to let Wittekind's committee of journalists bully him or inhibit him in any way. If they expected him to pretend to be objective after what he'd learned, he had no business working for people that wishy-washy. He began to suspect that the committee might be getting ready to issue a report that would be so inconclusive as to be taken for an exoneration by those who had reason to fear the unequivocal truth. Whatever they might decide about him, he told himself, he would take no part in any such report. If that is what it came down to, he would put together what he and Wittekind had dug up already and publish it on its own wherever he could. Those with an unconditional respect for the truth could draw their own conclusions. And the committee— to hell with the committee. Ripaldo suddenly felt a new surge of relief, another level of freedom, and that, he now realized, was of course what Wittekind had foreseen, the old hedonist crusader.

When he arrived at the place across from Lotte Kistner's apartment, he ordered a bottle of chilled wine and two glasses. He was in a very good mood, and the minute Lotte Kistner came in, she sensed it.

"So," she said, with a hint of a smile. "I can see that you're proud of yourself."

She sat down opposite him and used both hands to ease her dark hair back from her collar and flare it out. Ripaldo thought she looked gorgeous.

"Not exactly proud," he said. "Just relieved."

He handed her Schonfeld's journal.

"Well, you shouldn't be too proud," Lotte said. "Some would say what you did shows that you haven't learned as much as you might have from all this business about past history."

"At least I've learned that there are some things that should be beyond compromise."

"That's a good thing to have learned," Lotte said. "And this came from facing your enemy at a public festival in front of his admirers and many foreigners and speaking to him about terrible things he did half a century ago?"

"I suppose you could put it that way," Ripaldo said.

She had Schonfeld's journal in front of her and was leaning her chin on it. Her little smile was still there.

"That must have taken some courage," she said. "Of course it would also have taken some courage to walk away from that place and not do what you did even after you felt you had to do it."

"I don't follow. You mean just let the man get away with what he's been getting away with all these years now that I know the truth? Just forgive and forget?"

"No, I mean forgive without necessarily forgetting. Forgetting is of course very dangerous sometimes. But so is too much remembering."

"Well, so is too much forgiving. Especially when a person is a proven liar running for an important public office."

Lotte sighed. "I wasn't thinking only in political terms. I was actually thinking of your personal situation."

"Well, tell me about that," Ripaldo said. "It pleases me to think you could care about my personal situation."

Lotte set the journal down on the table, then pushed it aside as the waitress came up to pour their wine.

"I don't know," Lotte said. "These things are hard for me to judge. In political terms, I've seen the dangers of forgetting, especially in this country. But in personal terms, I've seen the dangers of remembering too long. Martin remembered too long."

"And you think that of me too?"

Lotte looked away. "I don't know you well enough. All I know is that a man who can do what you did must believe passionately in something. Maybe to the point of obsession."

"But is that so bad if what you're obsessed with is trying to uncover an evil that has been hidden too long?"

Lotte sighed again. "Let me try to put it another way. Maybe the time has come for you to stop worrying so much about what your enemy did and to worry more about yourself."

"Just leave him to heaven, or whatever you say here, and let him take up any public office he can get, is that it?"

"Just leave him to himself," Lotte said. "And think about yourself."

That made Ripaldo smile. "I'm not usually accused of being slow at that. I guess I can promise to think more about myself. Though I'd prefer to think more about you."

Lotte brushed her hair back again. She was looking at Ripaldo now, steadily, and her smile was gone. Then she looked down at her glass of wine.

"Let me tell you something," she said, twisting her glass. "Somebody, some philosopher or historian, has said that in every man there is an evil that can destroy him if he looks deep enough. I think this was said about Hitler and others like him, and maybe that's the way you feel about your enemy. But I like to think that in every man and every woman there is a good that can save you if you can only find it. Do you understand?"

"I think so," Ripaldo said. "You mean I should worry more about saving my own soul?"

Lotte shook her head. "I wouldn't put it in religious terms. I'm not religious in that sense. I mean, every man and every woman should try to come to some sort of personal recognition that allows you to free yourself. As Martin did in the end."

"By saying that my enemy, as you call him, had his war, as Martin had his and I had mine, and therefore that's the end of it? I don't think I can really accept that way of looking at things."

"Maybe that's the trouble," Lotte said. "Doesn't one have to arrive at the point where the enemy outside doesn't matter as much as the enemy inside? Which is maybe why obsessions are dangerous. Martin's or yours or anyone else's, mine included."

"I'll have to think about that," Ripaldo said. "How about taking this a bit farther over dinner? It's only fair that you tell me about your obsessions now that you know so much about mine."

Lotte reached over and touched his hand. "I don't think we're ready for that yet."

"Well when can I hope that we might be ready?"

Lotte took her hand back. Then she reached for Schonfeld's

journal and stood up.

"When the time comes, if it comes, I think you'll know it. And if you don't, it doesn't matter. That's the least important thing you have to worry about now."

"But you haven't finished your wine," Ripaldo said.

"You finish it for me. That way you may learn about my secret obsessions. Though they may not be exactly the ones you have in mind."

She eased her glass towards him, watching his face, then smiled at him and turned to go out.

After that too-quick encounter, Ripaldo returned to Vienna quite depressed. It seemed to him that he'd come to a dead end—with the investigation, the committee, even with Lotte Kistner. He'd planned to call Wittekind on arrival to find out where things stood exactly, but he was in no hurry to do that now. And as far as the American Embassy was concerned, he hadn't heard a word from them directly, no message when the police officer on duty in Salzburg gave him back his passport and wallet and pocket comb, no message at his hotel during the past two days. He told himself since they hadn't been the ones to come to his rescue in Salzburg, he didn't really owe them a thing, though as a matter of patriotic courtesy, he probably ought to give them a phone call at some point to thank them for bringing in Wittekind to bail him out and let it go at that.

It was early afternoon when Ripaldo reached his Vienna hotel. He decided that it might do him good to take a walk as far as the Schwartzenberg Park and the Belvedere Garden, and he managed to make it to the palace museum there with enough time before closing to pick up an image of Vienna in its more colorful days by way of Klimt and Schiele and Kokoschka. But it was walking the garden paths outside the museum that helped to bring him back to the green things of this world and a lighter mood. He sat on a bench outside until dusk came in to soften the palace's rococo facade, and during that time he found his spirit easing again enough to free itself of Vienna and its wartime ghosts. He decided that he would not only keep his distance from the local committee but he would tell Wittekind that, much as he regretted it, he was now ready to let Wittekind keep things going on his own, and the best of luck to him. One way or another, the Big O's political future now belonged to his own people more than to the rest of the world. Let them do with him as they chose since they were the ones who would have to live with their choice. And if the distinguished hypocrite continued to keep the charred bones of his past hidden from sight, Lotte Kistner probably had the best answer for that after all: leave the old sinner to himself.

Ripaldo now took stock. Things were certainly looking up. He had some money in his pocket, a valid passport, no job, but only one care in the world: his promise to Marina Angeloúdis.

When Ripaldo arrived in Panórama, there was a chill in the air. The heat wave that had surged in mid-August, burning the earth gray and coating the trees with dust, was dead now, and with the longer days came a coolness in the evening that anticipated the turn into September. He'd waited until close to dusk to go to Panórama because he didn't want to break into the siesta period, but by the time he got there, he found no one at home at Vassílis Angeloúdis' place. There was scaffolding on the roof, where they'd begun to add a new story. From a neighbor he learned that Marina had moved to the city to stay with her aged mother while the work on the house was going on but that he would probably find Vassílis as usual at his cafe in Hortiáti.

Ripaldo didn't go there right away. He wanted to have a look at the mountain slope beyond the top of the village, so he climbed the street that went by the few remnant houses of the old Arsaklí to the upper edge of Panórama, and he kept going up the steep mound of a hill that might have been an acropolis in ancient times if someone had thought to put a temple there. What he found instead, buried in the hillside, were two concrete pillboxes that the German army had left behind, one facing northwest and the other southwest. The pillboxes were full of trash from picnickers, plastic cups and water bottles, and here and there a dried turd. He stood on the roof of the one aimed at the northwest and looked across the valley below toward the village of Hortiáti in the distance. Partway across the valley there was a sheepfold, but there were no sheep grazing near it. He couldn't hear a thing up there whatever direction he turned.

He'd been disappointed to find that Marina wasn't at home, but now it seemed to him just as well. Whatever he might have told her could only work against the peacefulness he felt had come to that mountainside, her secret place and her lover's, and beyond that, her husband's place too. He knew now that he would not tell her what he had come there to reveal—all the missing history of Corporal Schonfeld after he'd left Arsaklí and then left Northern Greece to return to his pre-war life with another woman in another country. He would let that history end where Marina had seen it ending and where her memory still preferred to see it: near the Byzantine aqueduct on the road to Hortiáti that day in September, 1944. And he would let her husband be the one to tell her this, in a way that would give neither of them any pain but would free their American friend from further intrusion into their secret lives.

Ripaldo found Vassílis sitting at one of the two tables in his cafe that were occupied. He had his back turned to the door and was leaning toward the others, speaking softly but with conviction, so Ripaldo sat down at an empty table near the entrance and waited for an opening. One of the men at Vassílis' table interrupted him to say that a customer had come in—a tourist, Ripaldo heard the man say, looks like a German. Vassílis glanced at Ripaldo, then glanced again. He came over, wiping his hands on his apron. Then he embraced Ripaldo.

"So, my American friend," he said. "You came back. I knew you would."

"I told you I would," Ripaldo said. "I told Marina too."

Vassílis pulled out a chair and sat down.

"So," he said. "Did you find what you were looking for in Germany?"

"Austria," Ripaldo said. "I ended up not having to go to Germany. We found enough for our purposes in Austria."

"The officer? The tall one with the large nose and the big ears you were so interested in? Did you find him there?"

"Him and others. Which reminds me. I have a message for Marina. They told me she's staying with her mother while your house is under construction. I went by there on the way up here."

Vassílis eased back in his chair. "As you could see, we're doing a bit of adding on. A place to put Marina's mother so that she can stay with us. And a dowry for our youngest daughter. Who's getting a bit old now, but nevertheless."

"That's good," Ripaldo said. "Families are important. You people grow up knowing that, but we usually find it out after the first divorce or the second or when we're too old to get married and have children."

"Nonsense," Vassílis said. "You're never too old. And if you think you are, I've got a remedy for you. An *ouzo* glass of olive oil at night, followed by a glass of *ouzo*. Or maybe two."

"I'll keep that in mind," Ripaldo said.

Vassílis started to get up. "Now, what can I bring you?"

"First, before I forget, my message for Marina. Tell her that we found the officer she used to work for at the American School headquarters and he sends his best wishes. But unfortunately the Corporal was killed in action."

"What Corporal is that?"

"The medical soldier who fixed her cut fingers once. She remembered him being kind to her and to everyone else in that place."

"You have the name?"

"The name doesn't matter," Ripaldo said. "Just tell her the Corporal was killed in action after he was transferred from the American School headquarters. As some people suspected back then."

"And what about the officer with the large nose? Did you find out if he was in Arsaklí at the end of the war?"

"He was there all right. At the intelligence headquarters. So he knew about everything that was going on. Though exactly how much he was responsible for what went on remains unfinished business that is no longer my business. As far as my personal role is concerned, the case is closed."

"That's good news," Vassílis said. "So now you can forget about the war and your investigation and maybe stay with us a while?"

"Not quite yet," Ripaldo said. "There's still something I have to clear up in Austria. In Salzburg. Nothing to do with the war or the investigation."

"Salzburg," Vassílis said. "I don't know Salzburg. Of course I don't know Vienna either. Or even Belgrade. There's just too much north of here for a single life to know."

"Isn't that the truth," Ripaldo said.

"In any case, you'll have to tell me about Europe and what's really going on up there," Vassílis said. "But first let me get you something."

"I'll have an *ouzo*," Ripaldo said. "What the hell."

Vassílis smiled. "And some olive oil?"

"Not quite yet, my friend. Everything in its time."

When some of the older boy scouts in the front of the bus began to complain about the heat, the bus driver said of course he'd turned the air-conditioner off, way back when they'd come out above Panórama and headed across the level stretch toward the Asvestohórí crossroad, that's where the air outside had changed. It wasted fuel to use the air conditioner when you didn't really need it, the driver said, especially this late in September and this late in the day. Now tat the shadows were deepening on the mountainside, if they had a little patience and opened the windows, in a minute they'd feel the afternoon breeze coming down the ravine beyond Hortiáti village and probably complain about being too cold. Our driver is not only a poet of nature, one of the older boys said, but a philosopher, a defender of reason. Some of the boys up front found that their windows wouldn't stay open, so they began to egg the driver on until he swore at them, and that brought the scout master up front to make them quiet down. He bent down and spoke to the driver. That made the driver clam up. When they reached the crossroad and turned to head up toward Hortiáti village, the driver pulled the bus over on the gravel shoulder. This is as far as we go, the driver said, you walk the rest of the way, scout master's orders. There was a groan the length of the bus, and some of the boys went after the driver again. The scout master had to come up front and quiet them down. He told them they were lucky he hadn't made them walk all the way from Panórama, this was supposed to be a hike after all, what kind of sensitive plants were they anyway? The driver laughed, but nobody said anything. When the troop was finally out of the bus and lined up in twos, the scout master pulled the tallest boy out of line and told him to go back in and check the rear seats to make sure there weren't any lazy jokers hiding out back there. He said they were to stay in twos and keep their lines straight at least while they were on the shoulder of the highway, because he didn't want to have to pick up any bodies that had been knocked down by motorcy-

cle maniacs from the city who used that road to test their allotted time on this earth. The lines held well until the troop turned off the highway below the Byzantine aqueduct and cut across the fields to begin the climb up toward the village. Some stayed back to keep their own pace, but most went on up ahead with the scout master, who was in one of his story-telling moods now that they were safely off the gravel shoulder. He was telling those around him where the ambush had taken place and what that had brought on and what it was like to walk into that village after the Germans had set it on fire and nothing was left but charred walls and a charcoal smell. He said he'd been among the first from the city to walk into the place after the German army pulled out that year, the youngest member of the one small scout troop that had been organized at the end of the Occupation. The six of them had come up from the city that day through the village of Arsakli on their first outing of the year though it was already fall, and after that long a hike they had climbed up only as far as the village. It wasn't a thing he wanted to describe, he said, the feeling that place gave you, but it wasn't a thing you forgot either, not back then, not even fifty years later. That's why it was important for all of them to go up there and pay their respects. He shook his head, staring at the ground. Then he turned to see what had happened to the rest who'd fallen behind. The tail end of the troop was still down by the aqueduct. They'd discovered something there and two of them were playing catch with it, flipping it back and forth. It looked like some kind of wreath made of flowers that had gone dead. In the name of God, the scout master yelled down at them, don't you have any feeling for your own history? Leave that thing alone and let's get on up there before it gets too dark to see what these people have put up in their square to remind us about this Godforsaken place.